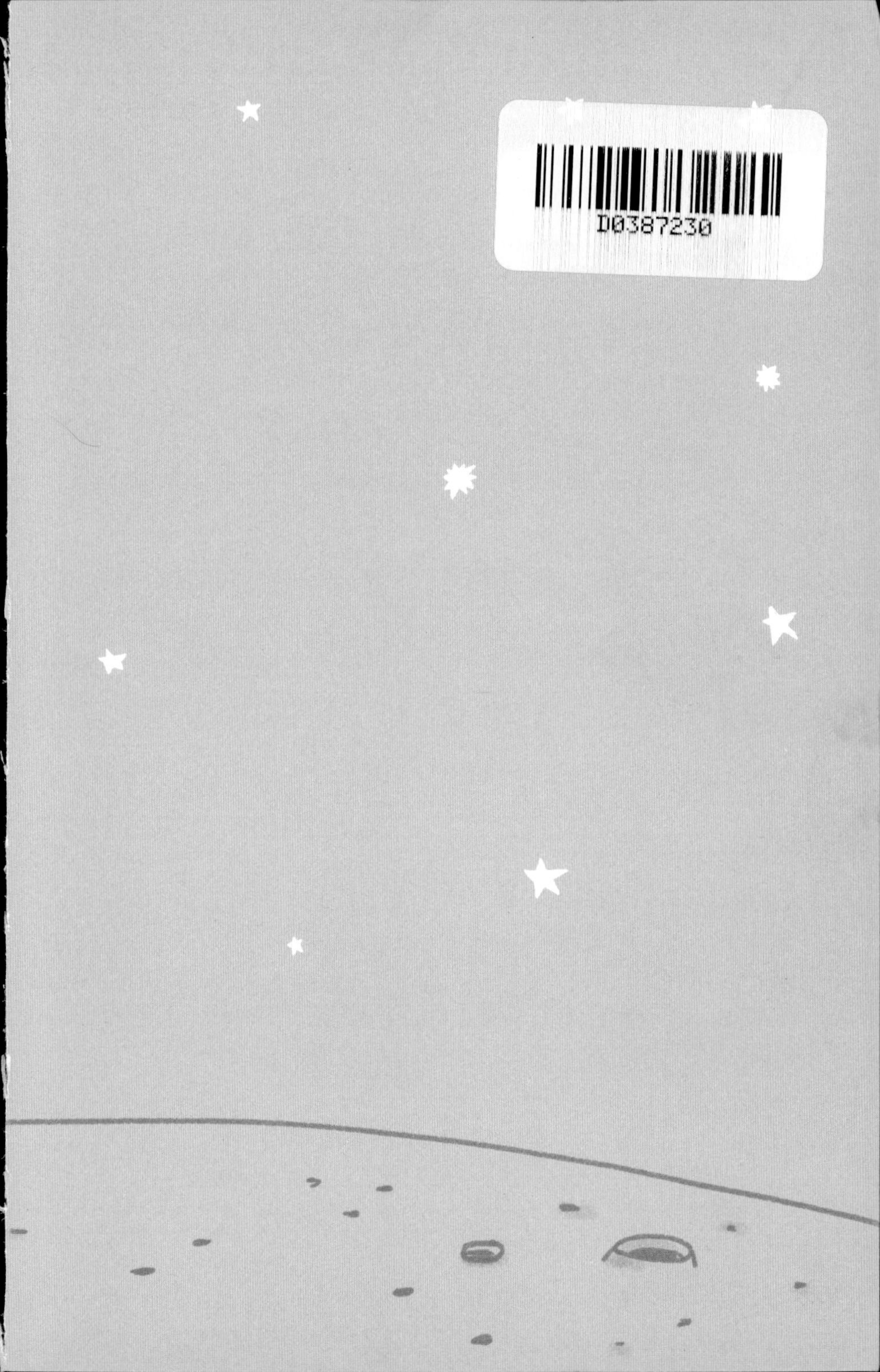

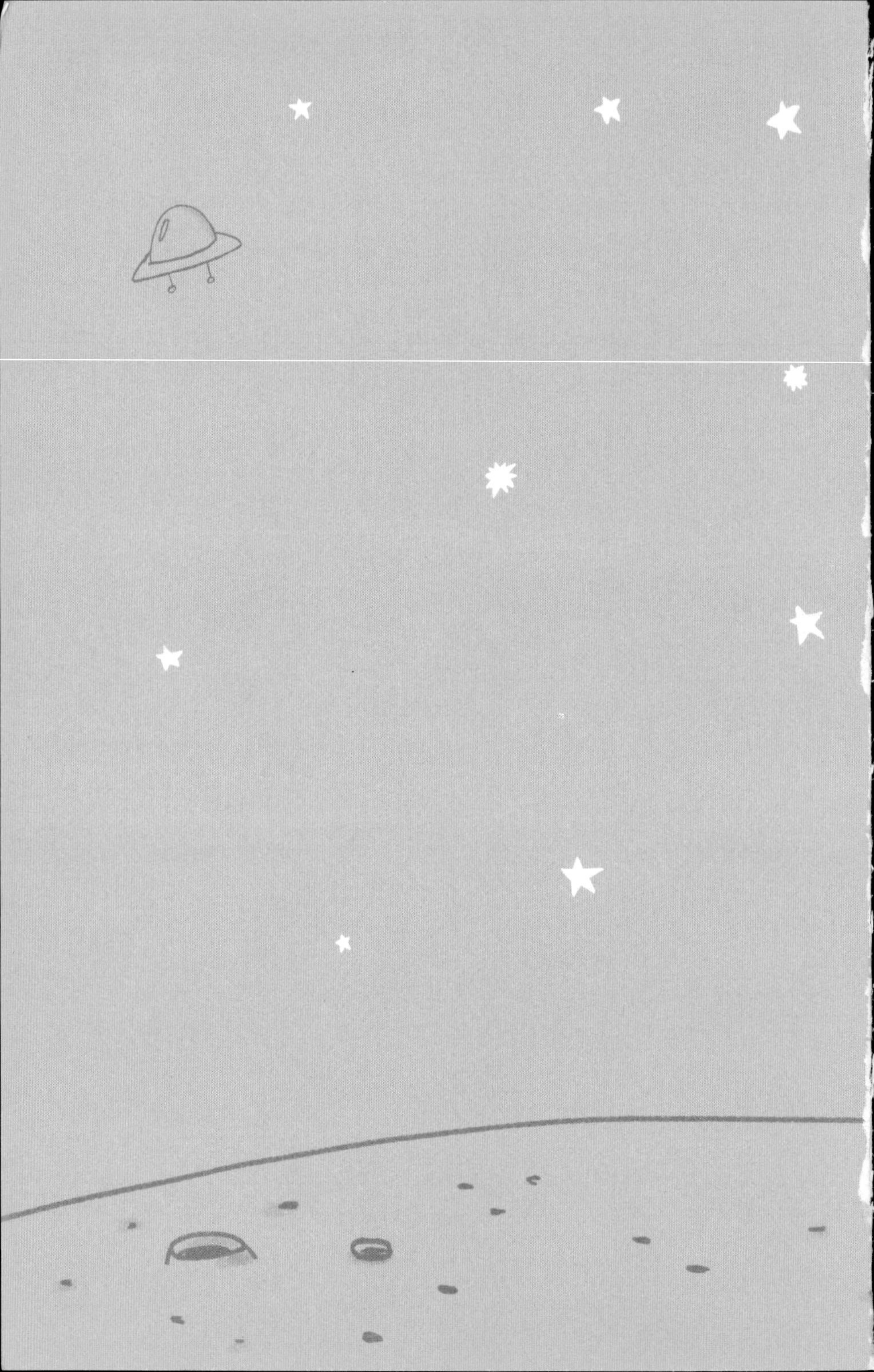

DOODLE ADVENTURES™

THE SEARCH FOR THE

SLIMY

SPACE

SLUGS!

DOODLE ADVENTURES™

THE SEARCH FOR THE SLIMY SPACE SLUGS!

MIKE LOWERY

WORKMAN PUBLISHING
NEW YORK

Library of Congress Cataloging-in-Publication Data is available.

ISBN 978-0-7611-8719-6

Workman books are available at special discounts when purchased in bulk for premiums and sales promotions as well as for fund-raising or educational use. Special editions or book excerpts can also be created to specification. For details, contact the Special Sales Director at the address below, or send an email to specialmarkets@workman.com.

Workman Publishing Co., Inc.
225 Varick Street
New York, NY 10014-4381
workman.com

WORKMAN is a registered trademark of Workman Publishing Co., Inc.
DOODLE ADVENTURES is a trademark of Workman Publishing Co., Inc.

Printed in China
First printing April 2016

10 9 8 7 6 5 4 3 2 1

FOR ALLISTER AND KATRIN,
WHO MAKE LIFE PRETTY AWESOME

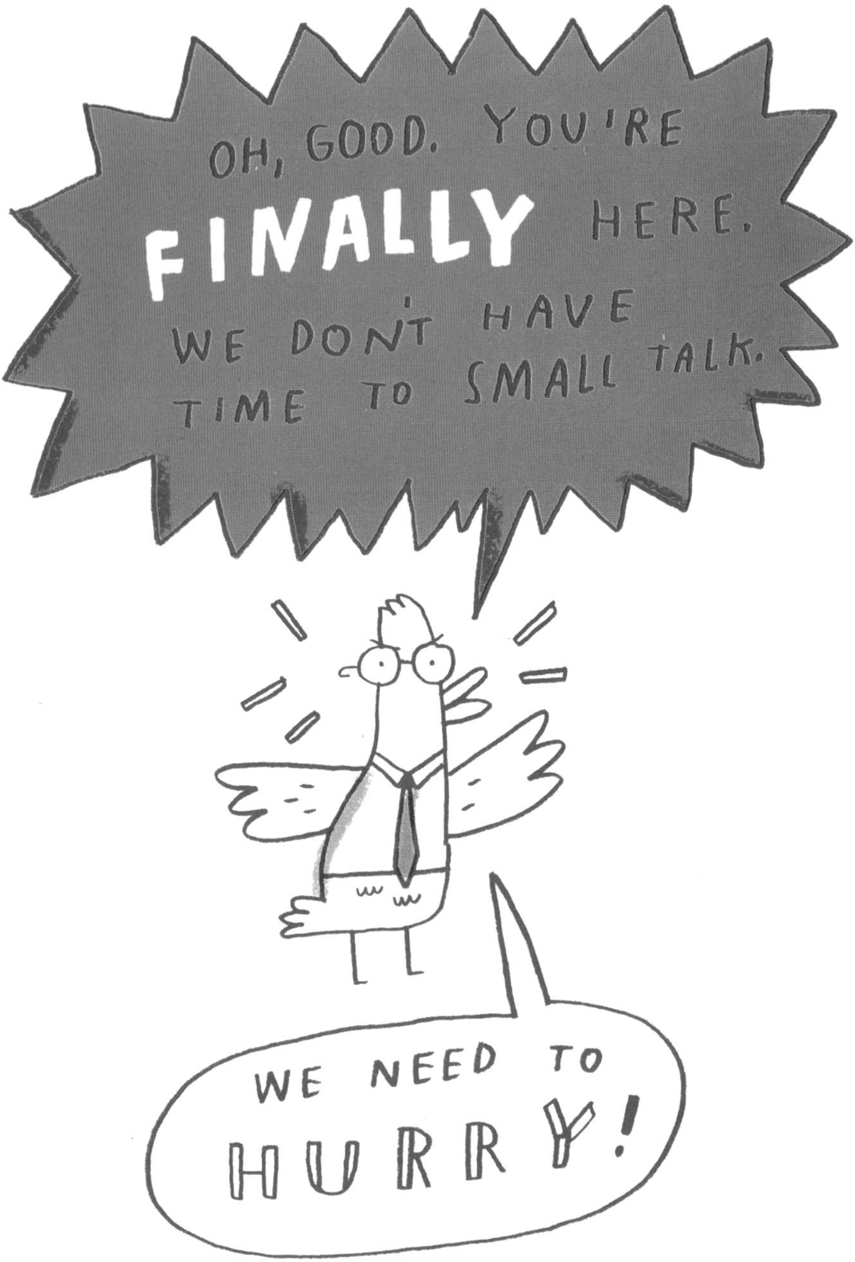
OH, GOOD. YOU'RE FINALLY HERE. WE DON'T HAVE TIME TO SMALL TALK.
WE NEED TO HURRY!

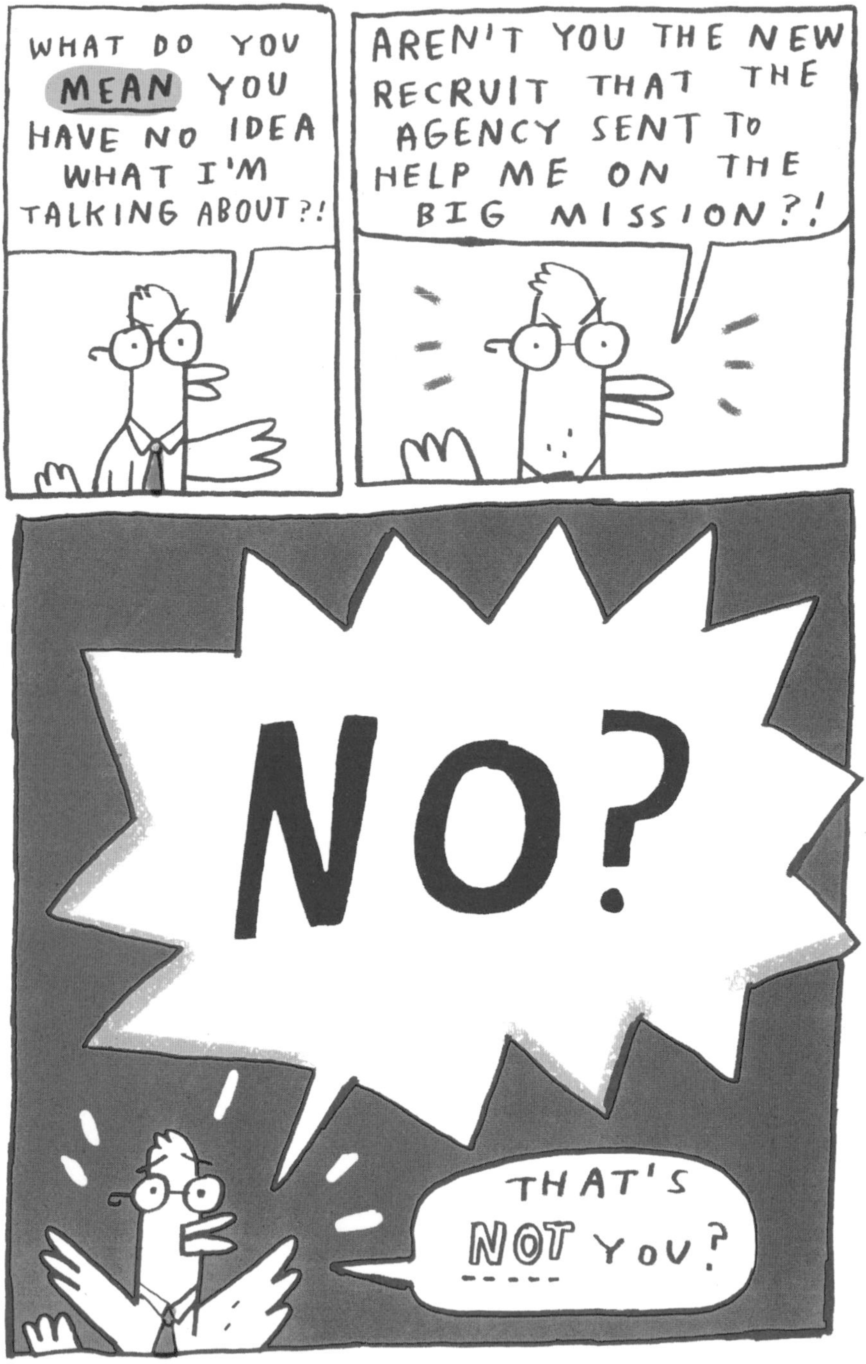
WHAT DO YOU MEAN YOU HAVE NO IDEA WHAT I'M TALKING ABOUT?!
AREN'T YOU THE NEW RECRUIT THAT THE AGENCY SENT TO HELP ME ON THE BIG MISSION?!
NO?
THAT'S NOT YOU?

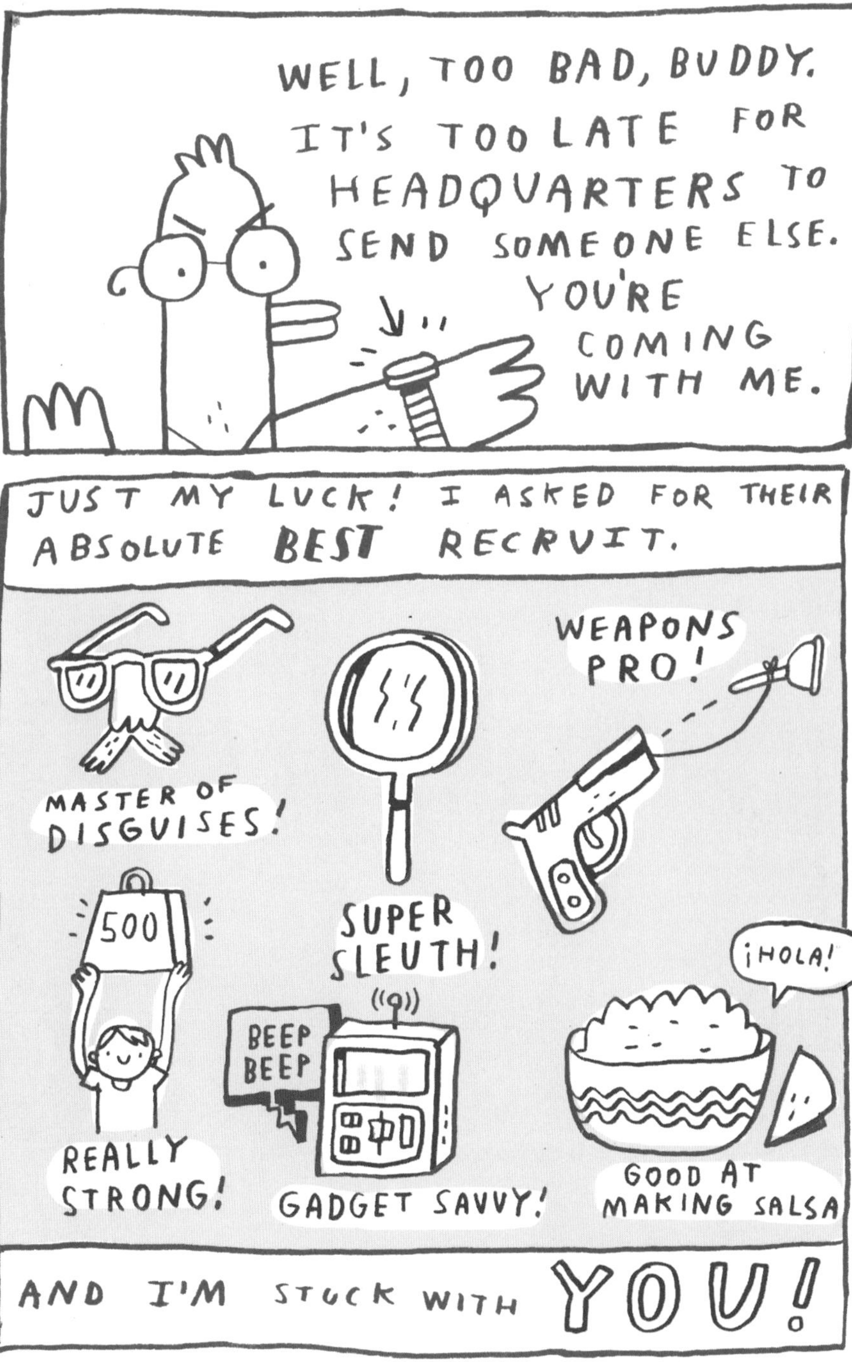
WELL, TOO BAD, BUDDY. IT'S TOO LATE FOR HEADQUARTERS TO SEND SOMEONE ELSE. YOU'RE COMING WITH ME.
JUST MY LUCK! I ASKED FOR THEIR ABSOLUTE BEST RECRUIT.
MASTER OF DISGUISES!
SUPER SLEUTH!
WEAPONS PRO!
500
REALLY STRONG!
BEEP BEEP
GADGET SAVVY!
¡HOLA!
GOOD AT MAKING SALSA
AND I'M STUCK WITH YOU!

OKAY, I'LL GET YOU UP TO SPEED, BUT YOU'RE REALLY GOING TO HAVE TO

LISTEN,

BECAUSE WE ARE IN A BIG HURRY.

IF THIS MISSION FAILS... WE CAN'T EVEN THINK ABOUT THAT. THE MISSION CAN'T

FAIL!

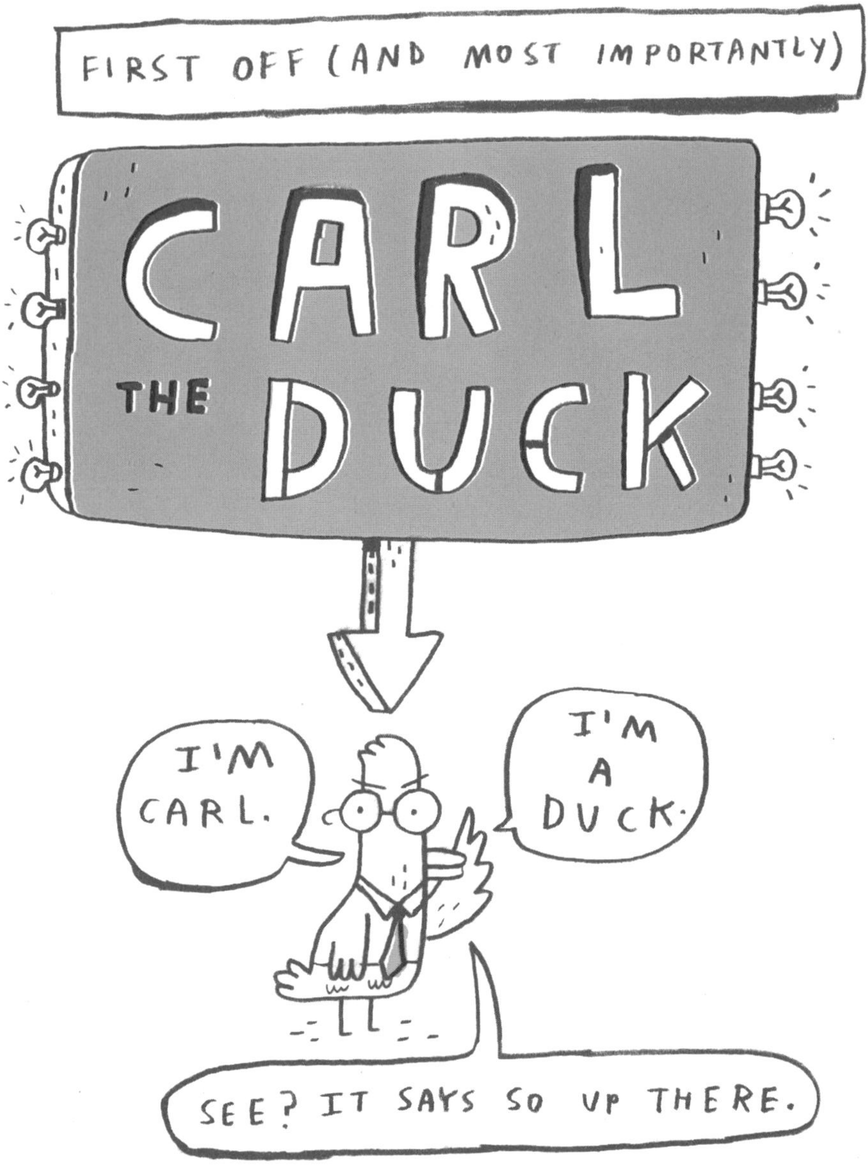
FIRST OFF (AND MOST IMPORTANTLY)
CARL THE DUCK
I'M CARL.
I'M A DUCK.
SEE? IT SAYS SO UP THERE.

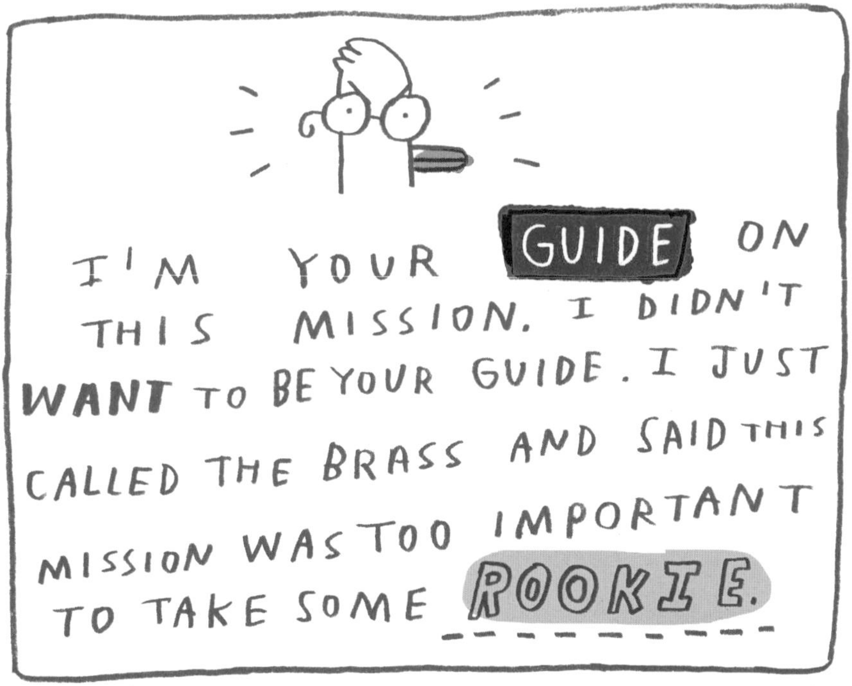
I'M YOUR GUIDE ON THIS MISSION. I DIDN'T WANT TO BE YOUR GUIDE. I JUST CALLED THE BRASS AND SAID THIS MISSION WAS TOO IMPORTANT TO TAKE SOME ROOKIE.

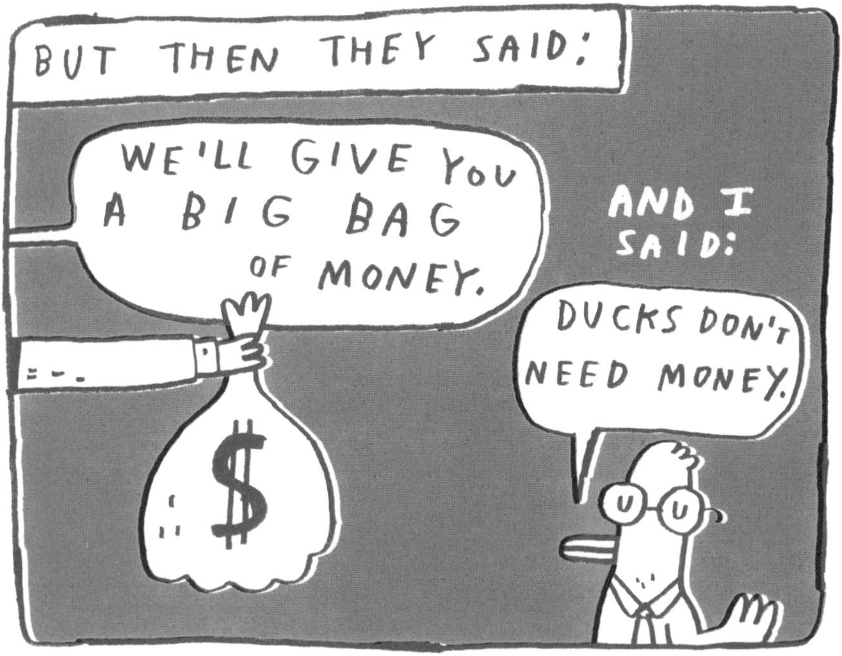
BUT THEN THEY SAID:
WE'LL GIVE YOU A BIG BAG OF MONEY.
AND I SAID:
DUCKS DON'T NEED MONEY.

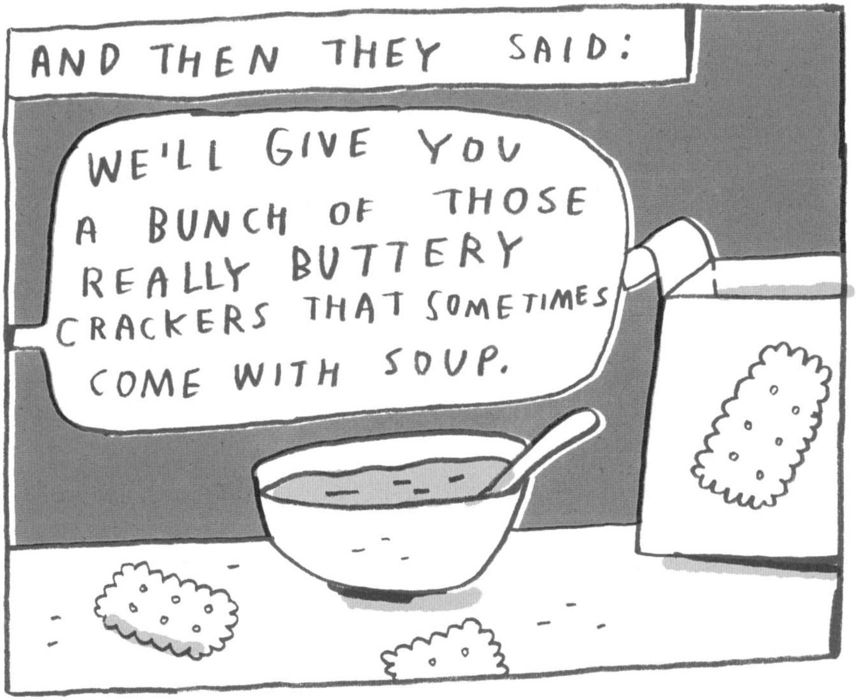
AND THEN THEY SAID:
WE'LL GIVE YOU A BUNCH OF THOSE REALLY BUTTERY CRACKERS THAT SOMETIMES COME WITH SOUP.

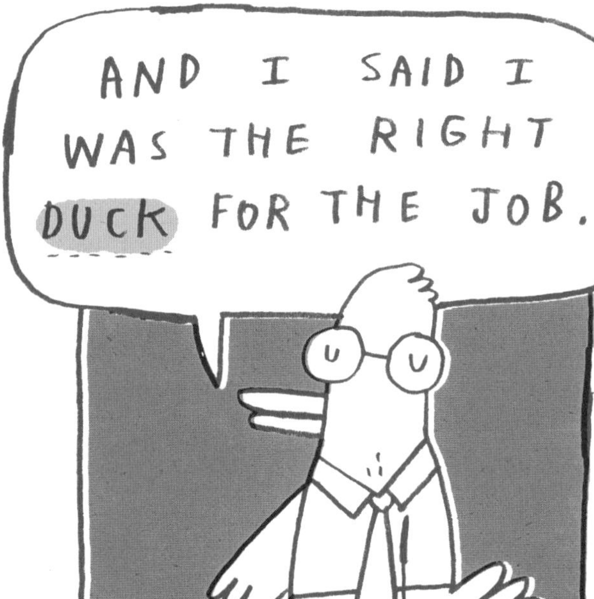
AND I SAID I WAS THE RIGHT DUCK FOR THE JOB.

THE BOOK THAT YOU'RE HOLDING IN YOUR HANDS RIGHT THIS SECOND IS DIFFERENT FROM <u>ANY</u> OTHER BOOK YOU'VE EVER HELD BEFORE.

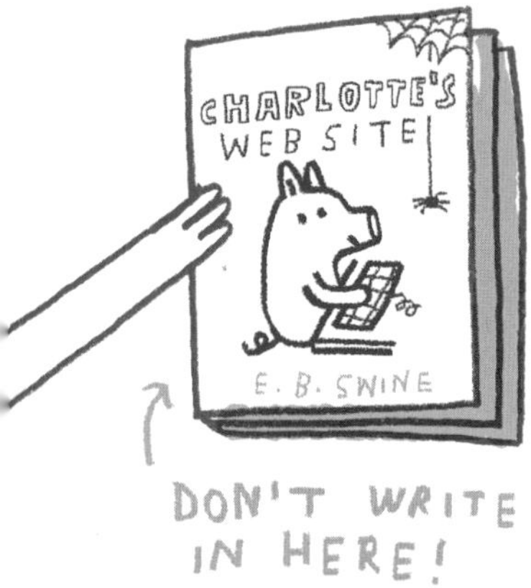
CHARLOTTE'S WEB SITE
E. B. SWINE
DON'T WRITE IN HERE!

YOU KNOW HOW YOUR PARENTS AND TEACHERS ARE ALWAYS SAYING **NOT** TO WRITE IN YOUR BOOKS??

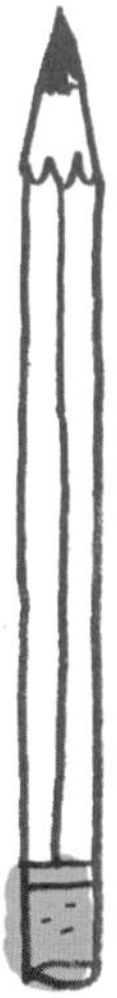

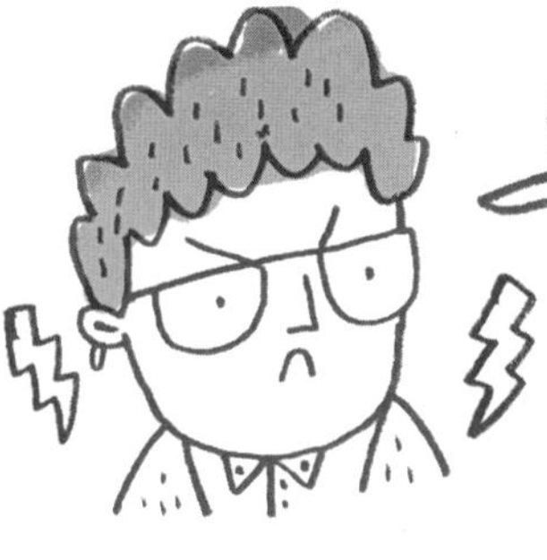
DON'T DO IT!

WELL...

YOU'VE <u>GOT</u> TO WRITE IN THIS ONE. IT'S REQUIRED. ABSOLUTELY <u>NECESSARY.</u>

LET'S START NOW. DRAW A
CAT WEARING SUNGLASSES. DRAW
IT QUICKLY. WE REALLY
HAVE TO HURRY.

COOL CAT'S
NAME : <u>B</u> <u>J</u> <u>B</u> _ _ _ _ _ _

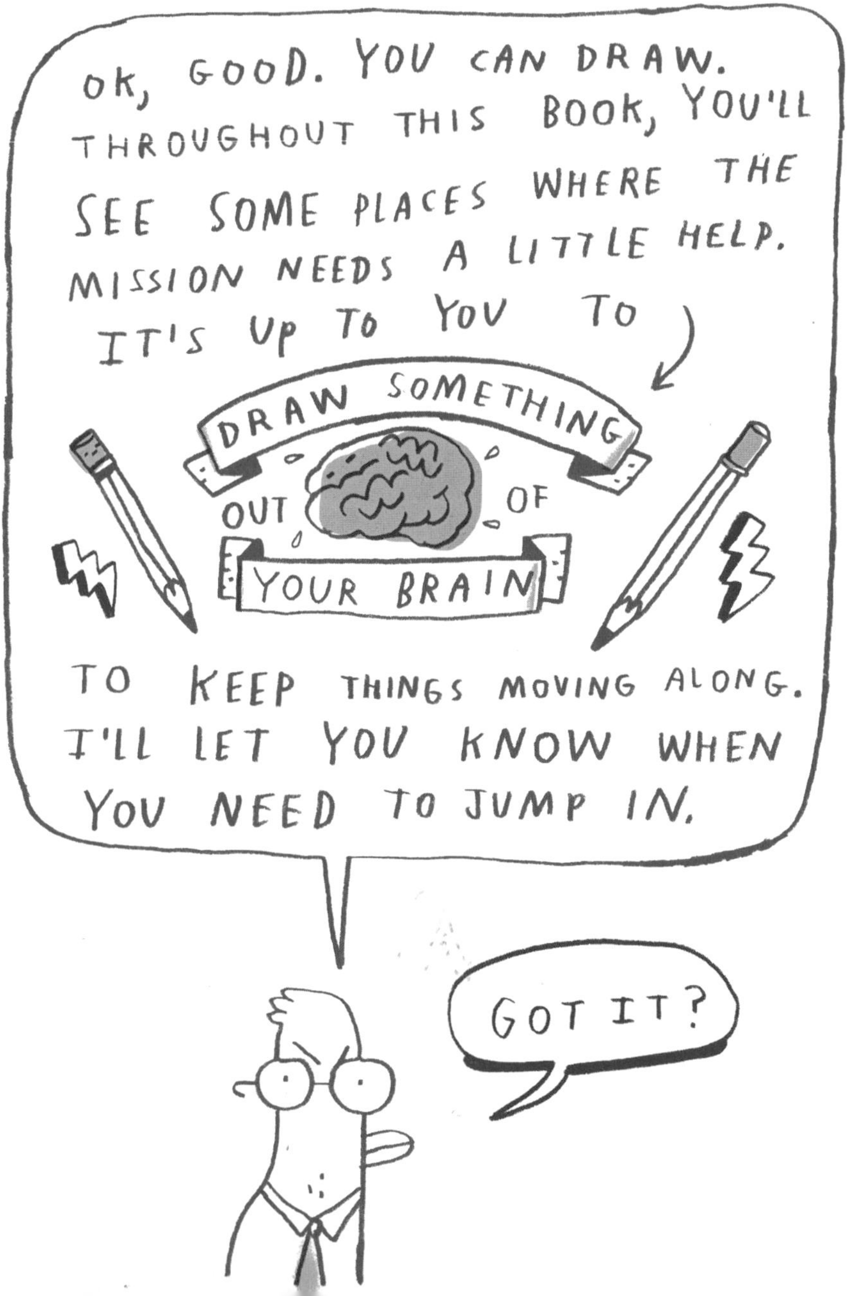
OK, GOOD. YOU CAN DRAW. THROUGHOUT THIS BOOK, YOU'LL SEE SOME PLACES WHERE THE MISSION NEEDS A LITTLE HELP. IT'S UP TO YOU TO
DRAW SOMETHING OUT OF YOUR BRAIN
TO KEEP THINGS MOVING ALONG. I'LL LET YOU KNOW WHEN YOU NEED TO JUMP IN.
GOT IT?

IF SO, YOU'LL NEED TO SIGN THIS
OATH SAYING YOU UNDERSTAND THE
TERMS AND CONDITIONS OF
THIS BOOK.

I, ___MILO___, AM A
(YOUR NAME)
PRETTY SMART KID AND CAN
DEFINITELY HANDLE THE TASKS
THAT THIS BOOK WILL ASK OF ME.
I AM AWARE THAT IT IS MY
RESPONSIBILITY TO DOODLE IN THE
BOOK (EVEN THOUGH LOTS OF FOLKS HAVE
TOLD ME TO NEVER, EVER DRAW IN
MY BOOKS BECAUSE WE WANT TO KEEP
OUR (NICE) THINGS (NICE) OR WHATEVER).
I SOLEMNLY SWEAR TO COMPLETELY

FINISH THIS BOOK TO GET
OUR HEROES HOME SAFE
AT THE END.
SIGNED, MILO

(QUILL PEN NOT REQUIRED)

NOW, BEFORE YOU ARE ALLOWED TO GO ON AN OFFICIAL MISSION, YOU NEED TO FILL OUT SOME PAPERWORK.

NEWLY EMPLOYED RECRUIT DOCUMENT ("NERD" FOR SHORT)

DRAW A PHOTO OF YOURSELF

AGENT NAME: Foot Lick er Poxll

AGENT HOMETOWN: _____

AGE: 10   HAIR COLOR: BIP

FAVORITE CANDY: Jolly Rances

IF YOU COULD HAVE ANY SUPERPOWER, IT WOULD BE:

(DRAW YOURSELF USING THAT POWER)

OFFICIAL USE ONLY   DA #0013A

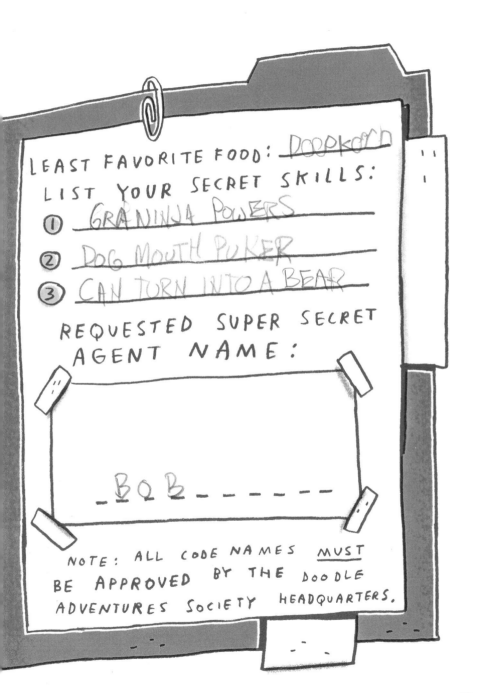

LEAST FAVORITE FOOD: Poopkorn

LIST YOUR SECRET SKILLS:
① GRANINJA POWERS
② DOG MOUTH PUKER
③ CAN TURN INTO A BEAR

REQUESTED SUPER SECRET AGENT NAME:

_ B O B _ _ _ _ _ _ _

NOTE: ALL CODE NAMES MUST BE APPROVED BY THE DOODLE ADVENTURES SOCIETY HEADQUARTERS.

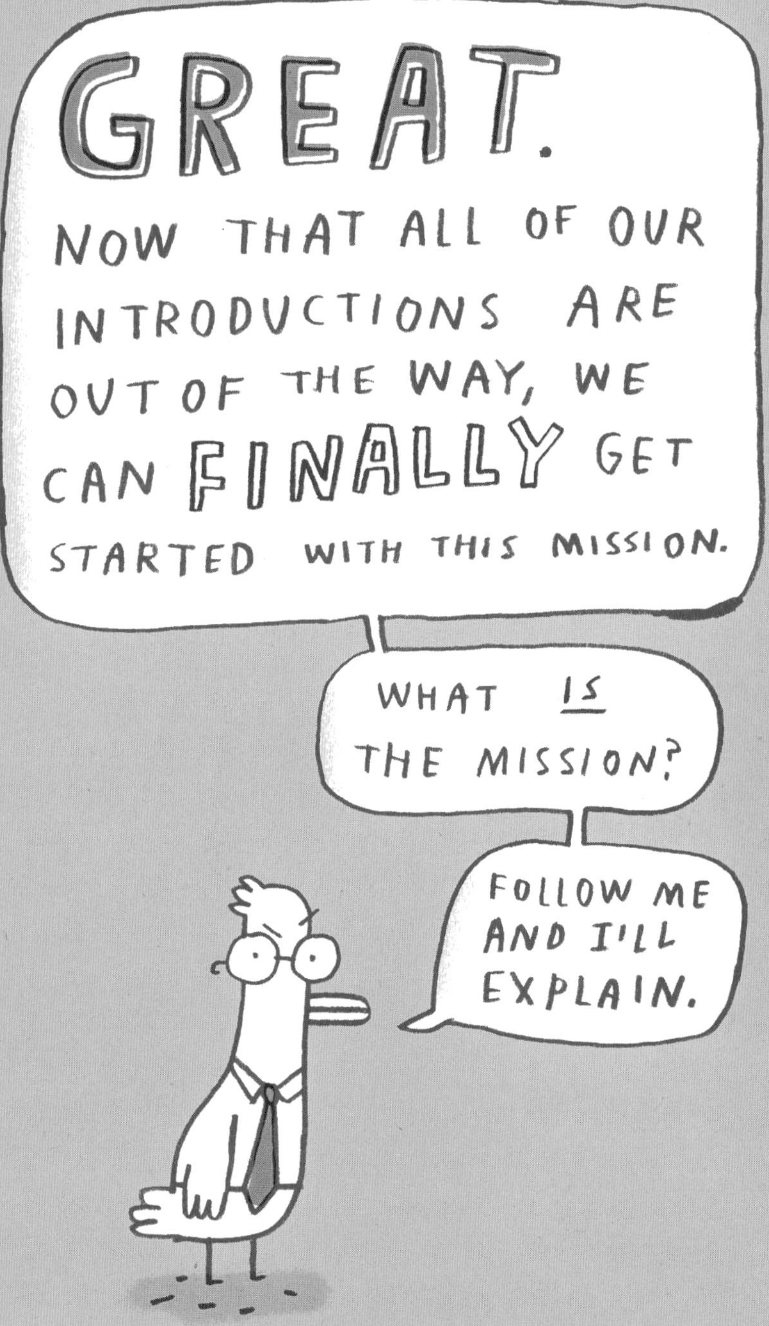
GREAT.
NOW THAT ALL OF OUR INTRODUCTIONS ARE OUT OF THE WAY, WE CAN FINALLY GET STARTED WITH THIS MISSION.
WHAT IS THE MISSION?
FOLLOW ME AND I'LL EXPLAIN.

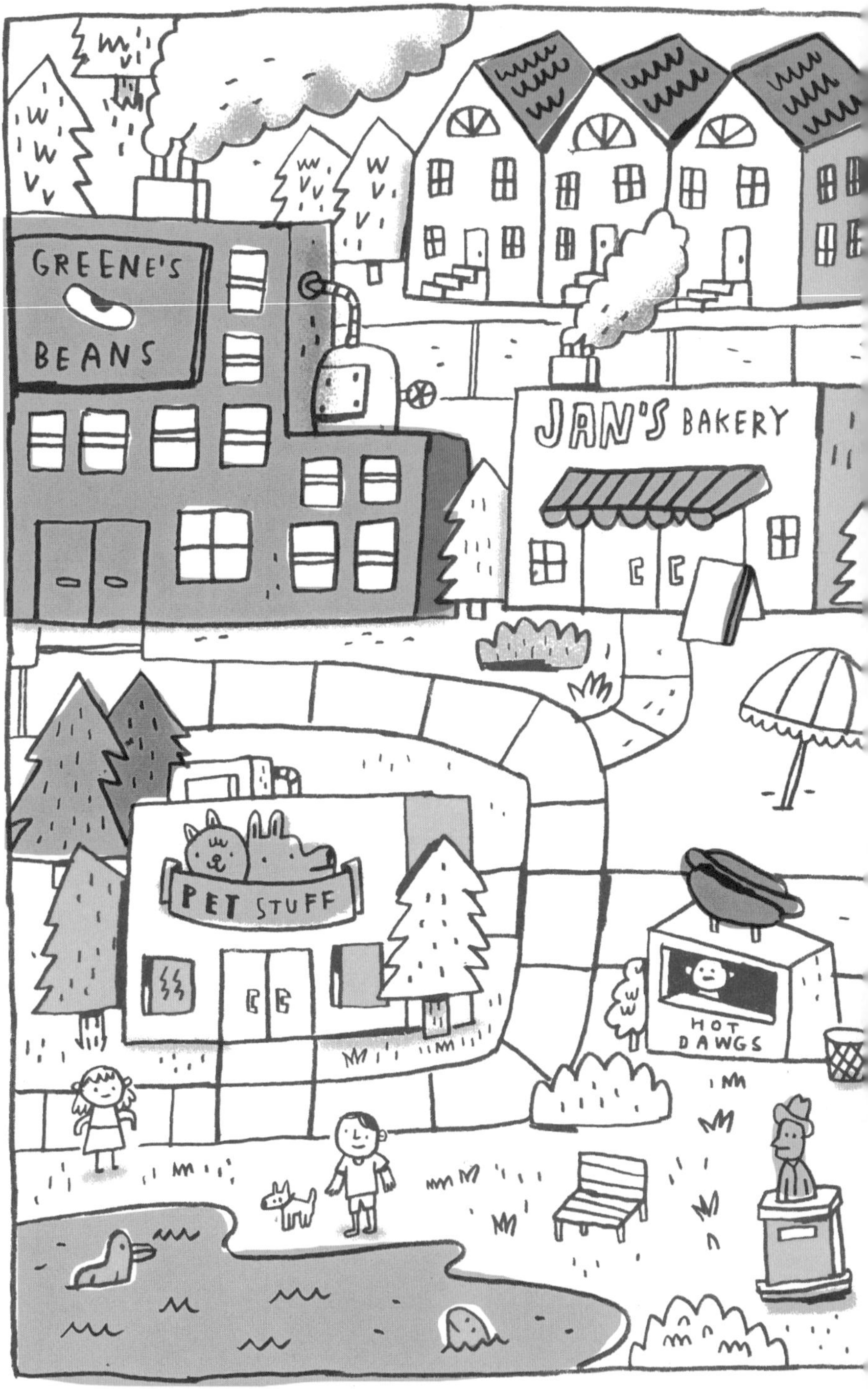
GREENE'S
BEANS
JAN'S BAKERY
PET STUFF
HOT
DAWGS

DRAW SOME OF THE PLACES IN THIS TOWN.

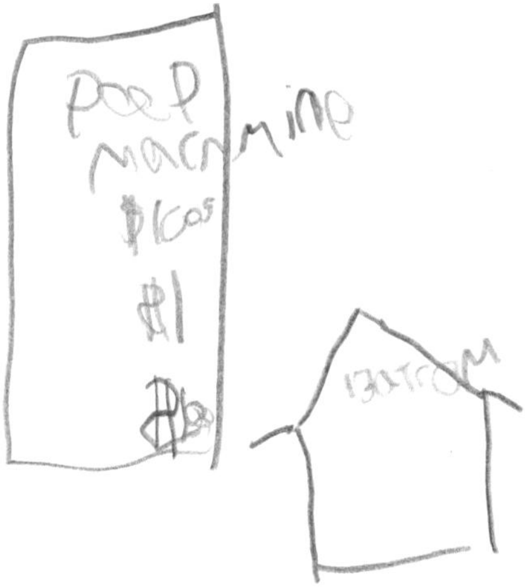

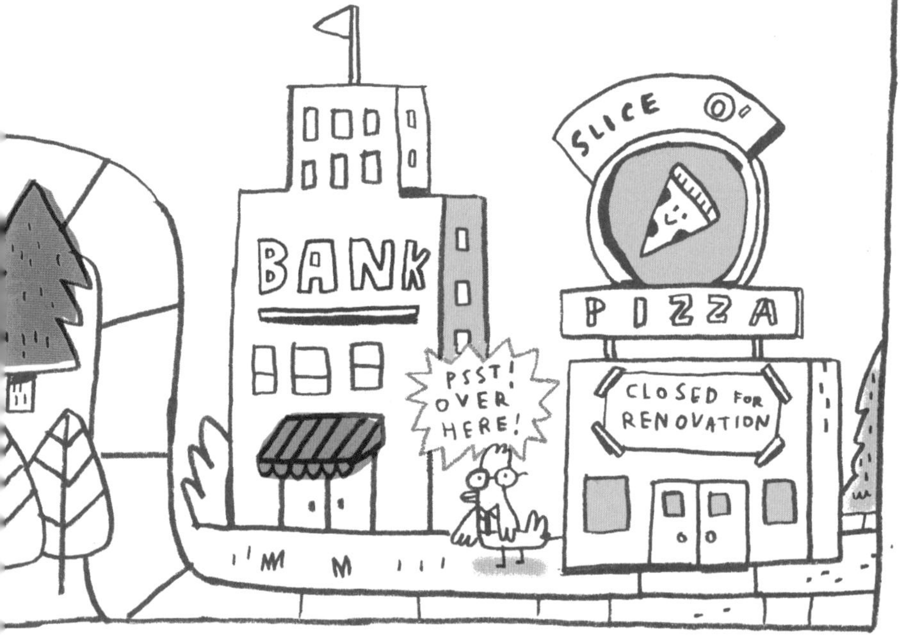

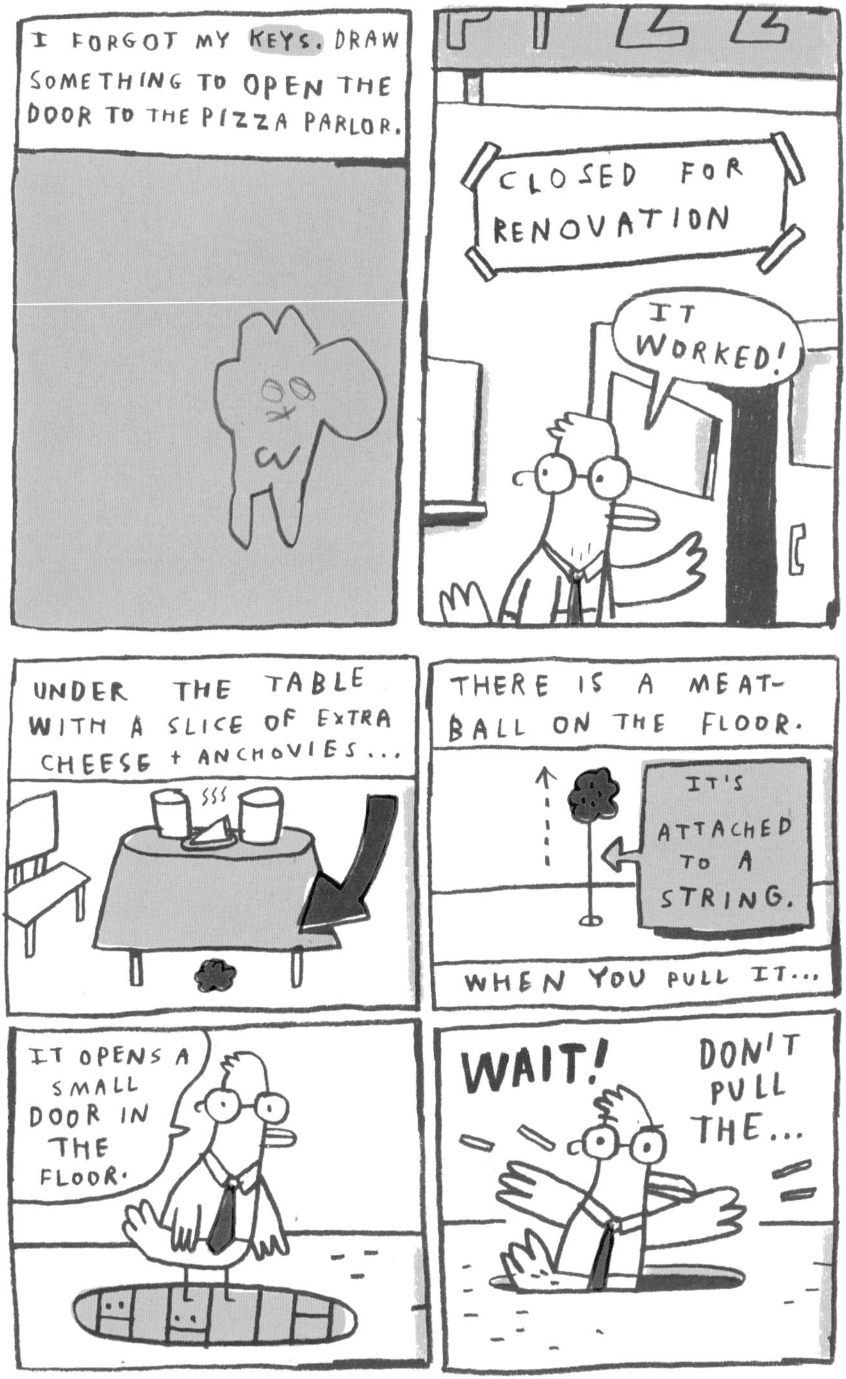
I FORGOT MY KEYS. DRAW SOMETHING TO OPEN THE DOOR TO THE PIZZA PARLOR.
CLOSED FOR RENOVATION
IT WORKED!
UNDER THE TABLE WITH A SLICE OF EXTRA CHEESE + ANCHOVIES...
THERE IS A MEAT-BALL ON THE FLOOR.
IT'S ATTACHED TO A STRING.
WHEN YOU PULL IT...
IT OPENS A SMALL DOOR IN THE FLOOR.
WAIT!
DON'T PULL THE...

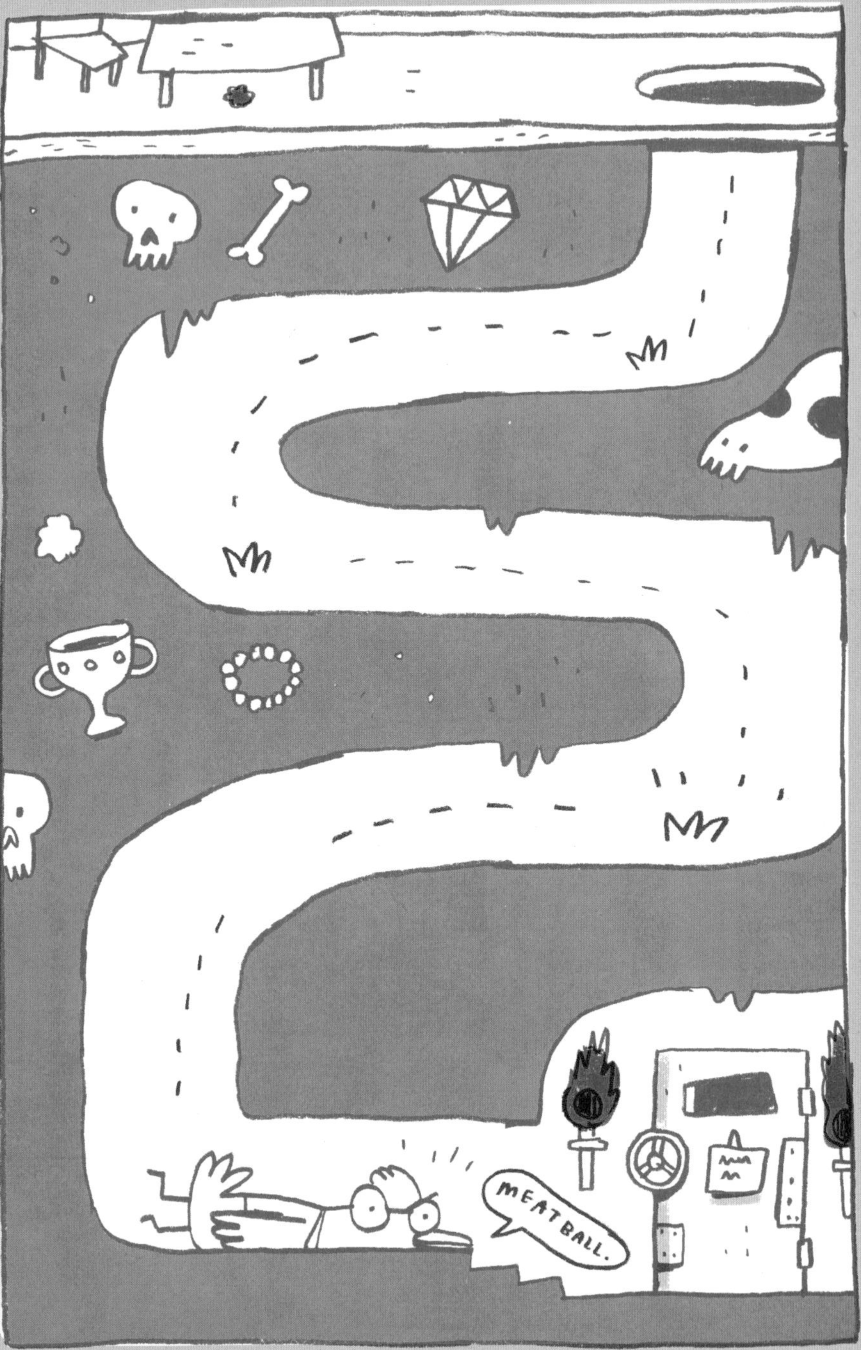
MEATBALL.

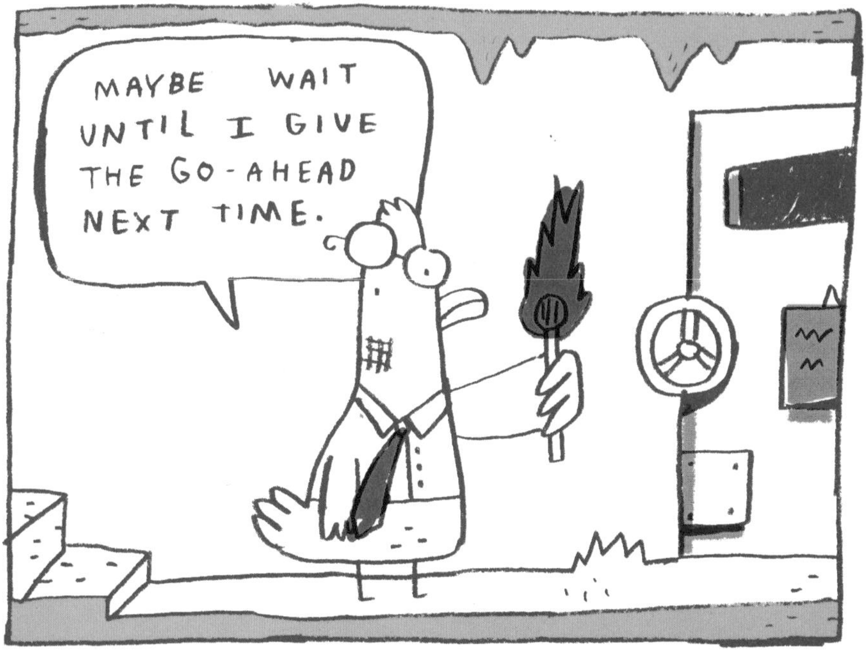
MAYBE WAIT UNTIL I GIVE THE GO-AHEAD NEXT TIME.

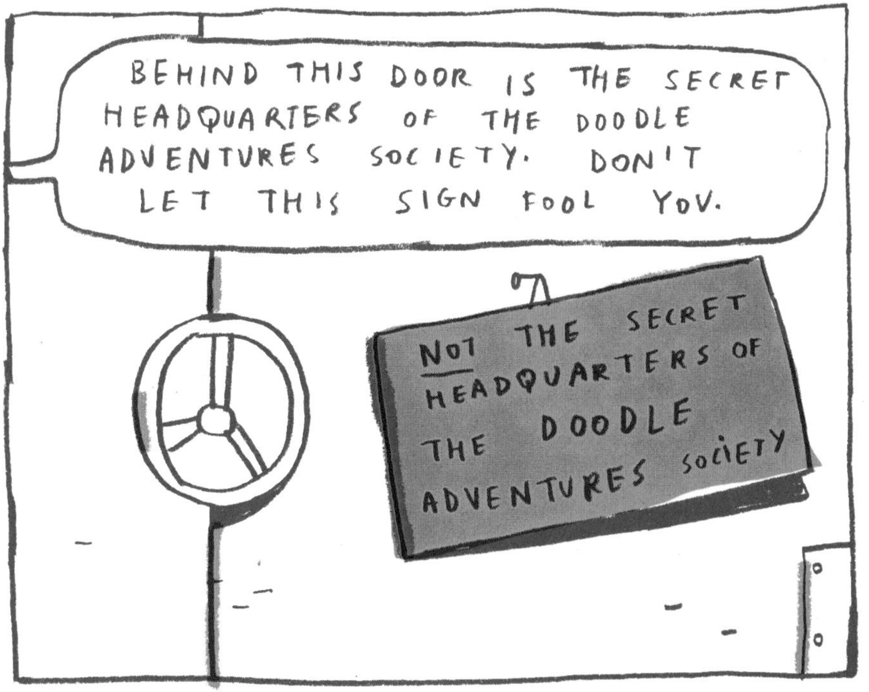
BEHIND THIS DOOR IS THE SECRET HEADQUARTERS OF THE DOODLE ADVENTURES SOCIETY. DON'T LET THIS SIGN FOOL YOU.
NOT THE SECRET HEADQUARTERS OF THE DOODLE ADVENTURES SOCIETY

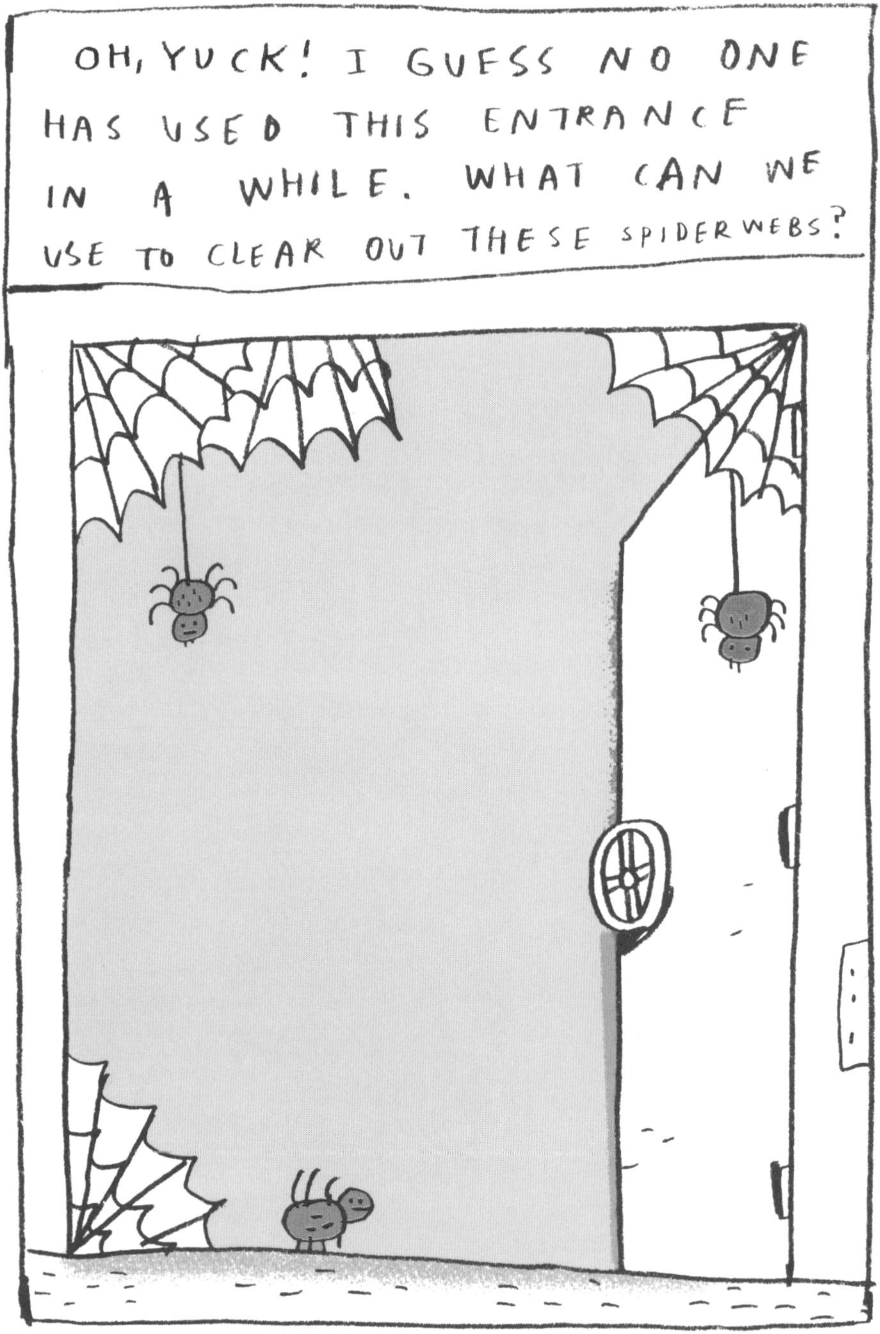
OH, YUCK! I GUESS NO ONE HAS USED THIS ENTRANCE IN A WHILE. WHAT CAN WE USE TO CLEAR OUT THESE SPIDERWEBS?

WELCOME TO THE HEADQUARTERS OF A SOCIETY THAT IS SO SECRET SOME OF OUR MEMBERS DON'T EVEN KNOW THEY ARE MEMBERS. THE DA SOCIETY IS MADE UP OF ONLY THE MOST PRESTIGIOUS AND SKILLED EXPLORERS ON THE PLANET.

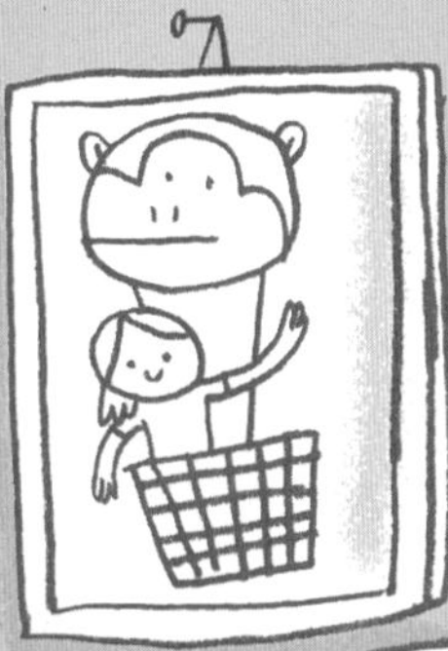

MARCIA PRIDDY

THE FIRST PERSON TO FLY AROUND THE WORLD IN A HOT AIR BABOON.

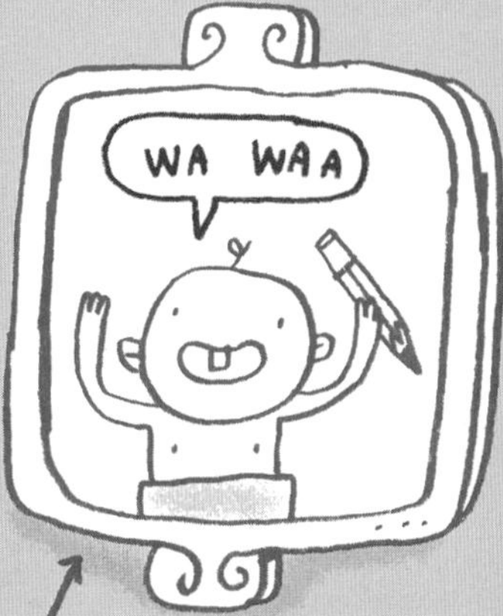
WA WAA

ALLISTER J. LINGUINI

DISCOVERED THE FOUNTAIN OF YOUTH IN 1743.

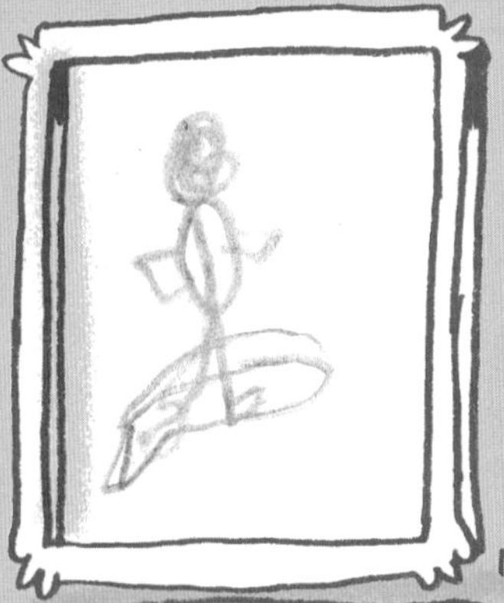

CALLIE THRASHER

A SURFING EXPLORER WHO ONCE PUNCHED A SHARK IN THE FACE. SHE APOLOGIZED, AND NOW THEY'RE BFFS.

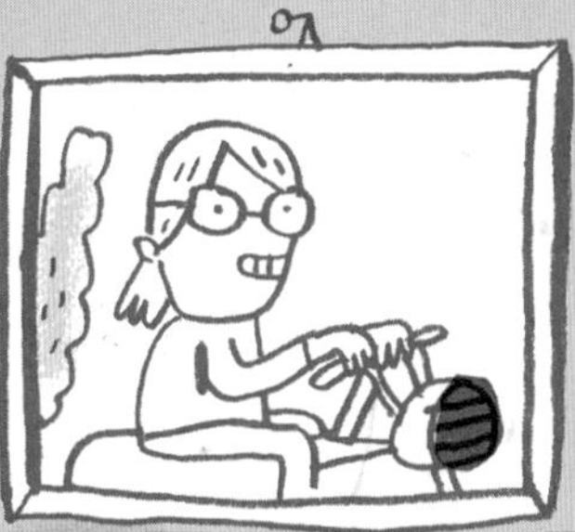

KATHLEEN WHEELIE

JUMPED OVER THE BLAND CANYON ON A MOTORCYCLE.

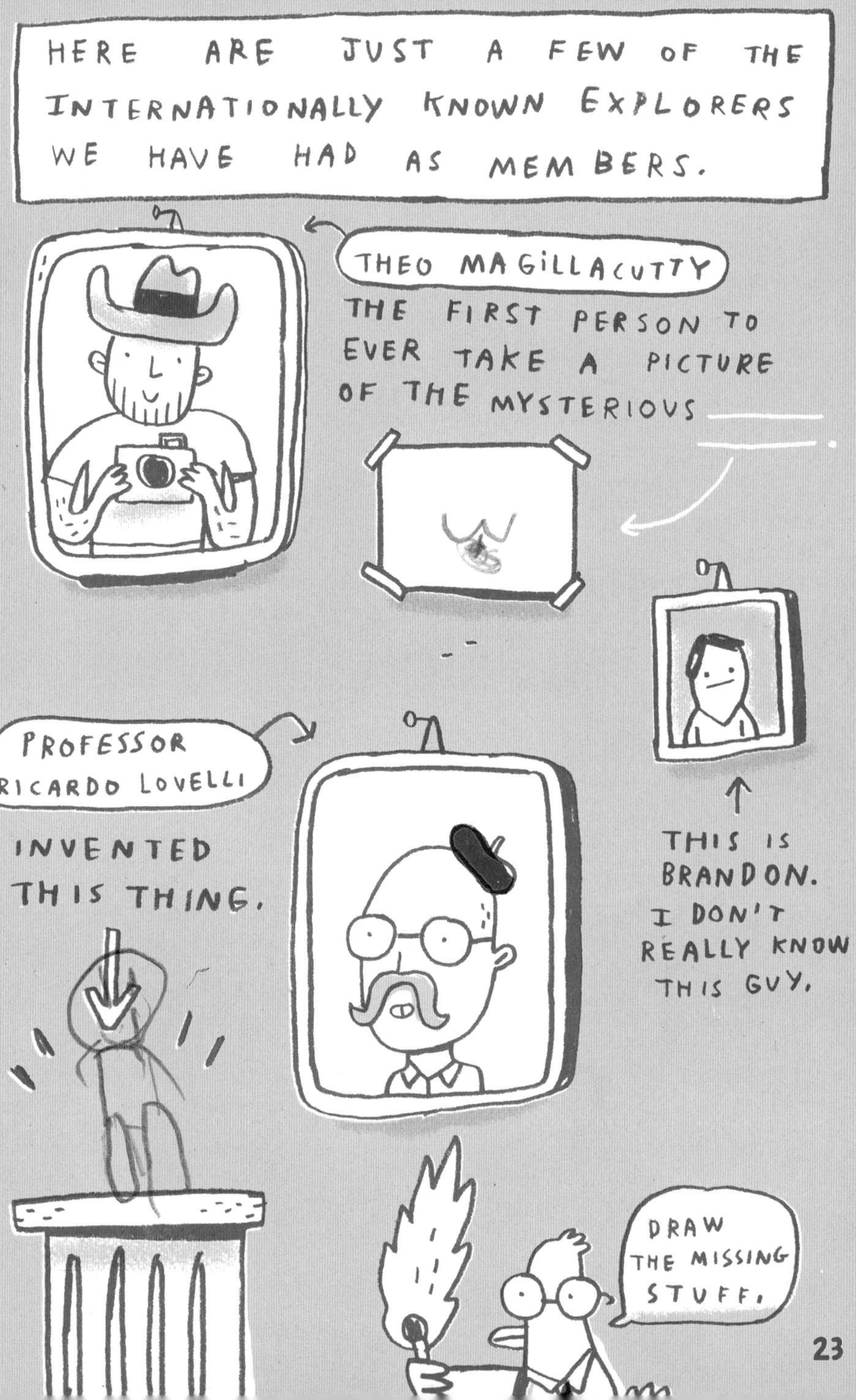
HERE ARE JUST A FEW OF THE INTERNATIONALLY KNOWN EXPLORERS WE HAVE HAD AS MEMBERS.
THEO MAGILLACUTTY
THE FIRST PERSON TO EVER TAKE A PICTURE OF THE MYSTERIOUS ________.
PROFESSOR RICARDO LOVELLI
INVENTED THIS THING.
THIS IS BRANDON. I DON'T REALLY KNOW THIS GUY.
DRAW THE MISSING STUFF.

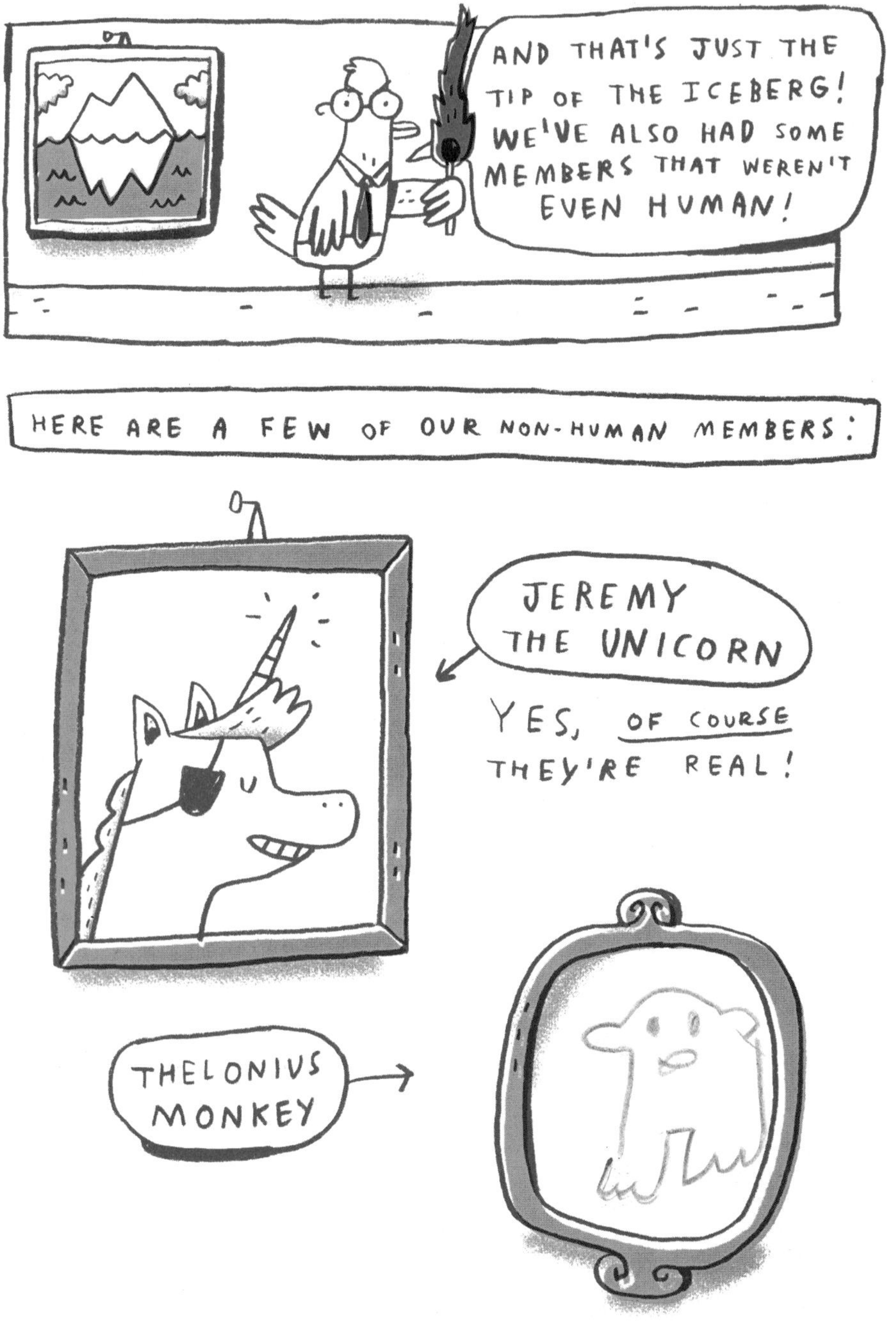
AND THAT'S JUST THE TIP OF THE ICEBERG! WE'VE ALSO HAD SOME MEMBERS THAT WEREN'T EVEN HUMAN!
HERE ARE A FEW OF OUR NON-HUMAN MEMBERS:
JEREMY THE UNICORN
YES, OF COURSE THEY'RE REAL!
THELONIUS MONKEY

SALLY THE NARWHAL

THE UNICORN OF THE SEA!

SIR ALEXANDER STIGLIANO

THE TINY LADYBUG EXPLORER.

IF YOU THOUGHT ONLY HUMANS CAN BE ADVENTURERS, THEN YOU PROBABLY FORGOT YOUR GUIDE IS A TALKING DUCK!

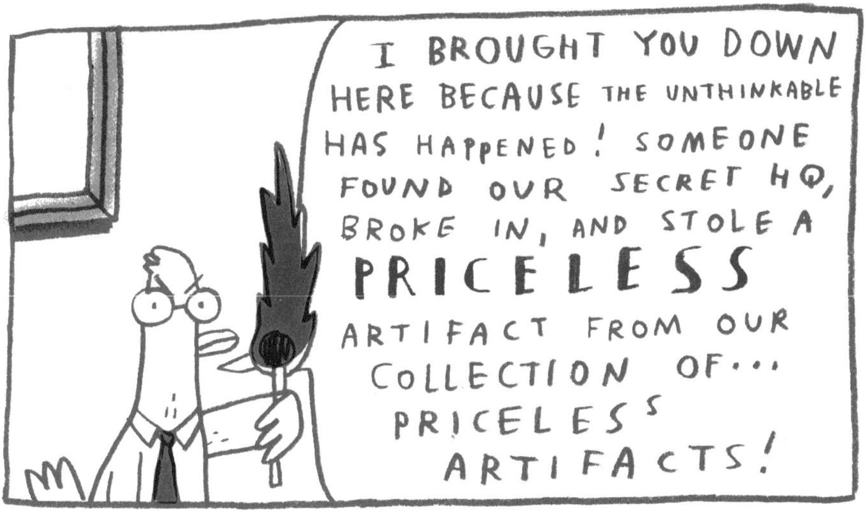
I BROUGHT YOU DOWN HERE BECAUSE THE UNTHINKABLE HAS HAPPENED! SOMEONE FOUND OUR SECRET HQ, BROKE IN, AND STOLE A PRICELESS ARTIFACT FROM OUR COLLECTION OF... PRICELESS ARTIFACTS!

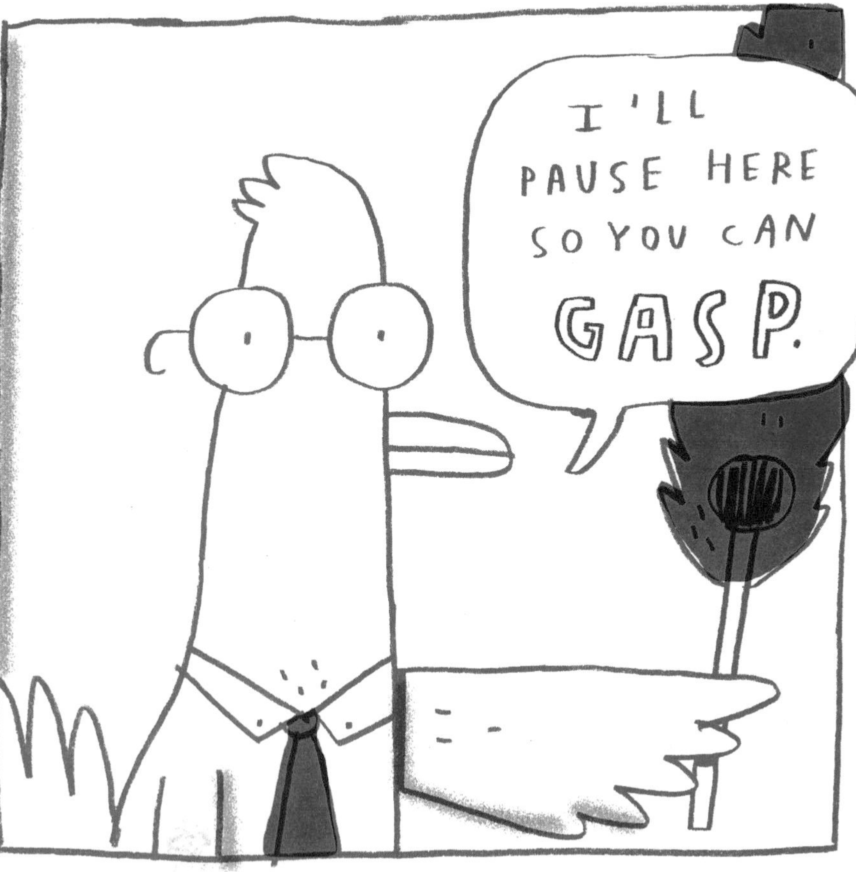
I'LL PAUSE HERE SO YOU CAN GASP.

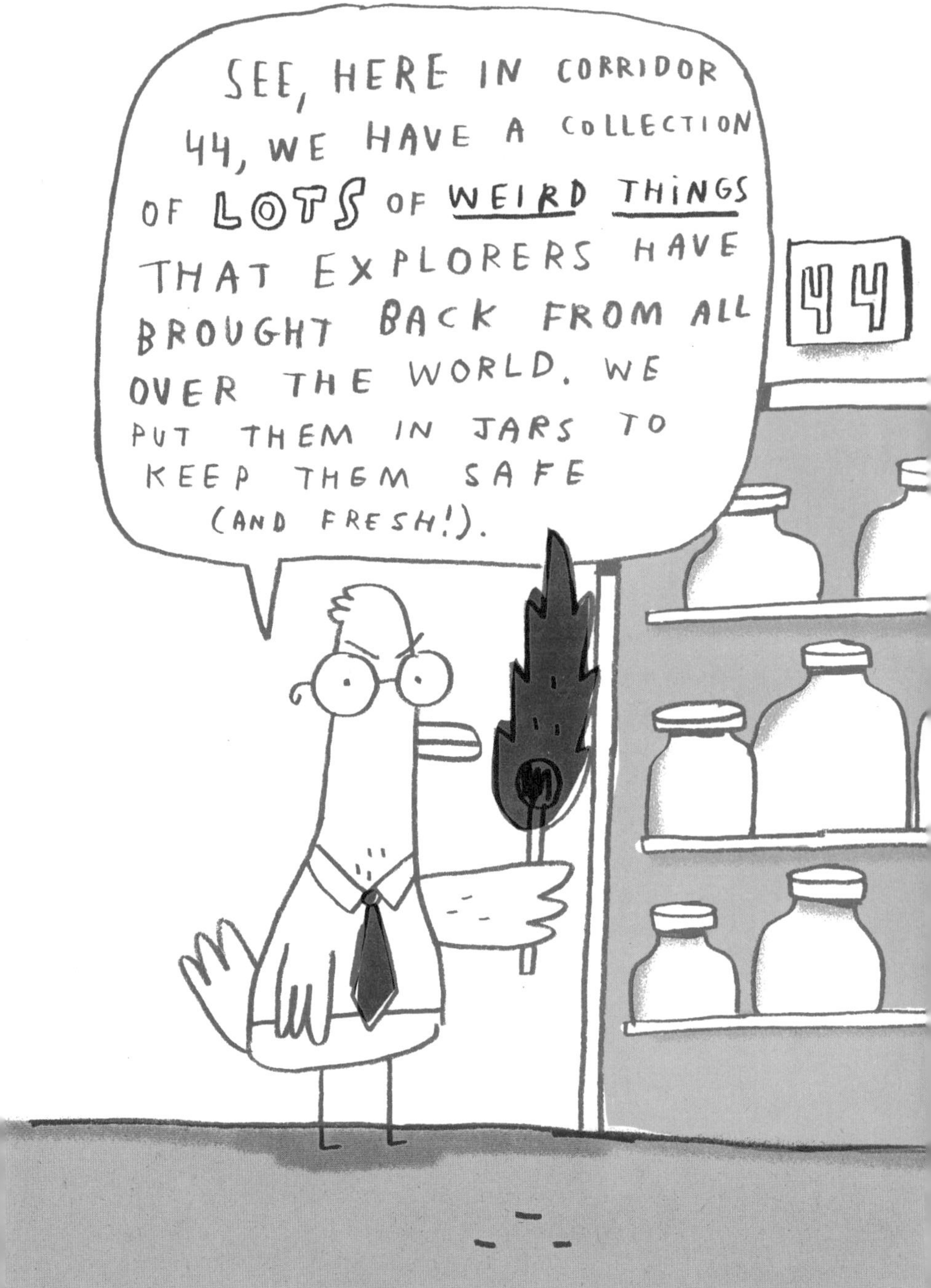
SEE, HERE IN CORRIDOR 44, WE HAVE A COLLECTION OF LOTS OF WEIRD THINGS THAT EXPLORERS HAVE BROUGHT BACK FROM ALL OVER THE WORLD. WE PUT THEM IN JARS TO KEEP THEM SAFE (AND FRESH!).
44

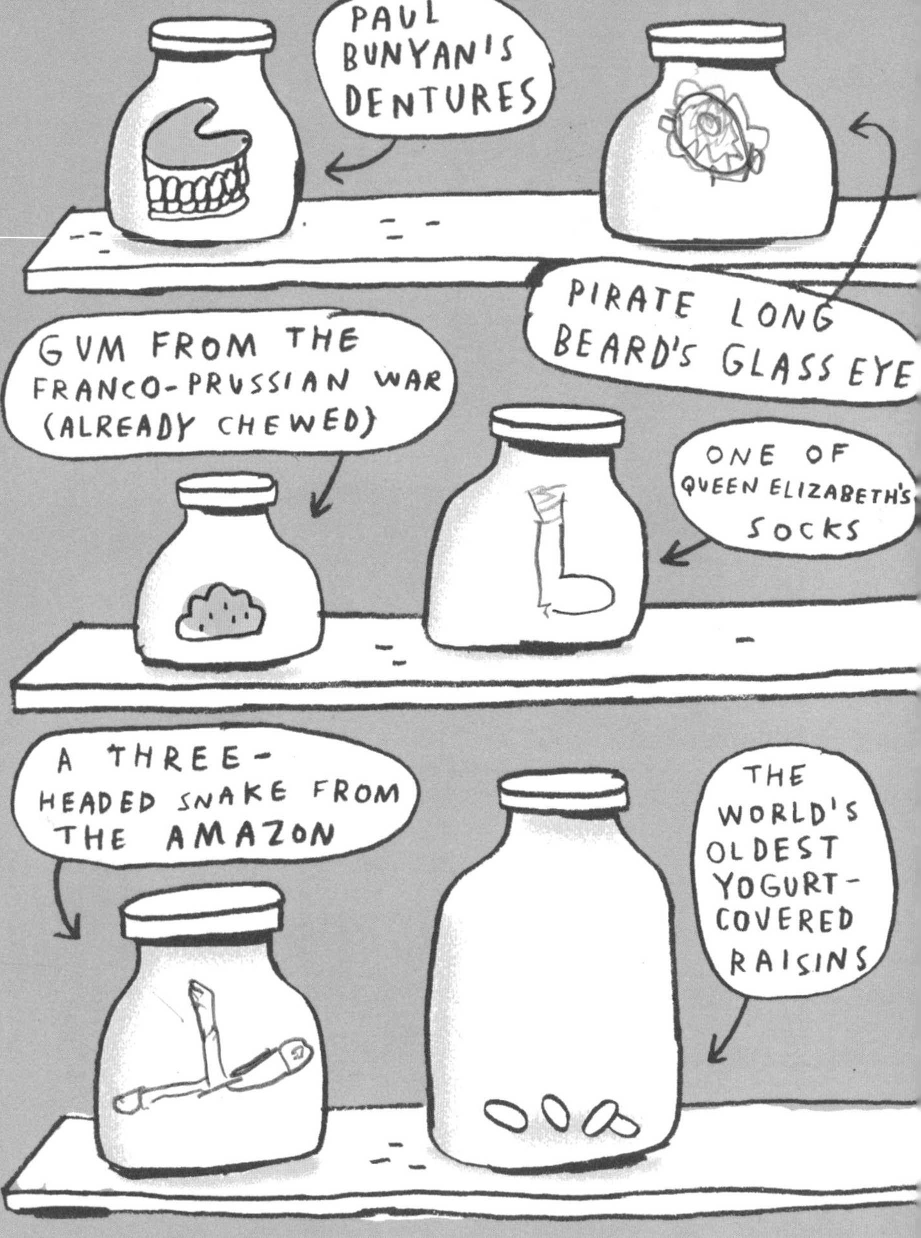
PAUL BUNYAN'S DENTURES
PIRATE LONG BEARD'S GLASS EYE
GUM FROM THE FRANCO-PRUSSIAN WAR (ALREADY CHEWED)
ONE OF QUEEN ELIZABETH'S SOCKS
A THREE-HEADED SNAKE FROM THE AMAZON
THE WORLD'S OLDEST YOGURT-COVERED RAISINS

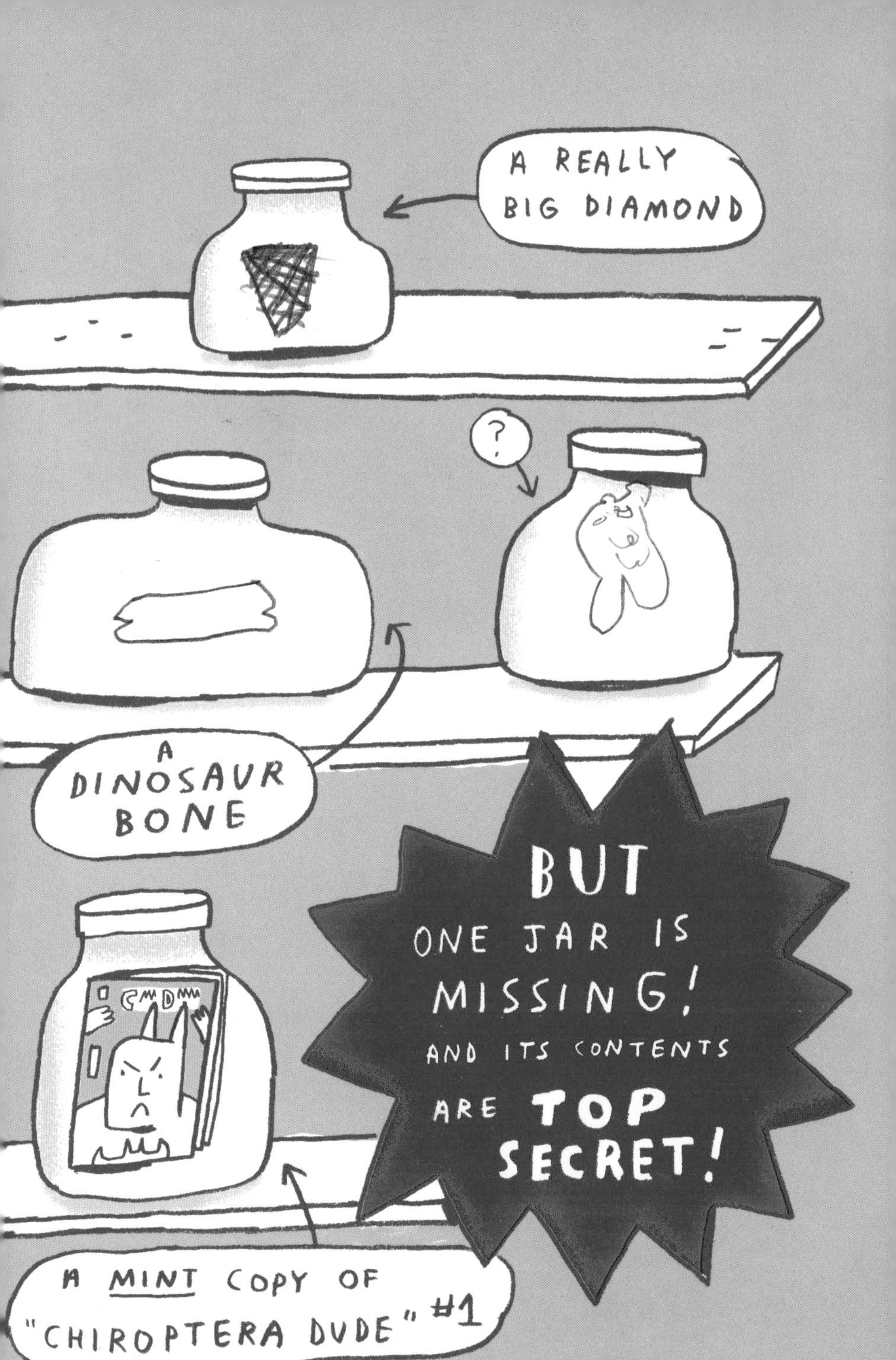

A REALLY BIG DIAMOND
?
A DINOSAUR BONE
BUT ONE JAR IS MISSING! AND ITS CONTENTS ARE TOP SECRET!
A MINT COPY OF "CHIROPTERA DUDE" #1

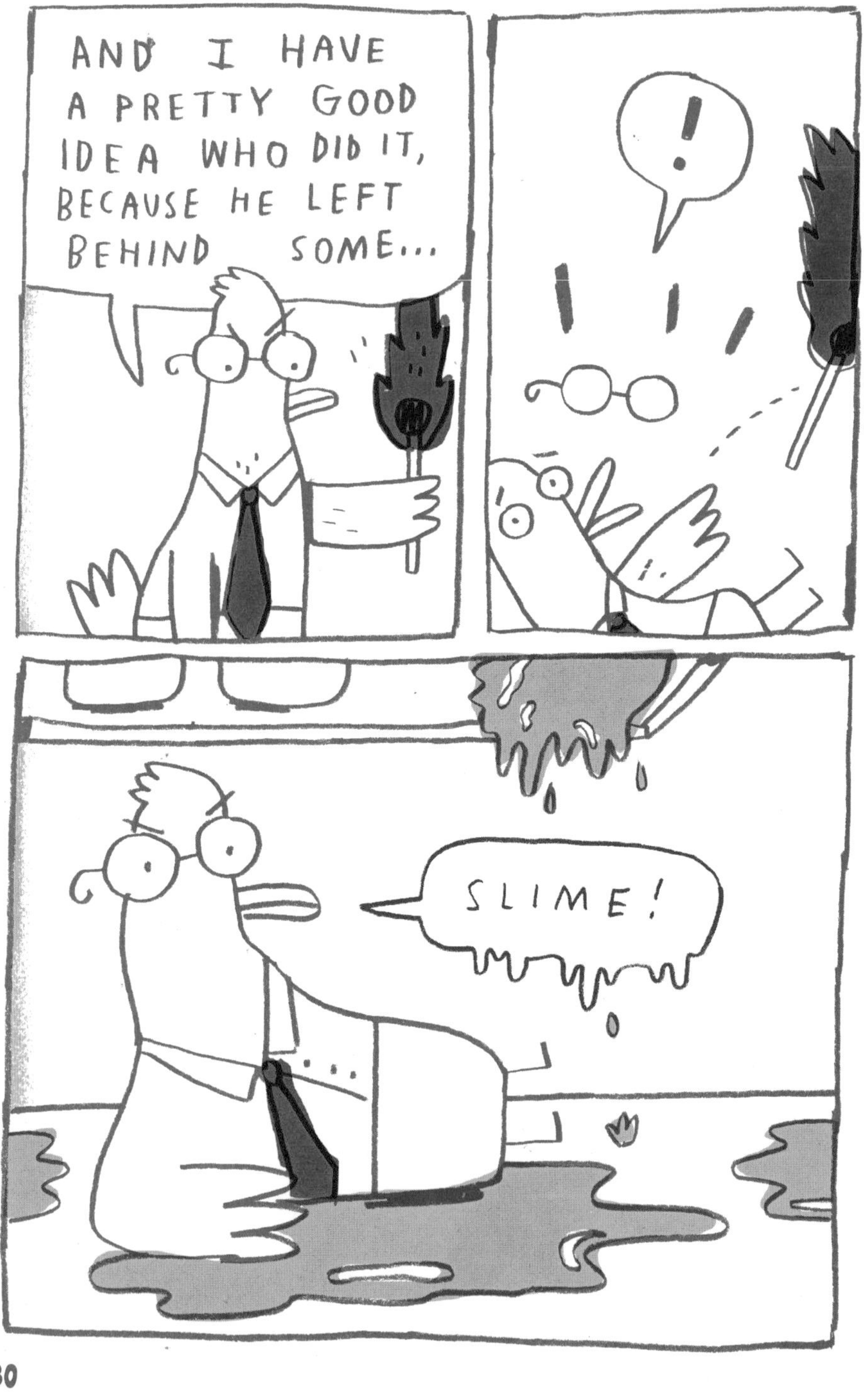
AND I HAVE A PRETTY GOOD IDEA WHO DID IT, BECAUSE HE LEFT BEHIND SOME...
!
SLIME!

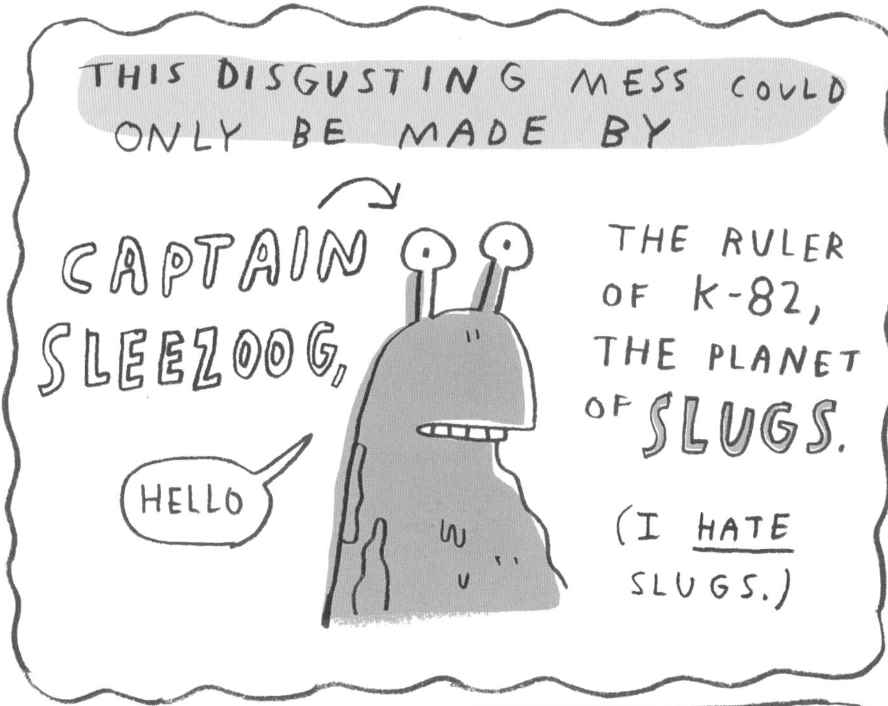
THIS DISGUSTING MESS COULD ONLY BE MADE BY
CAPTAIN SLEEZOOG,
HELLO
THE RULER OF K-82, THE PLANET OF SLUGS.
(I HATE SLUGS.)

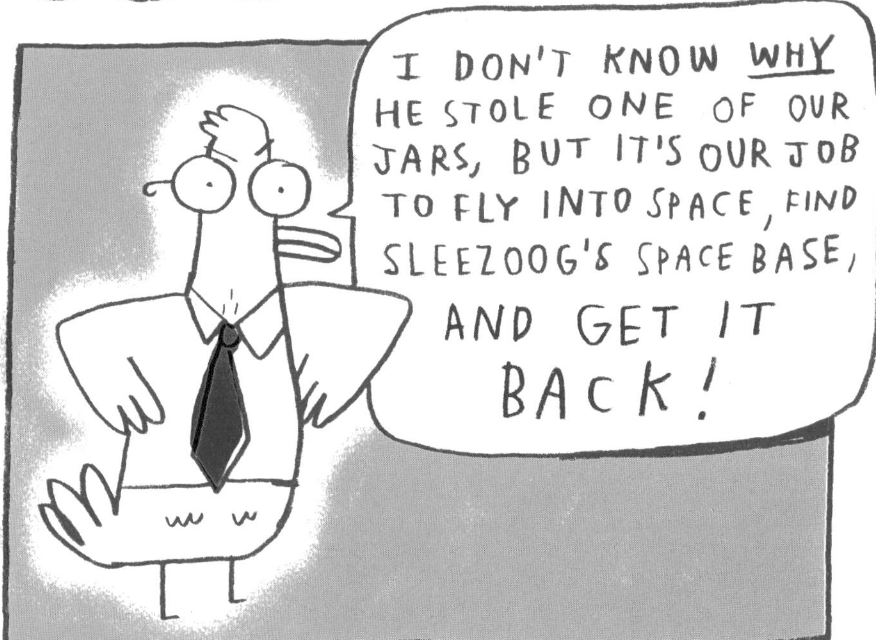
I DON'T KNOW WHY HE STOLE ONE OF OUR JARS, BUT IT'S OUR JOB TO FLY INTO SPACE, FIND SLEEZOOG'S SPACE BASE, AND GET IT BACK!

NOW THAT YOU KNOW THE DETAILS OF THE MISSION, WHAT DO YOU SAY? WILL YOU JOIN ME?

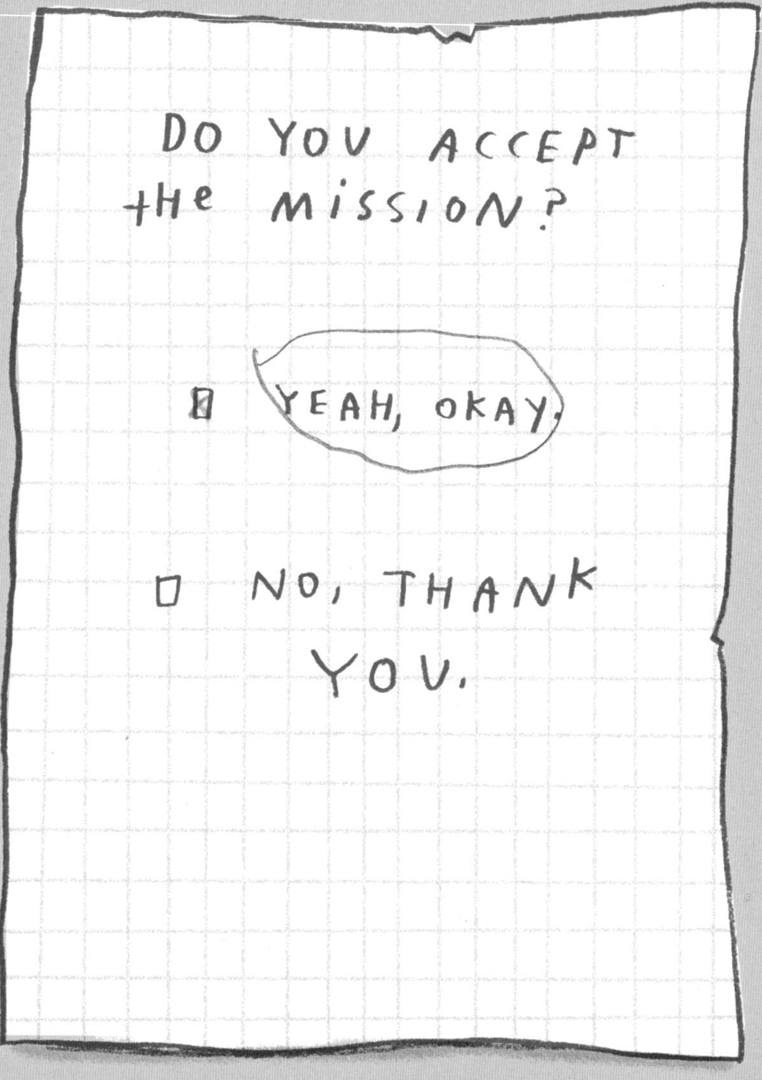
DO YOU ACCEPT the MISSION?
☐ YEAH, OKAY.
☐ NO, THANK YOU.

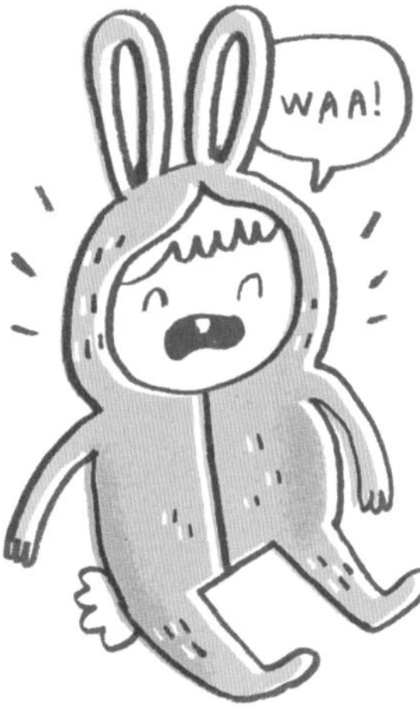
WAA!

IF YOU MARKED **NO**, YOU ARE ALLOWED TO PUT ON SOME FLUFFY BUNNY PAJAMAS RIGHT NOW AND DRINK SOME WARM MILK AND GO STRAIGHT TO BED, BECAUSE YOU ARE A **BIG BABY**.

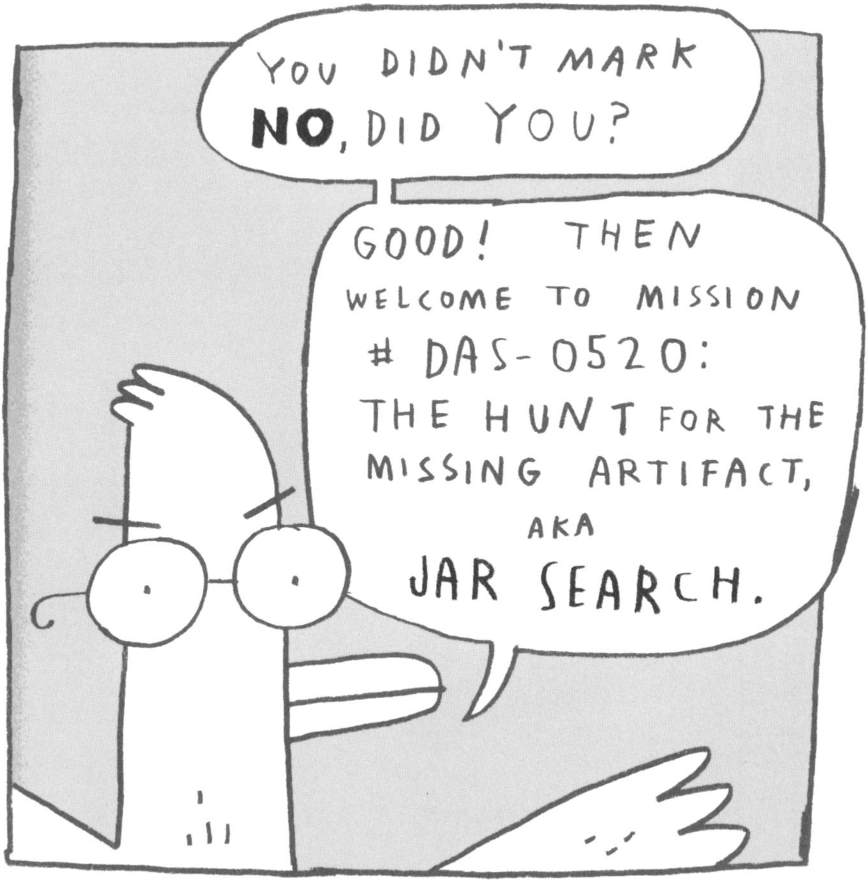
YOU DIDN'T MARK **NO**, DID YOU?
GOOD! THEN WELCOME TO MISSION # DAS-0520: THE HUNT FOR THE MISSING ARTIFACT, AKA JAR SEARCH.

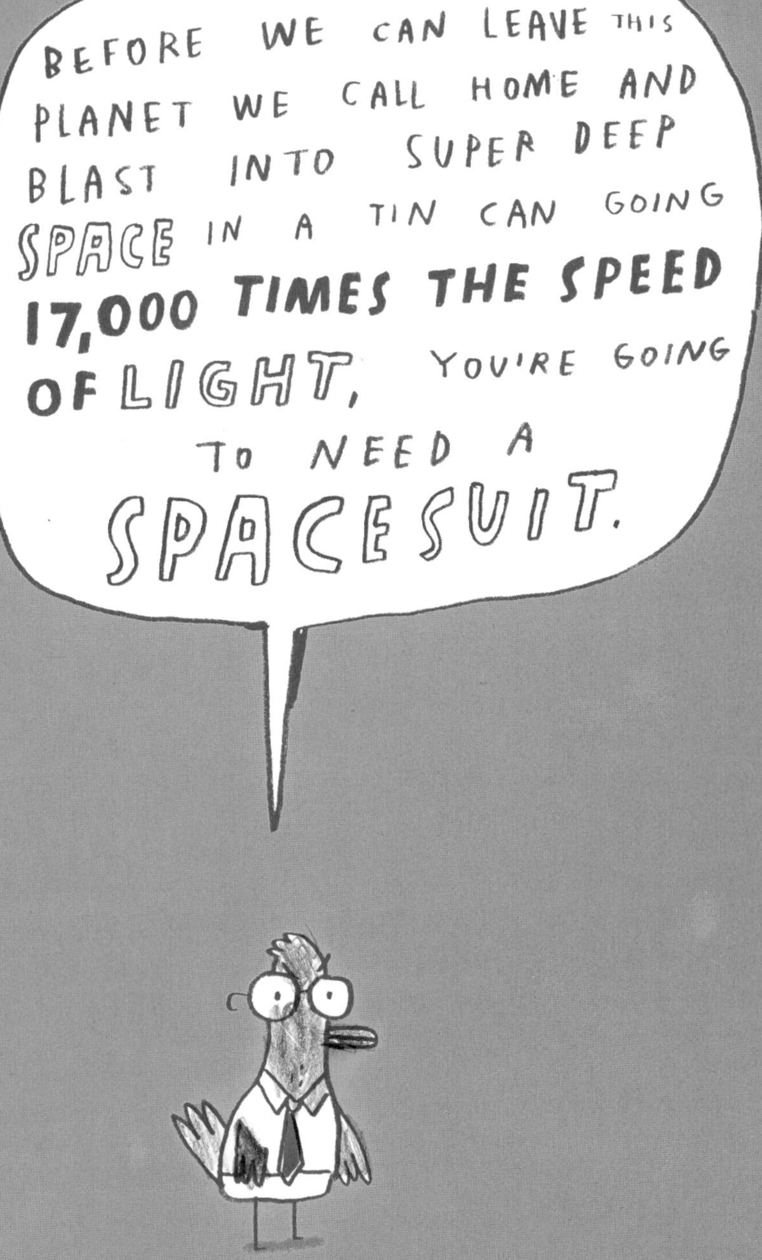
BEFORE WE CAN LEAVE THIS PLANET WE CALL HOME AND BLAST INTO SUPER DEEP SPACE IN A TIN CAN GOING 17,000 TIMES THE SPEED OF LIGHT, YOU'RE GOING TO NEED A SPACESUIT.

USE SOME OF THE OBJECTS FROM THIS PAGE TO COMPLETE YOUR SUIT (OR JUST MAKE THE WHOLE THING UP).

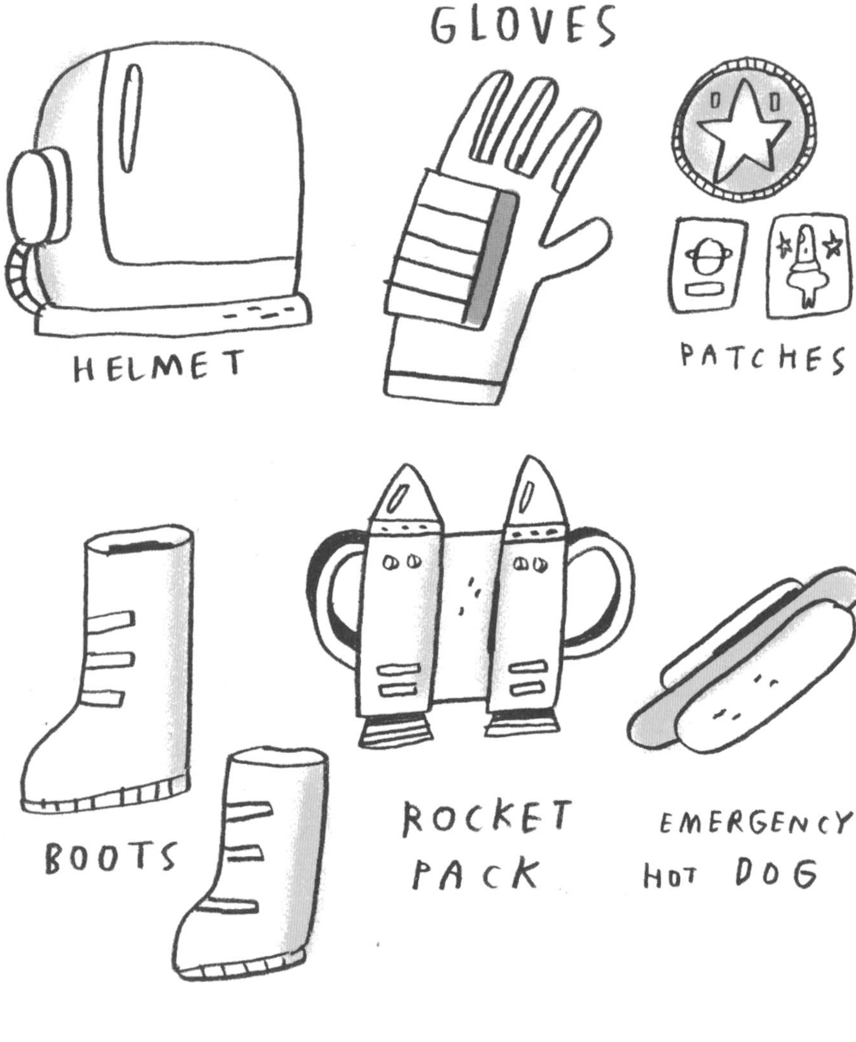
GLOVES
HELMET
PATCHES
BOOTS
ROCKET PACK
EMERGENCY HOT DOG

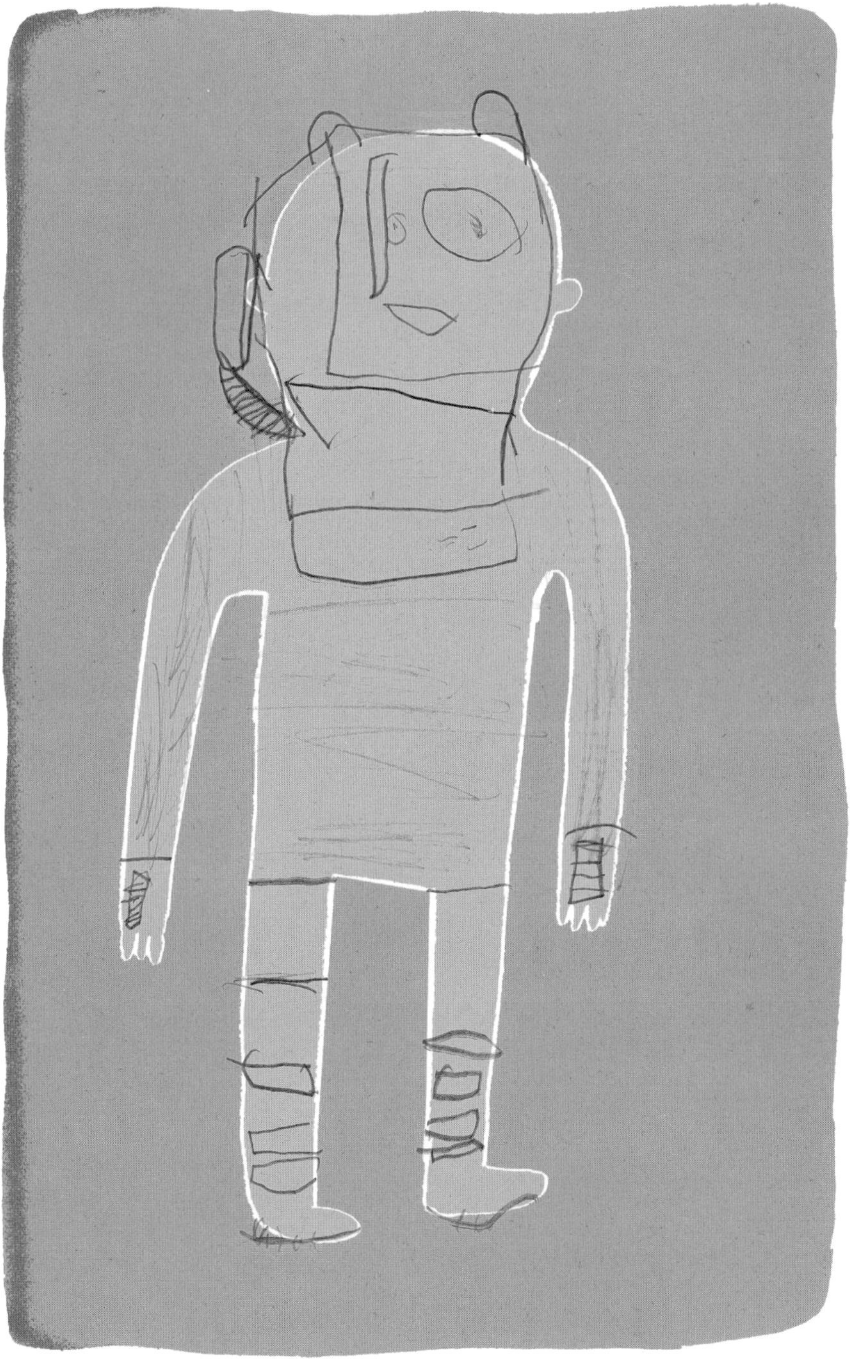

NEXT, WE NEED TO PACK ALL OF OUR SUPPLIES FOR SUCH A LONG TRIP.

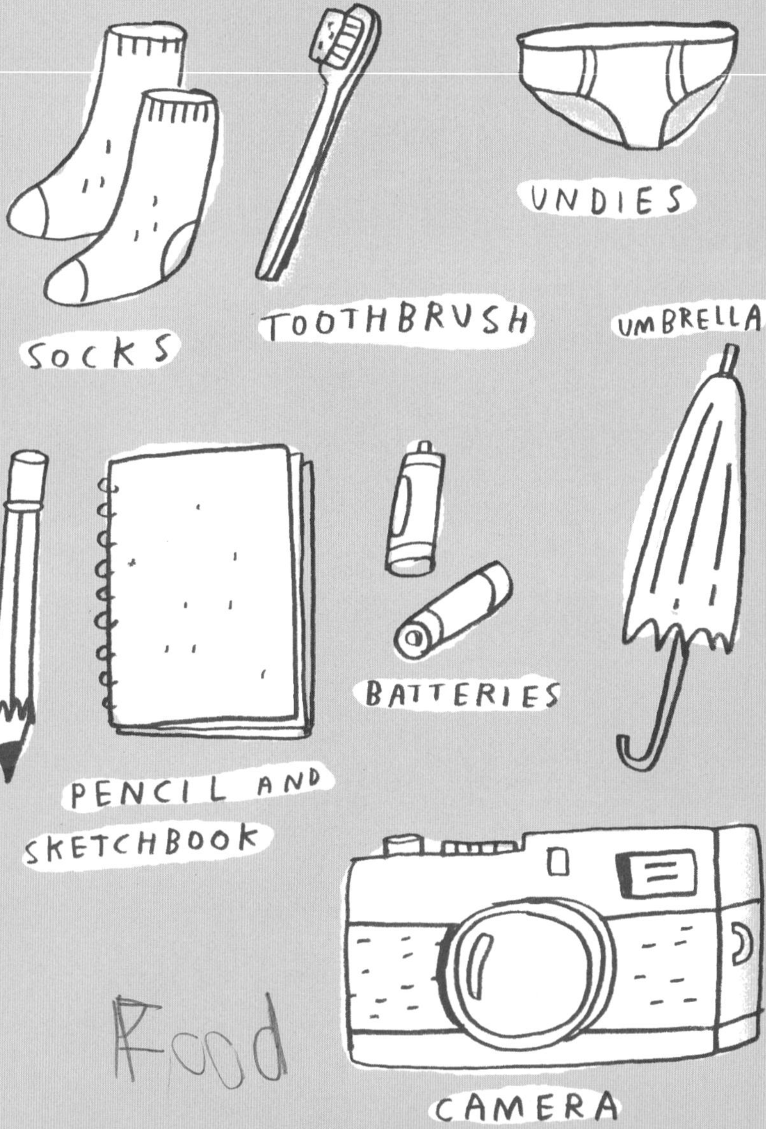
UNDIES
SOCKS
TOOTHBRUSH
UMBRELLA
BATTERIES
PENCIL AND SKETCHBOOK
Food
CAMERA

WHAT ELSE SHOULD WE BRING?

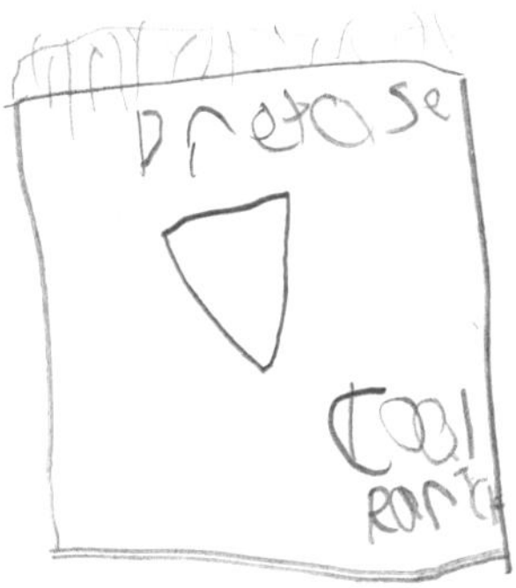

Cool

Closse

DON'T FORGET THE SNACKS!

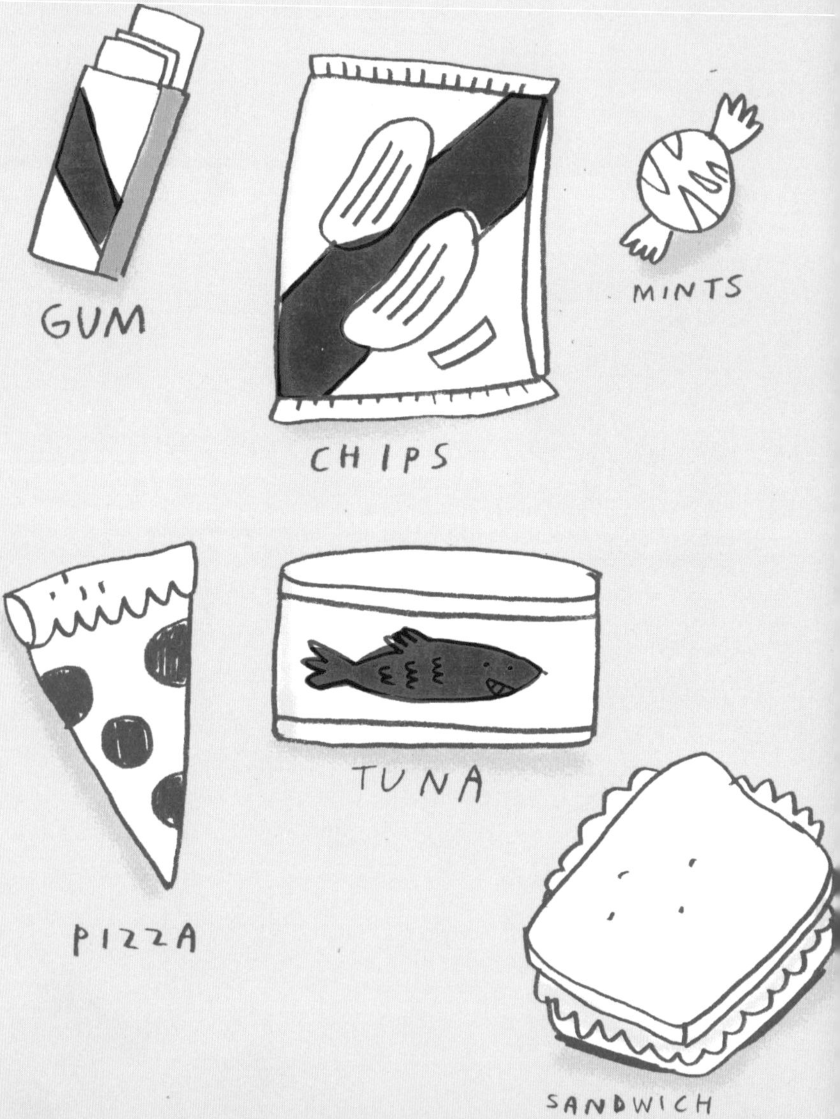
GUM
CHIPS
MINTS
PIZZA
TUNA
SANDWICH

WHAT WOULD YOU LIKE
TO BRING TO EAT?

AND MOST IMPORTANTLY WE NEED...

A ROCKET SHIP!

HOW MANY OF THESE ITEMS CAN YOU USE IN YOUR ROCKET DESIGN?

LIGHTBULB

BOLTS

BANDAGES

TAPE

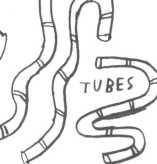

TUBES

FISHBOWL

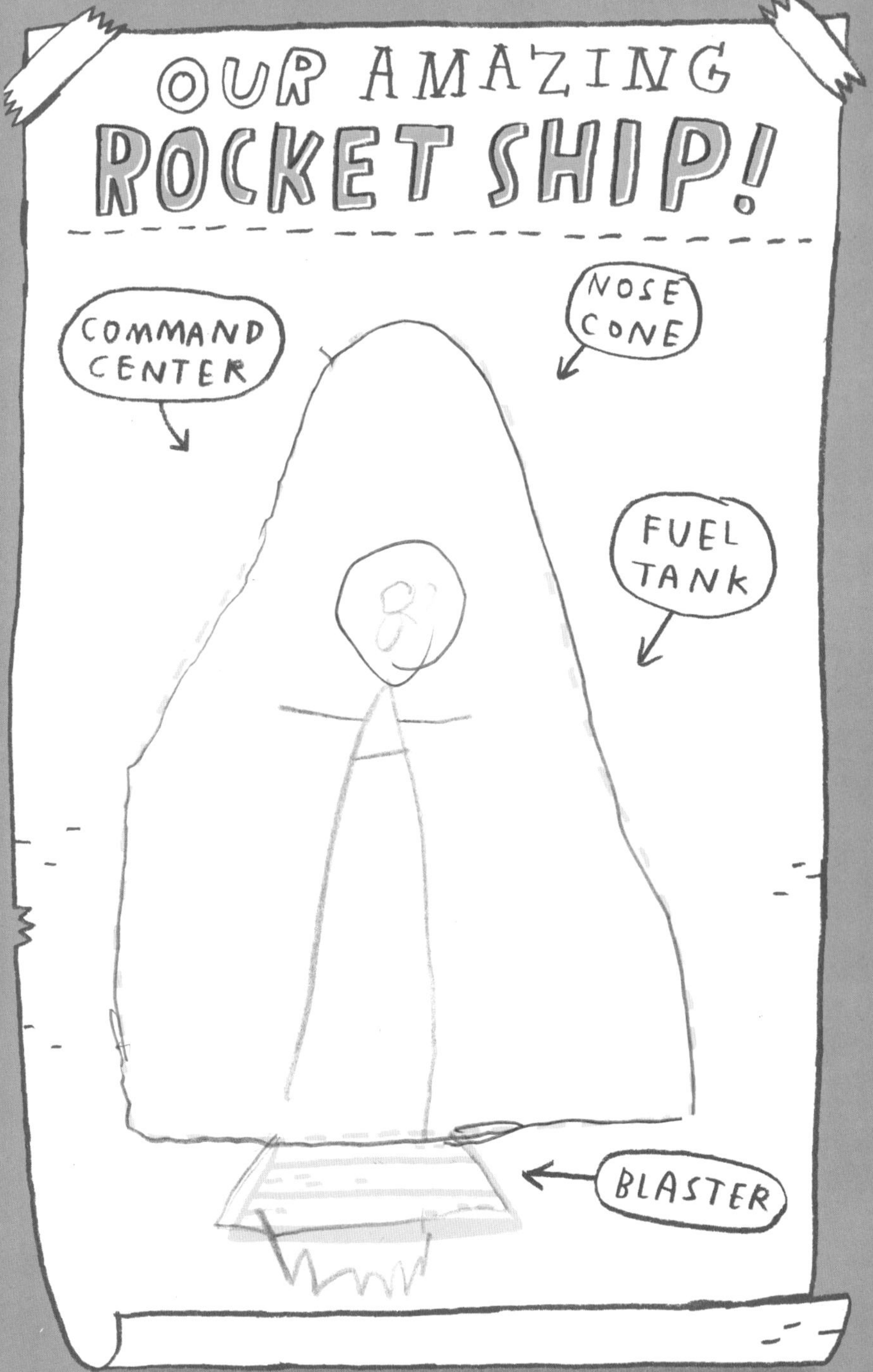
OUR AMAZING
ROCKET SHIP!
COMMAND CENTER
NOSE CONE
FUEL TANK
BLASTER

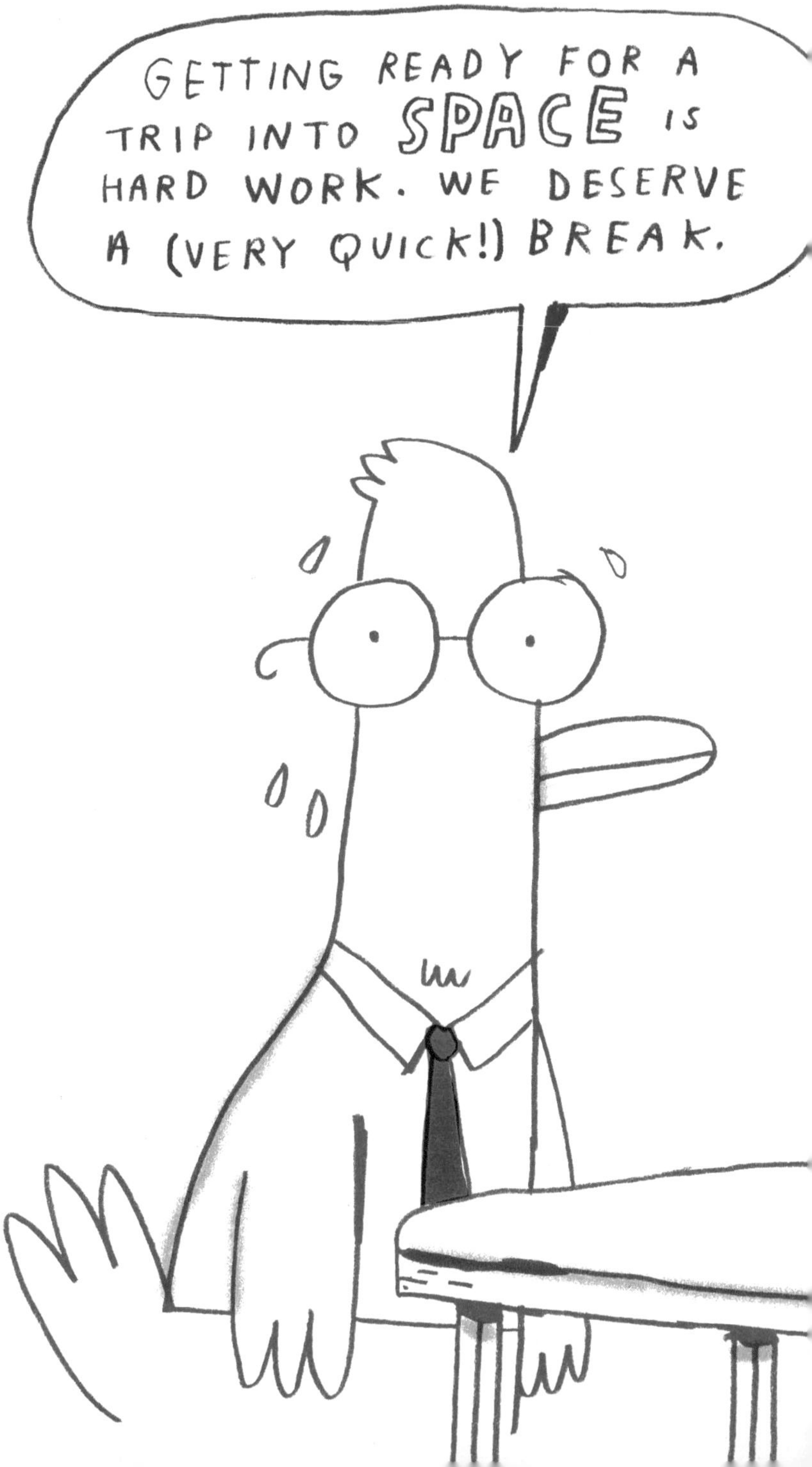
GETTING READY FOR A TRIP INTO SPACE IS HARD WORK. WE DESERVE A (VERY QUICK!) BREAK.

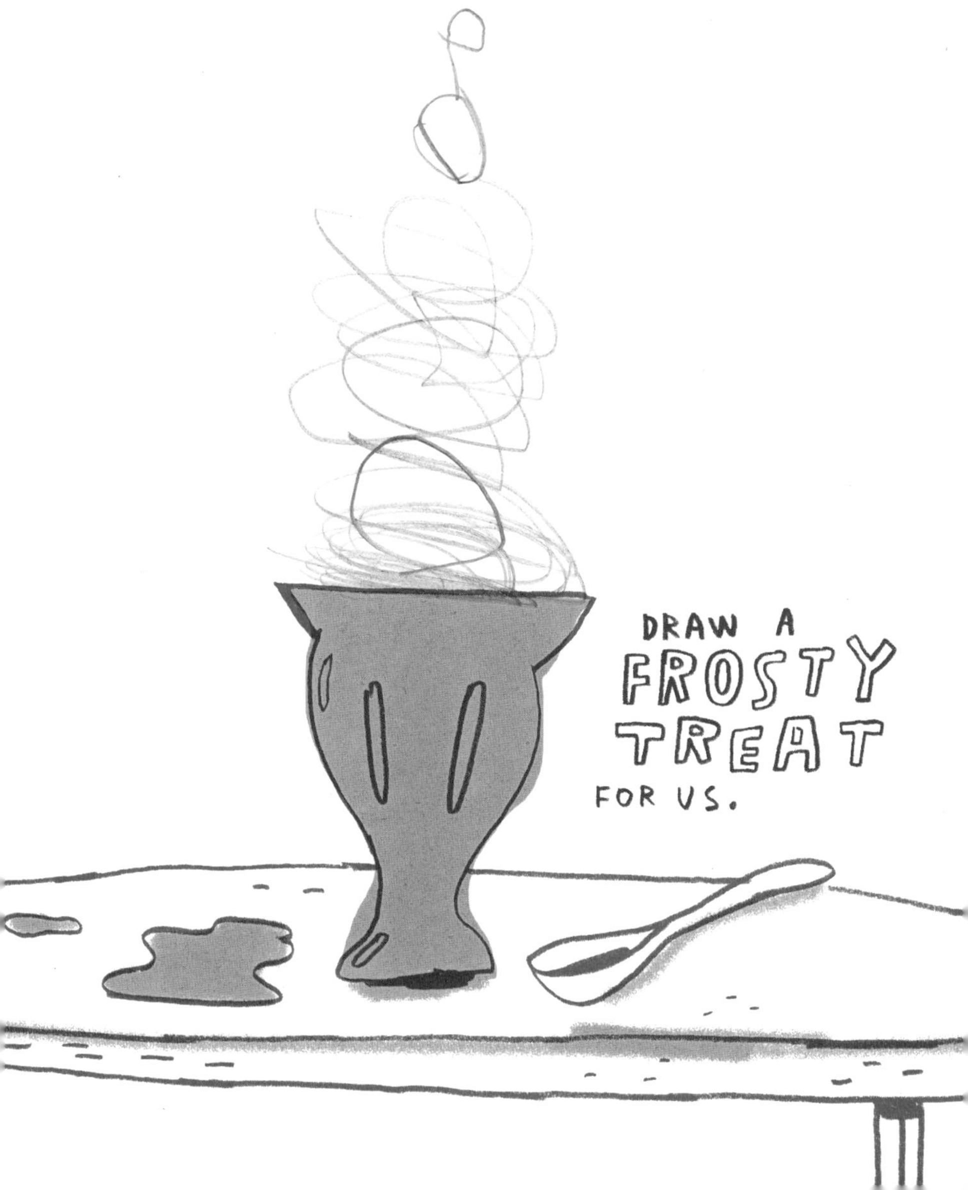
DRAW A
FROSTY
TREAT
FOR US.

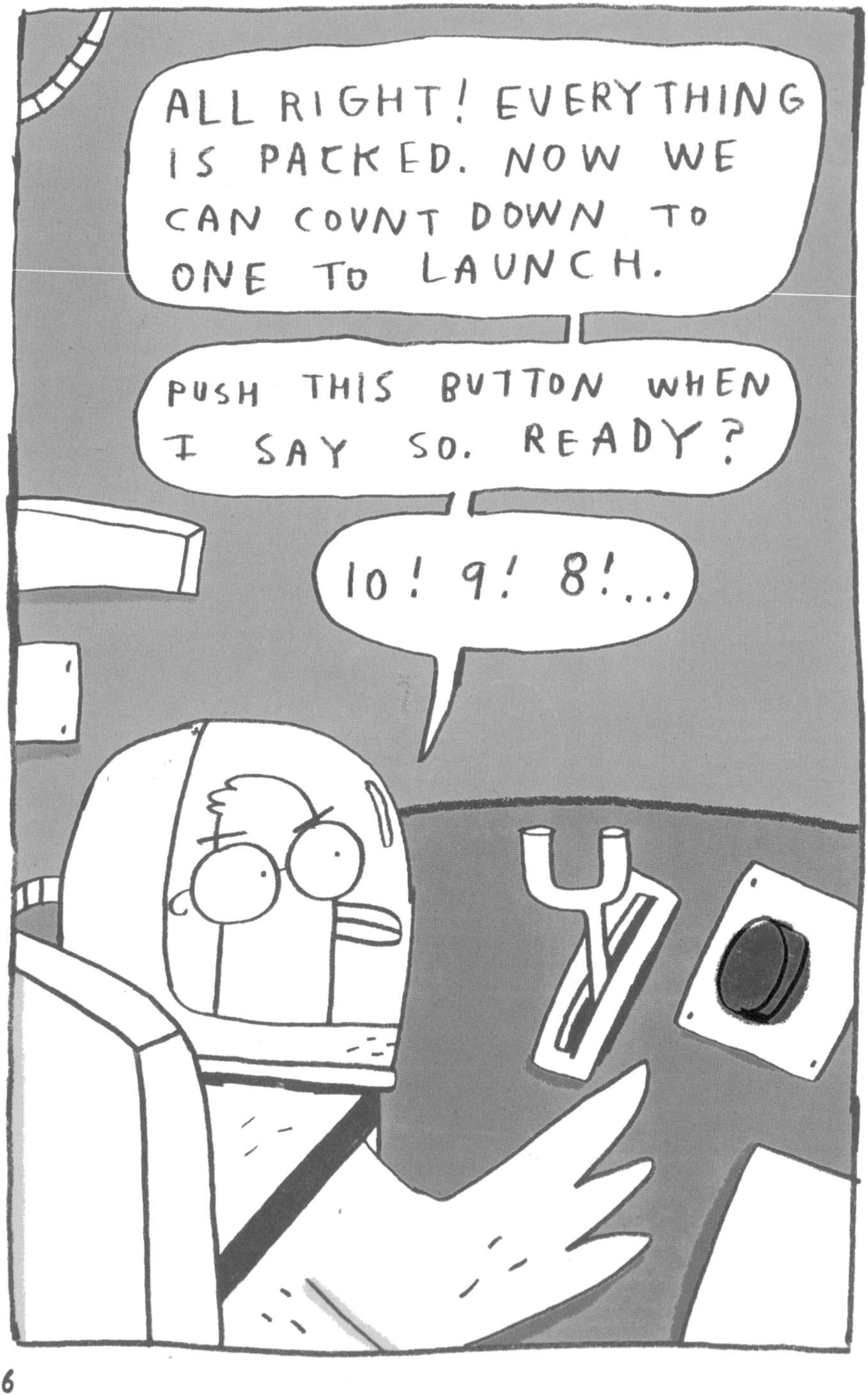
ALL RIGHT! EVERYTHING IS PACKED. NOW WE CAN COUNT DOWN TO ONE TO LAUNCH.
PUSH THIS BUTTON WHEN I SAY SO. READY?
10! 9! 8!...

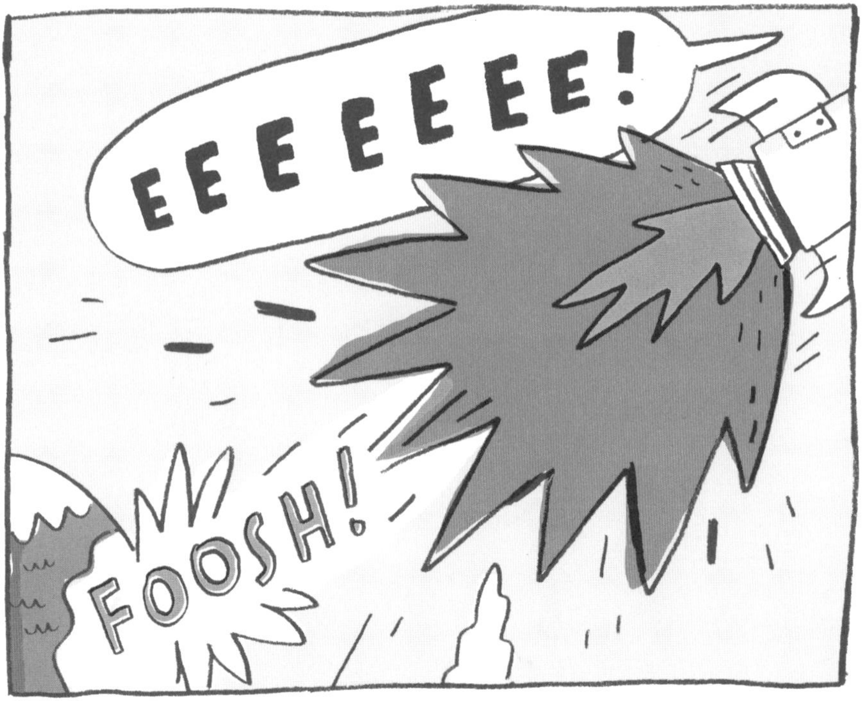
EEEEEEEE!
FOOSH!

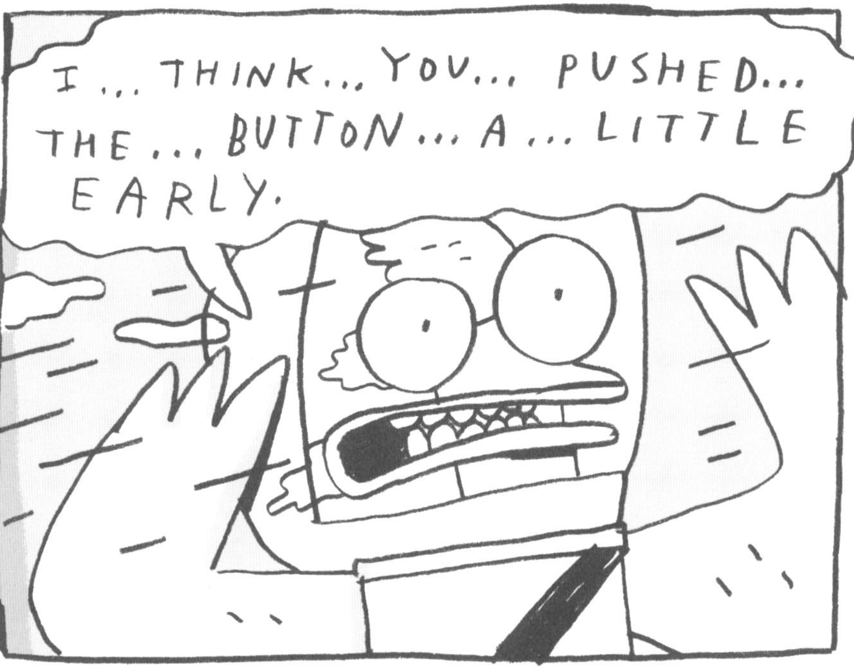
I ... THINK ... YOU ... PUSHED ... THE ... BUTTON ... A ... LITTLE EARLY.

LOOK AT THAT INCREDIBLE VIEW!

DRAW OUR VIEW OF OUTER SPACE.

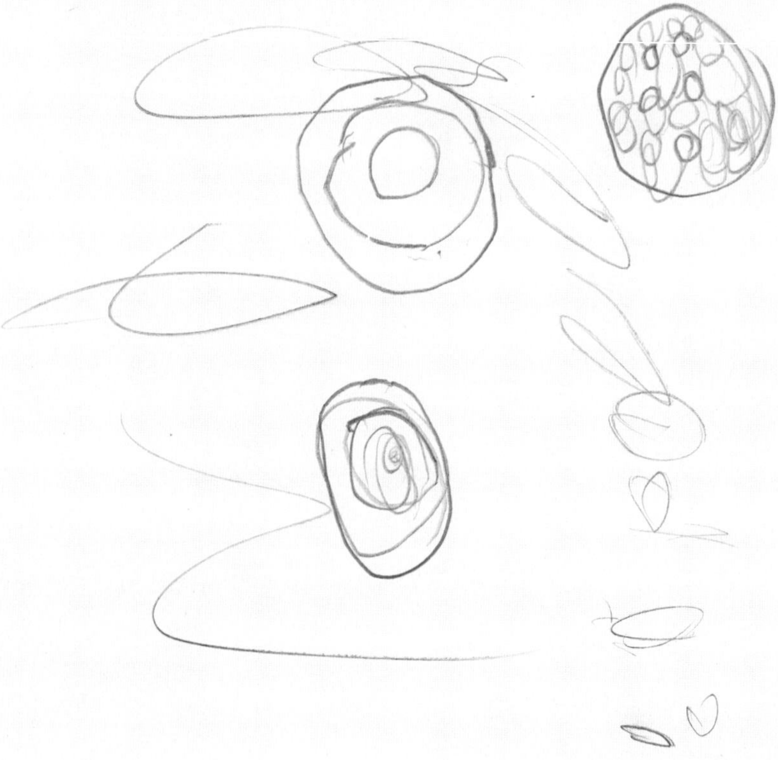

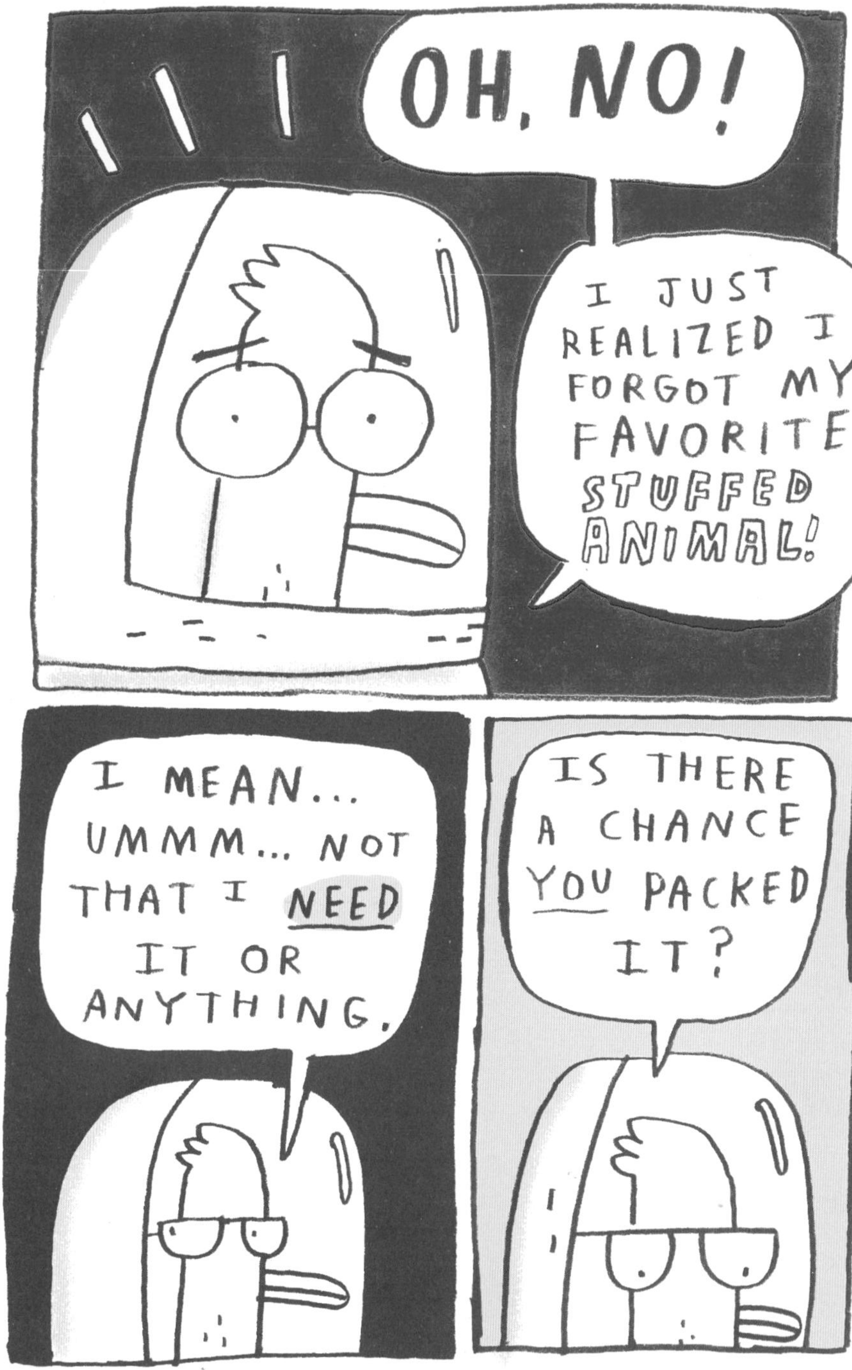
OH, NO!
I JUST REALIZED I FORGOT MY FAVORITE STUFFED ANIMAL!
I MEAN... UMMM... NOT THAT I NEED IT OR ANYTHING.
IS THERE A CHANCE YOU PACKED IT?

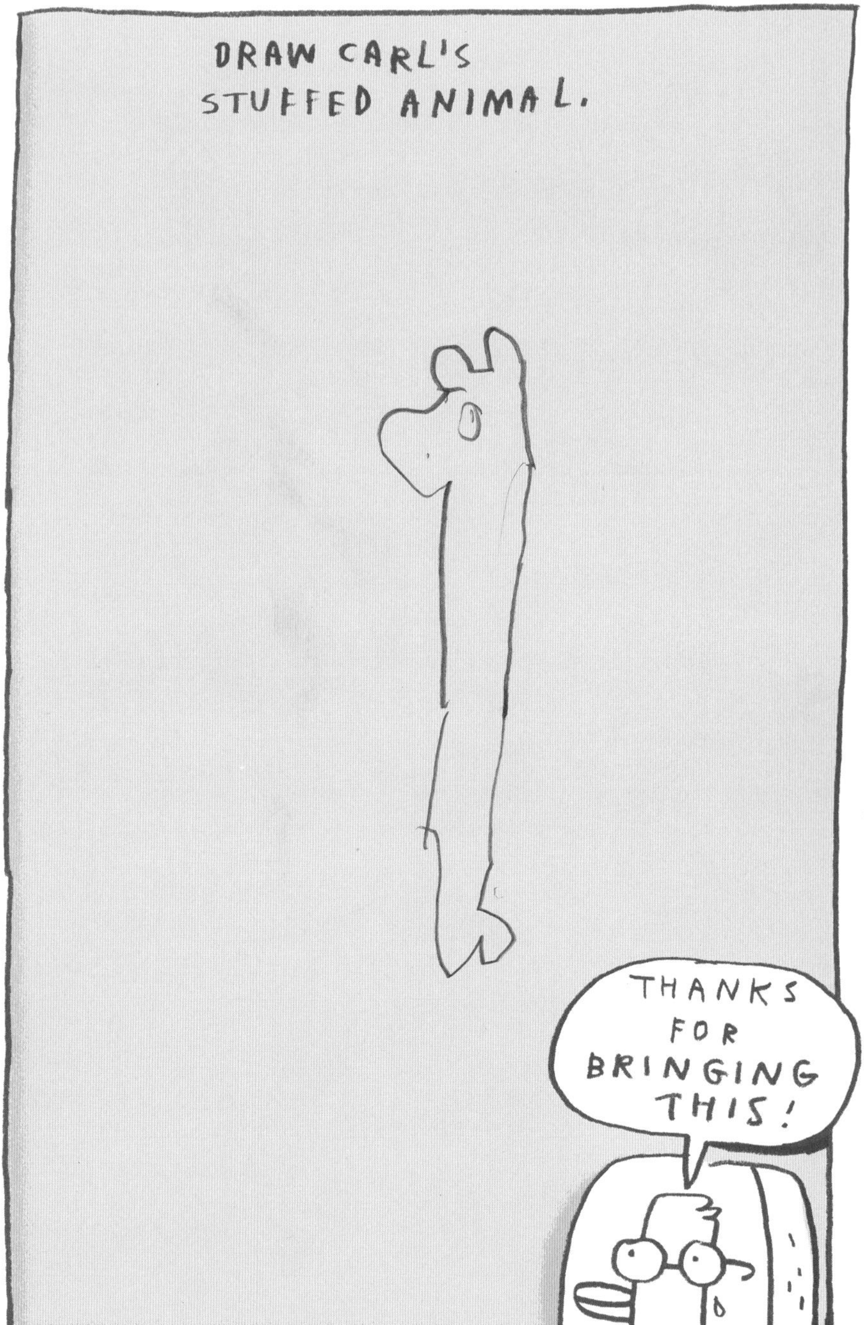
DRAW CARL'S STUFFED ANIMAL.
THANKS FOR BRINGING THIS!

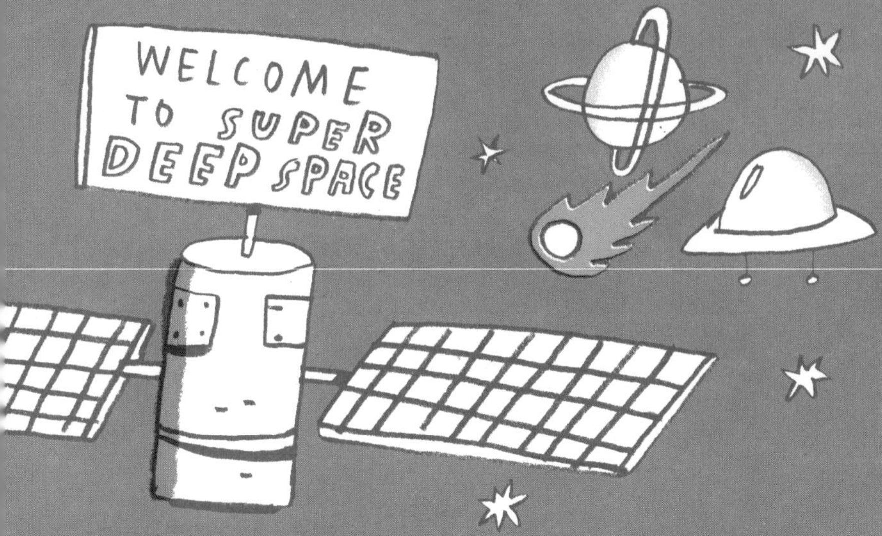
WELCOME
TO SUPER
DEEP SPACE

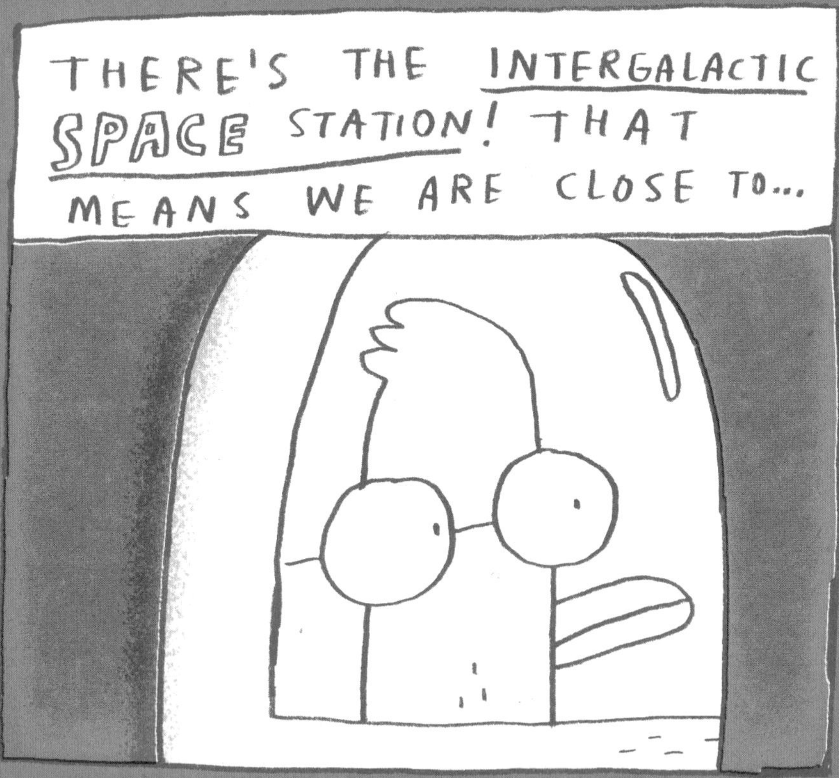
THERE'S THE INTERGALACTIC SPACE STATION! THAT MEANS WE ARE CLOSE TO...

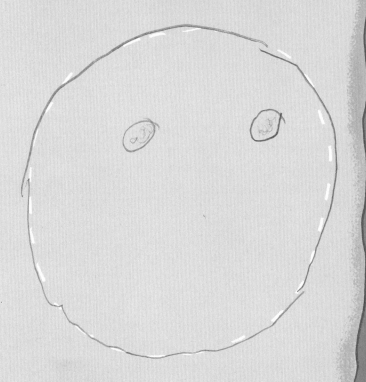

K-82!

DRAW THE **SLUG** PLANET.

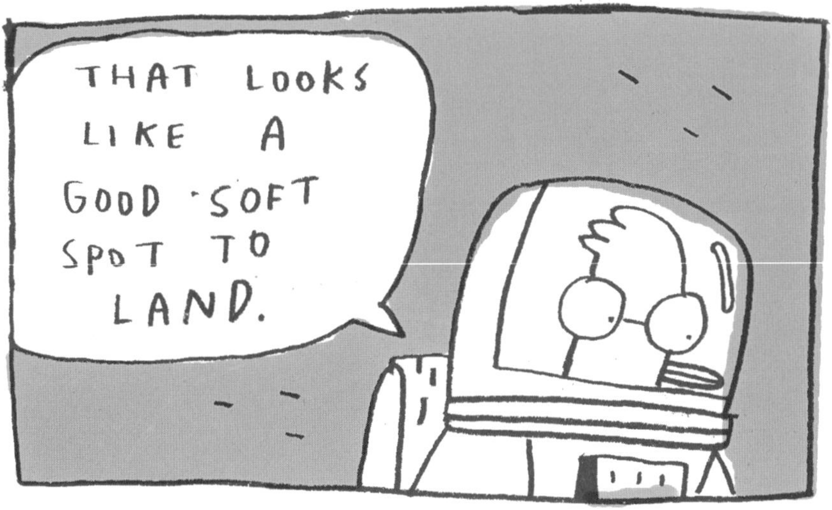
THAT LOOKS LIKE A GOOD SOFT SPOT TO LAND.

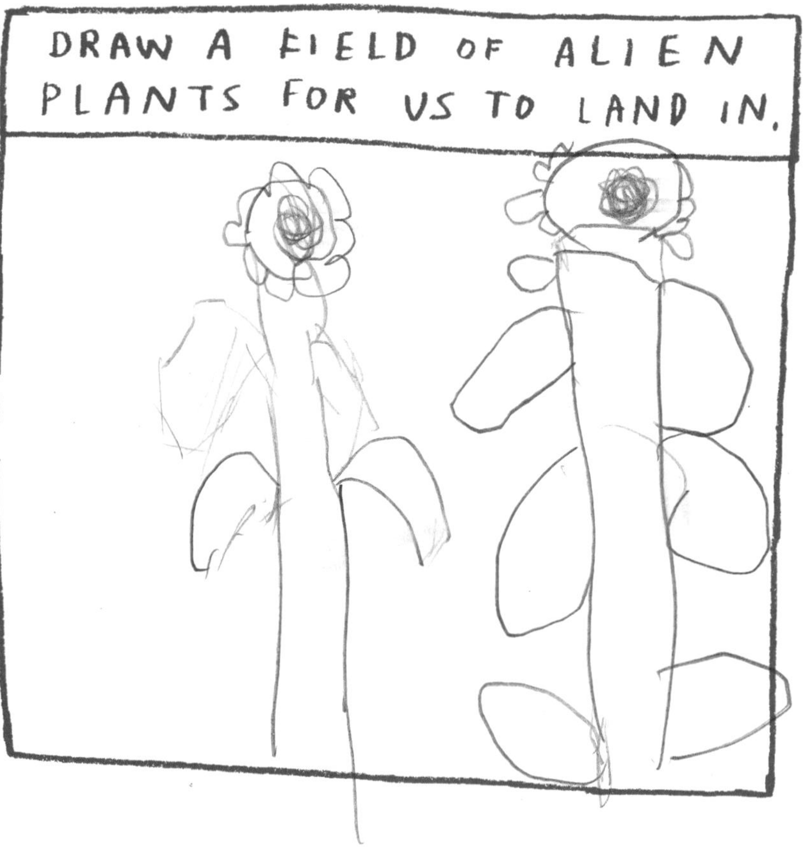
DRAW A FIELD OF ALIEN PLANTS FOR US TO LAND IN.

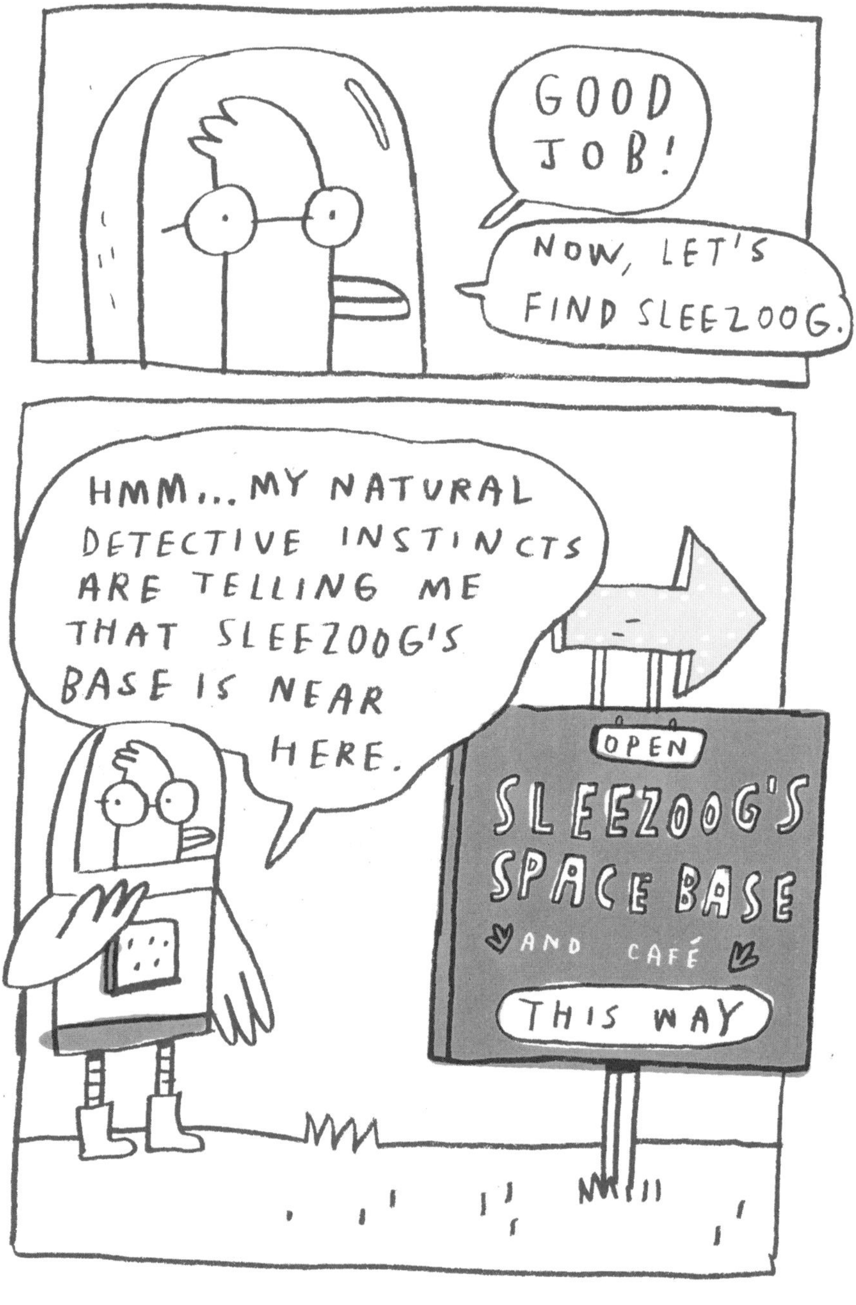
GOOD JOB!
NOW, LET'S FIND SLEEZOOG.
HMM... MY NATURAL DETECTIVE INSTINCTS ARE TELLING ME THAT SLEEZOOG'S BASE IS NEAR HERE.
OPEN
SLEEZOOG'S SPACE BASE
AND CAFÉ
THIS WAY

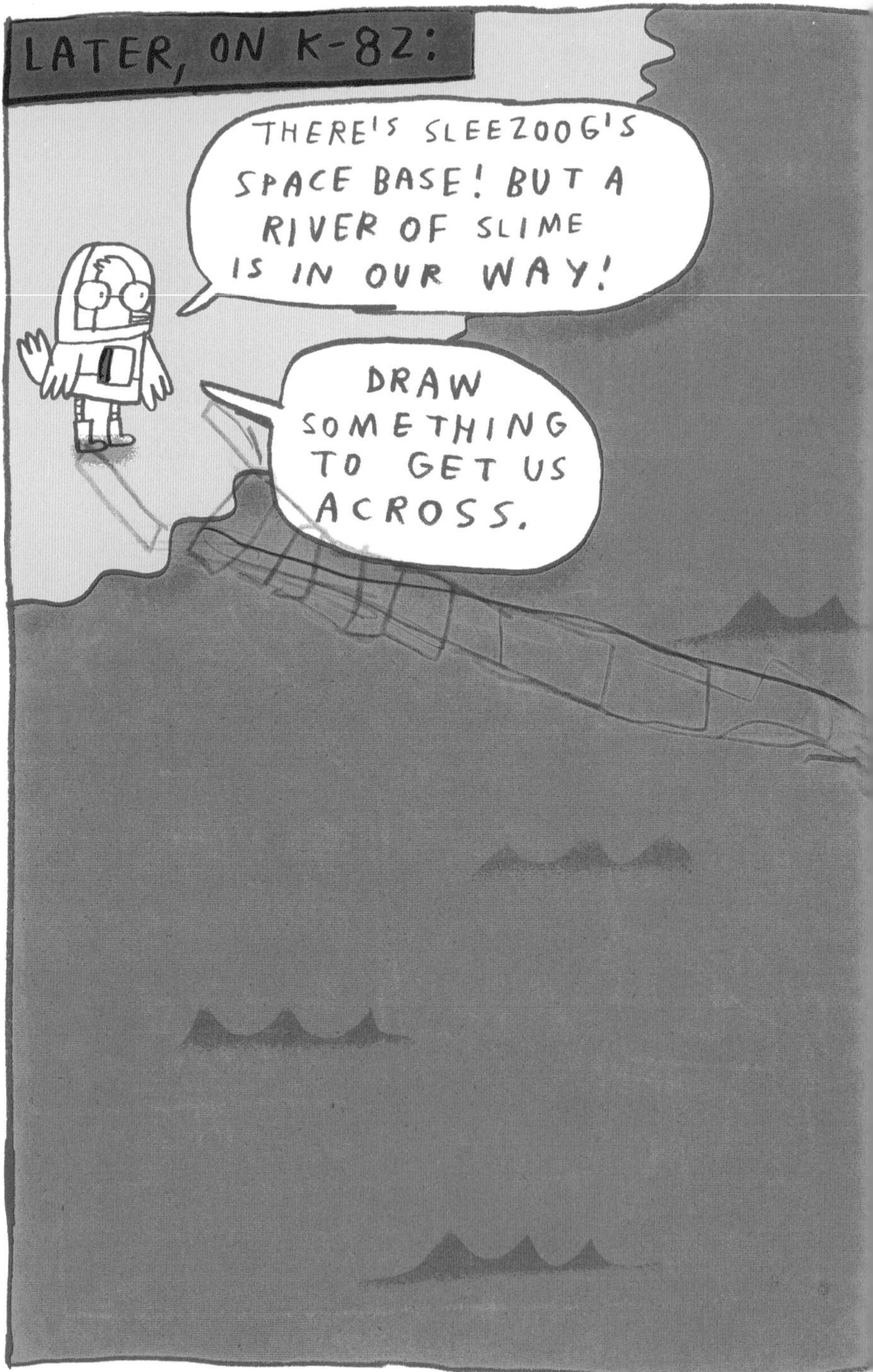
LATER, ON K-82:
THERE'S SLEEZOOG'S SPACE BASE! BUT A RIVER OF SLIME IS IN OUR WAY!
DRAW SOMETHING TO GET US ACROSS.

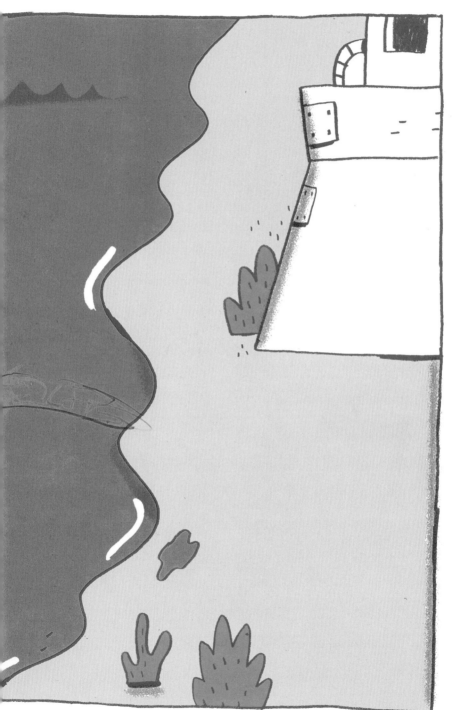

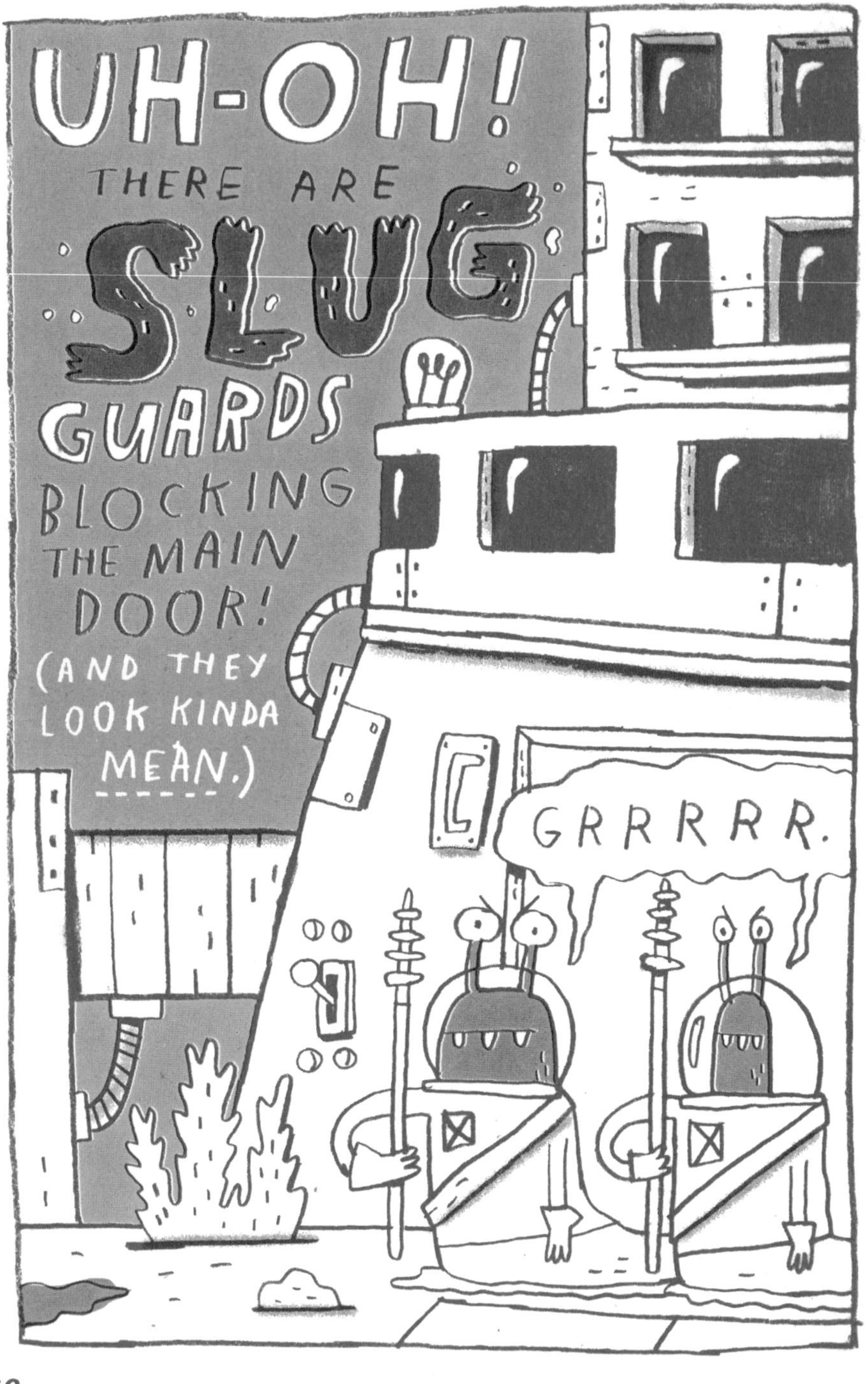
UH-OH!
THERE ARE
SLUG
GUARDS
BLOCKING
THE MAIN
DOOR!
(AND THEY
LOOK KINDA
MEAN.)
GRRRRR.

DRAW SOMETHING SALTY
(SLUGS **HATE** SALT!)

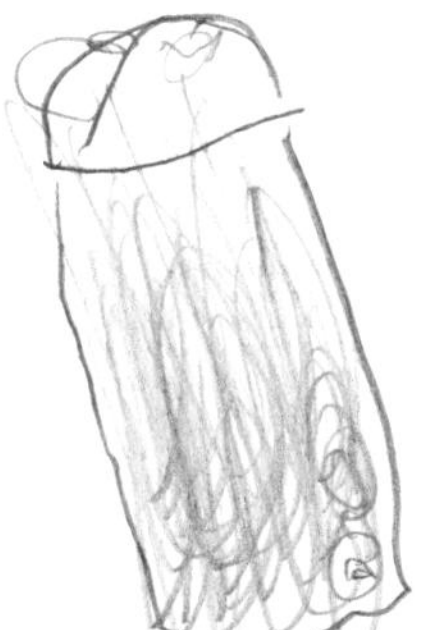

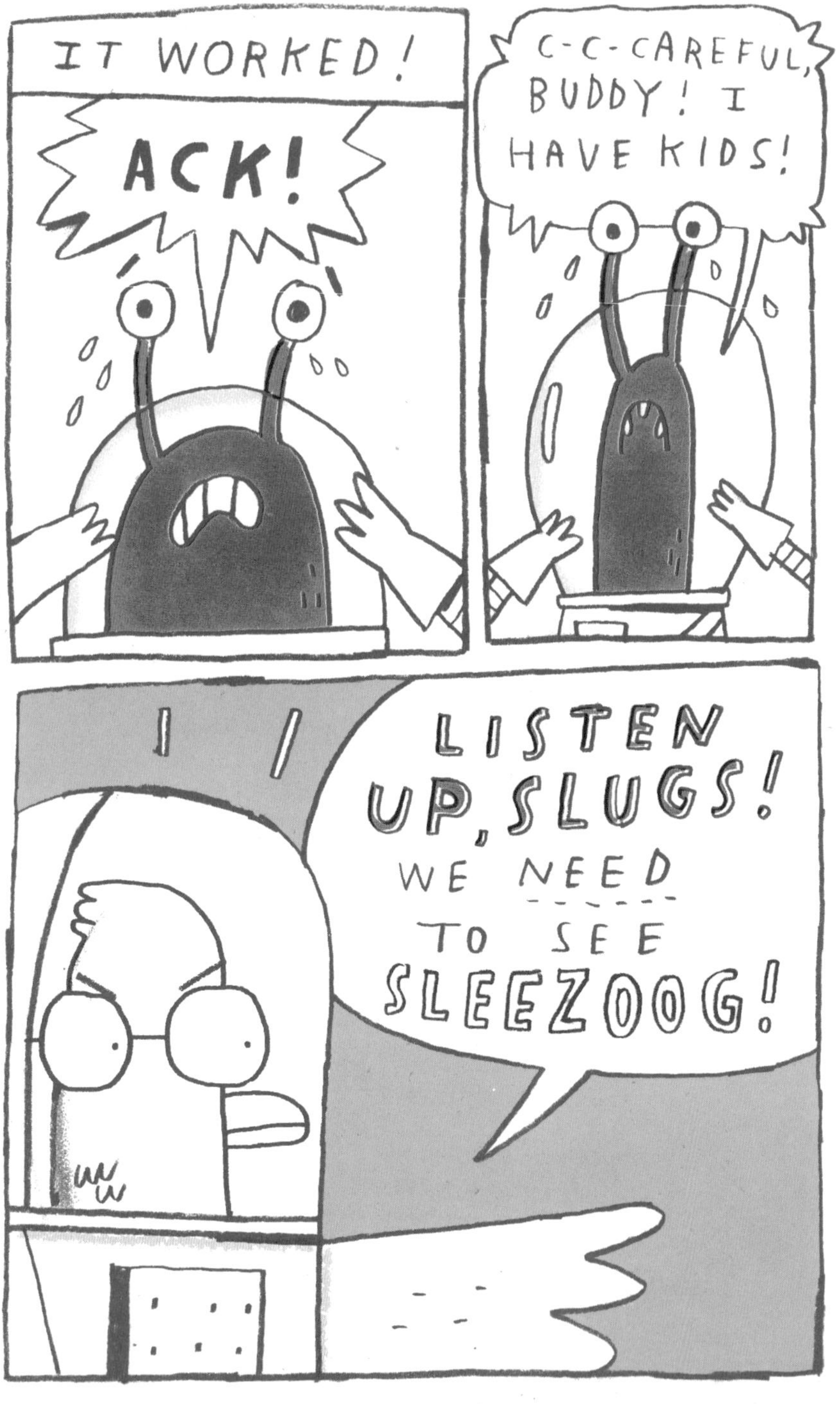
IT WORKED!
ACK!
C-C-CAREFUL, BUDDY! I HAVE KIDS!
LISTEN UP, SLUGS! WE NEED TO SEE SLEEZOOG!

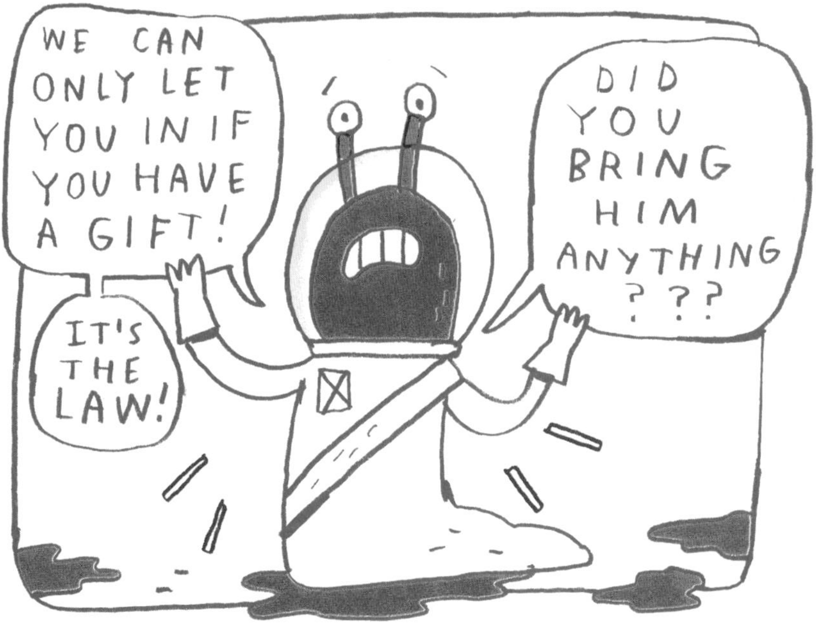
WE CAN ONLY LET YOU IN IF YOU HAVE A GIFT!
IT'S THE LAW!
DID YOU BRING HIM ANYTHING???

DRAW A PRESENT FOR SLEEZOOG.

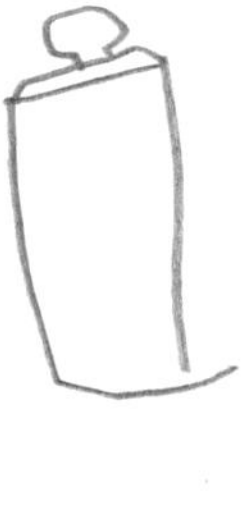

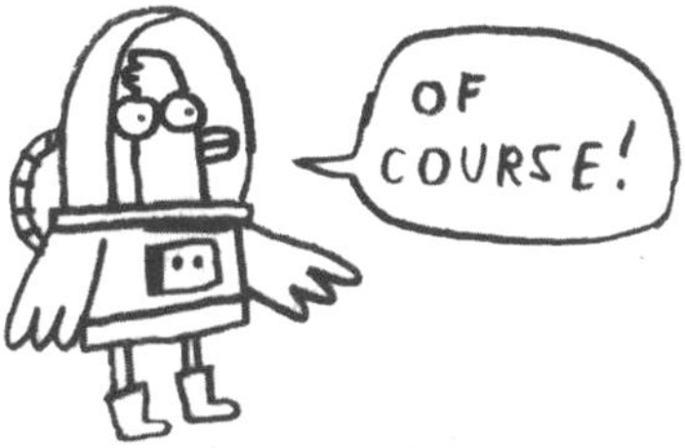
OF COURSE!

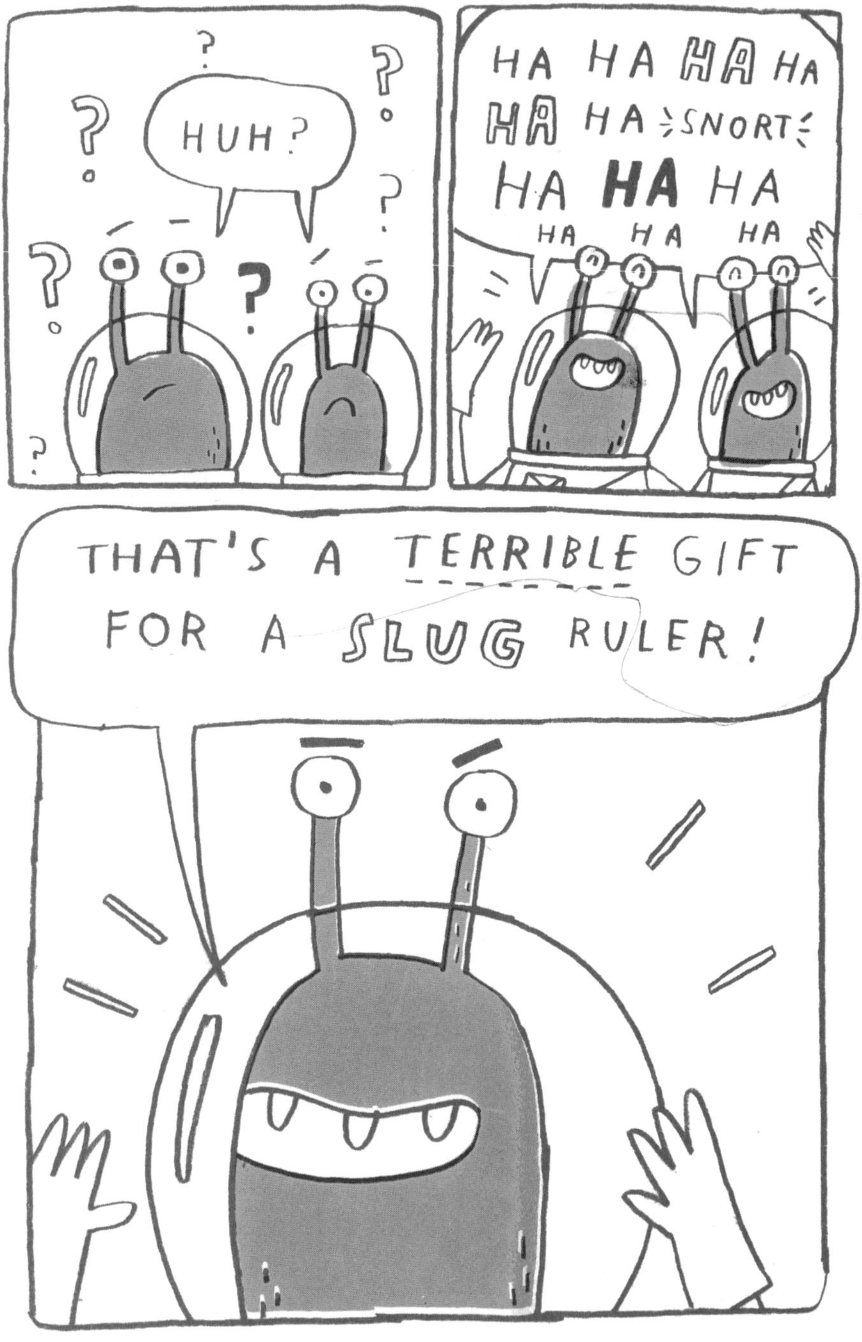
HUH?
HA HA HA HA HA HA ≥SNORT≤ HA HA HA
HA HA HA
THAT'S A TERRIBLE GIFT FOR A SLUG RULER!

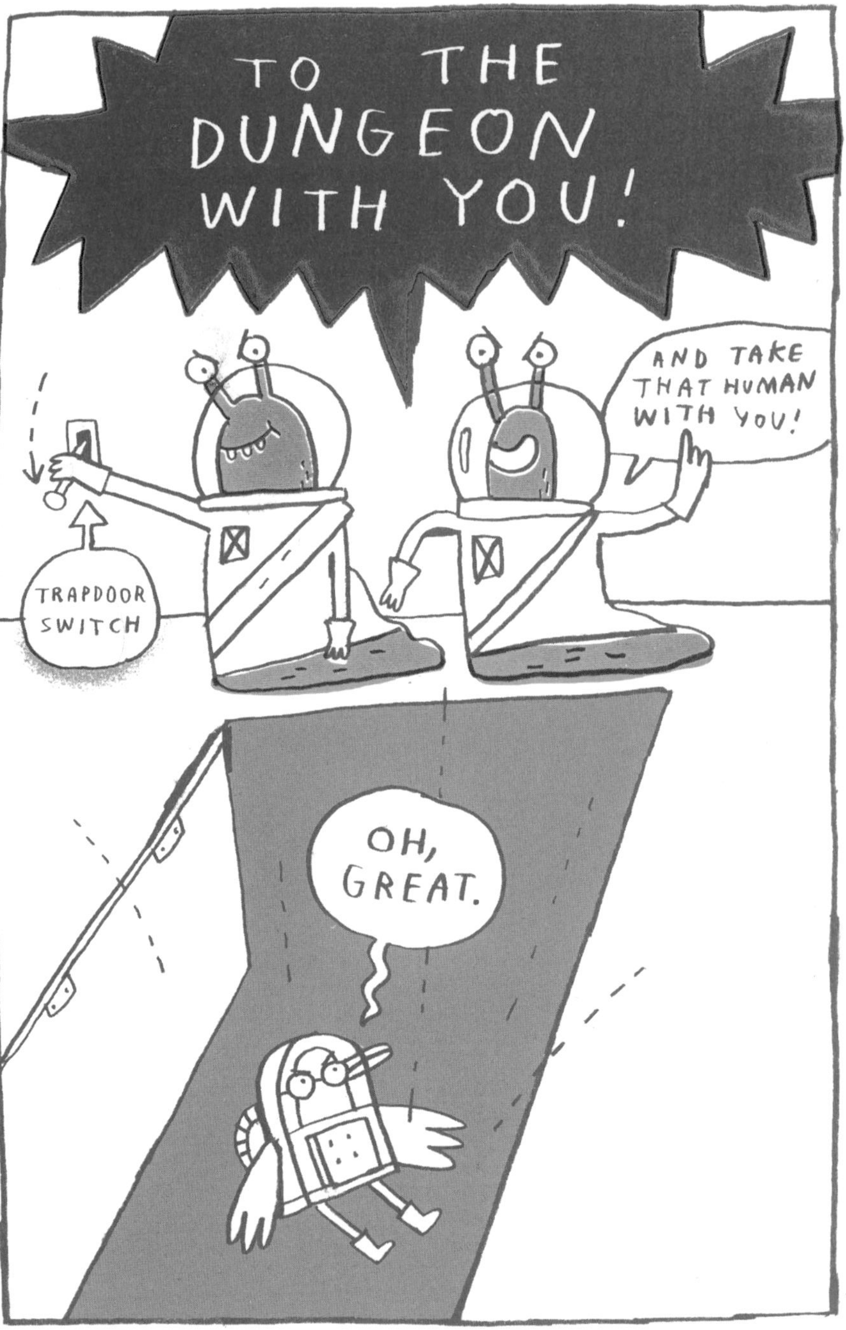
TO THE DUNGEON WITH YOU!
AND TAKE THAT HUMAN WITH YOU!
TRAPDOOR SWITCH
OH, GREAT.

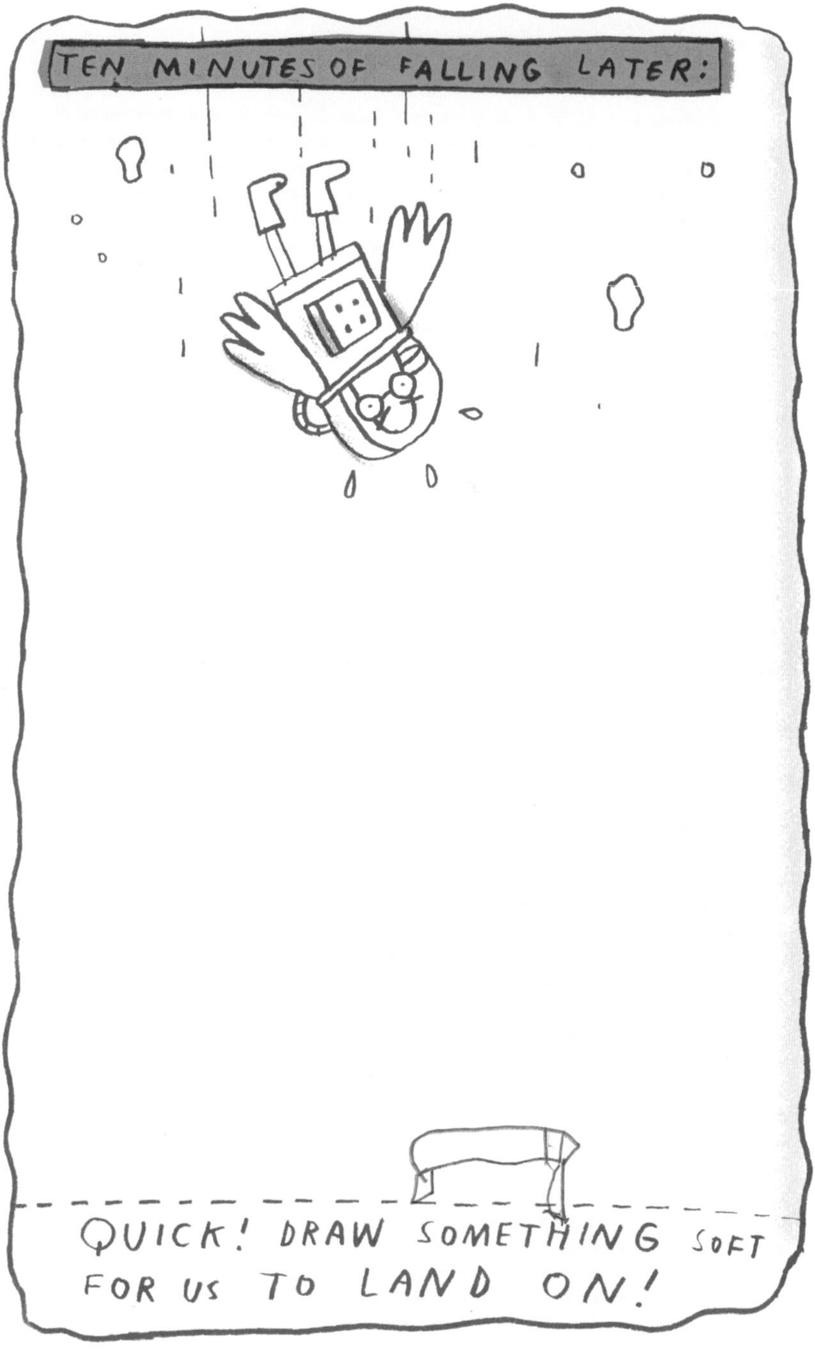
TEN MINUTES OF FALLING LATER:
QUICK! DRAW SOMETHING SOFT FOR US TO LAND ON!

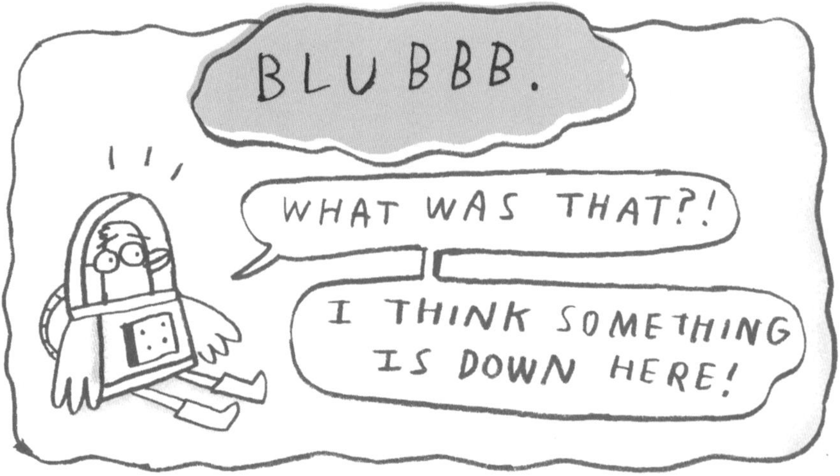
BLUBBB.
WHAT WAS THAT?!
I THINK SOMETHING IS DOWN HERE!

DRAW SOMETHING TO LIGHT UP THE DARK DUNGEON.

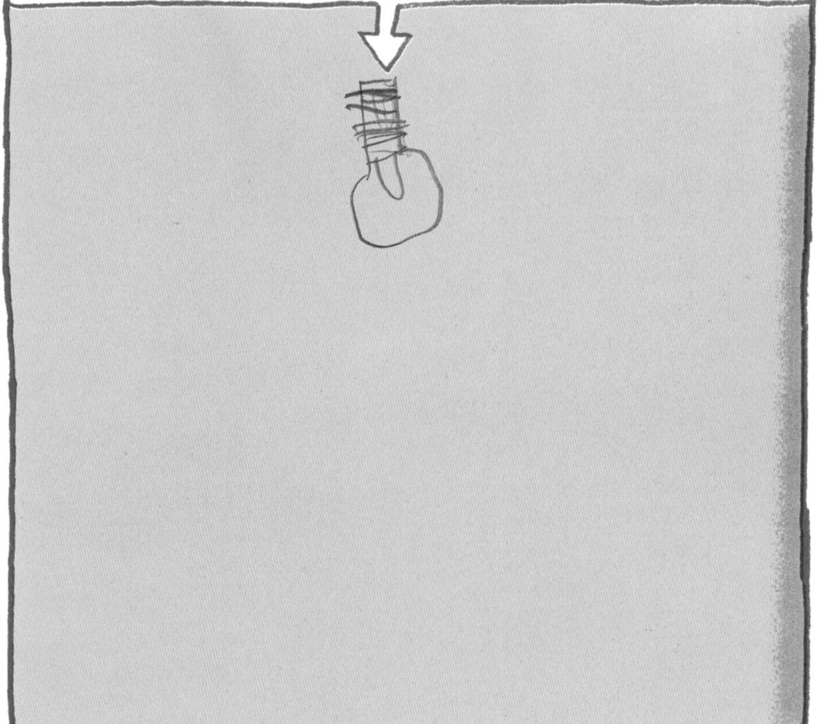

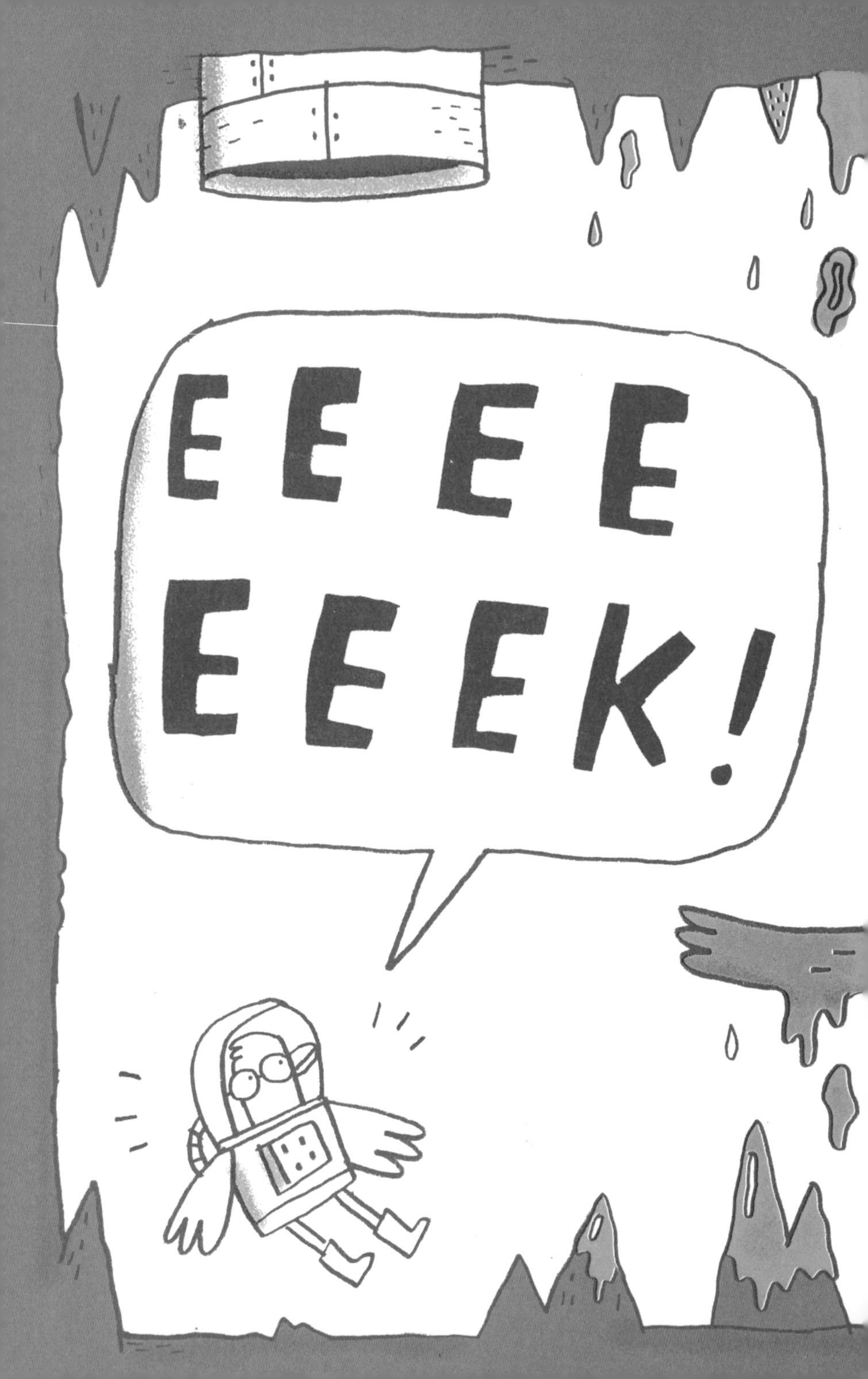
EEEE EEEK!

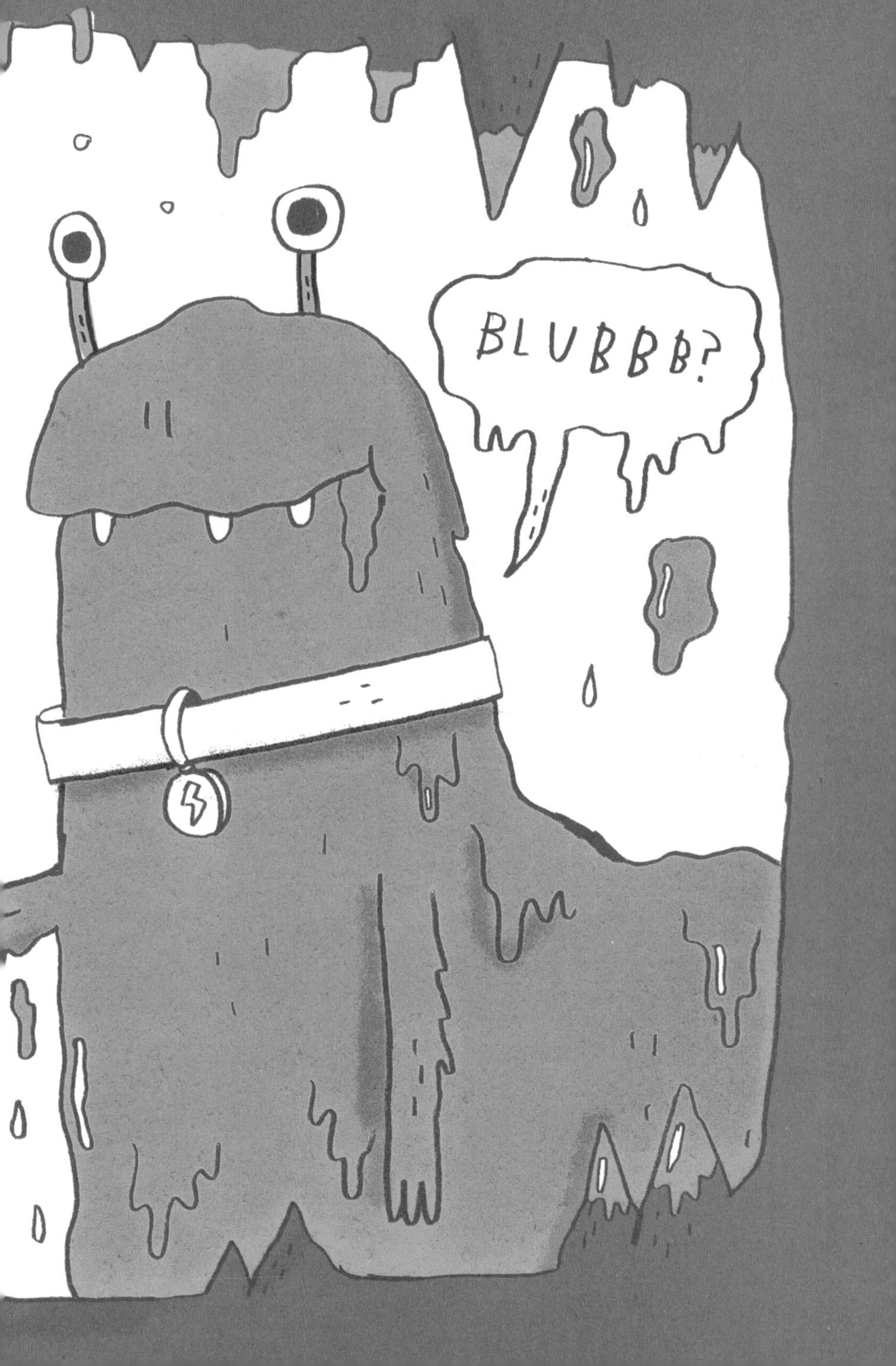
BLUBBB?

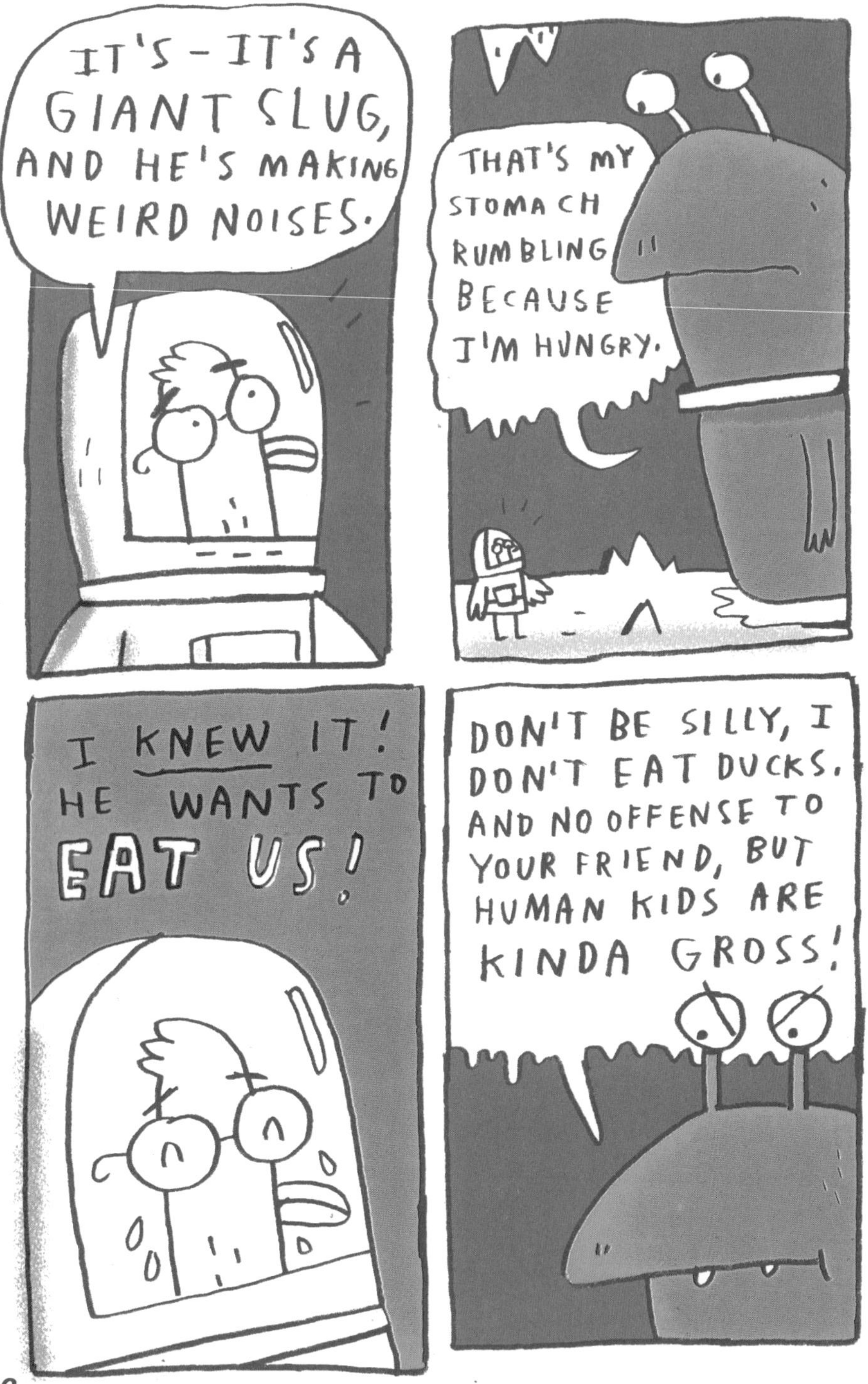
IT'S - IT'S A GIANT SLUG, AND HE'S MAKING WEIRD NOISES.
THAT'S MY STOMACH RUMBLING BECAUSE I'M HUNGRY.
I KNEW IT! HE WANTS TO EAT US!
DON'T BE SILLY, I DON'T EAT DUCKS. AND NO OFFENSE TO YOUR FRIEND, BUT HUMAN KIDS ARE KINDA GROSS!

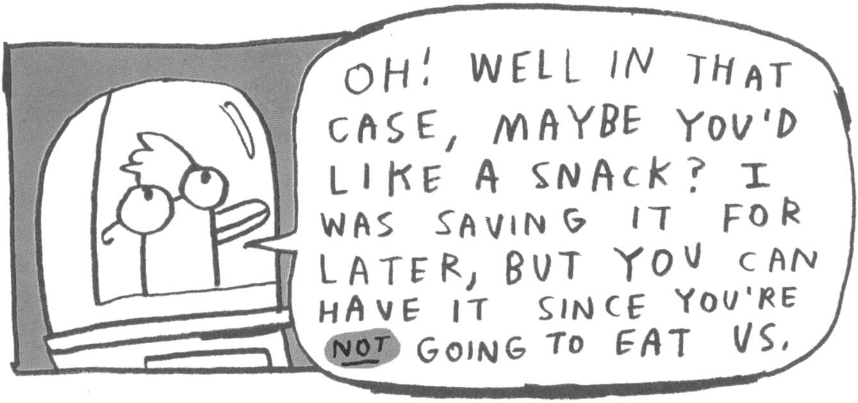
OH! WELL IN THAT CASE, MAYBE YOU'D LIKE A SNACK? I WAS SAVING IT FOR LATER, BUT YOU CAN HAVE IT SINCE YOU'RE NOT GOING TO EAT US.

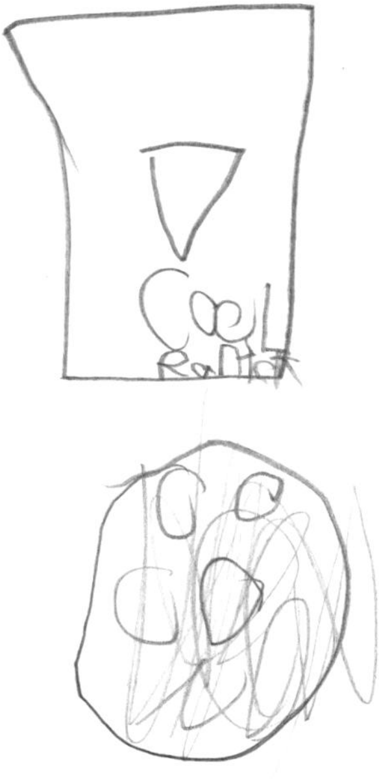

DRAW THE MOST DELICIOUS THING YOU CAN THINK OF.

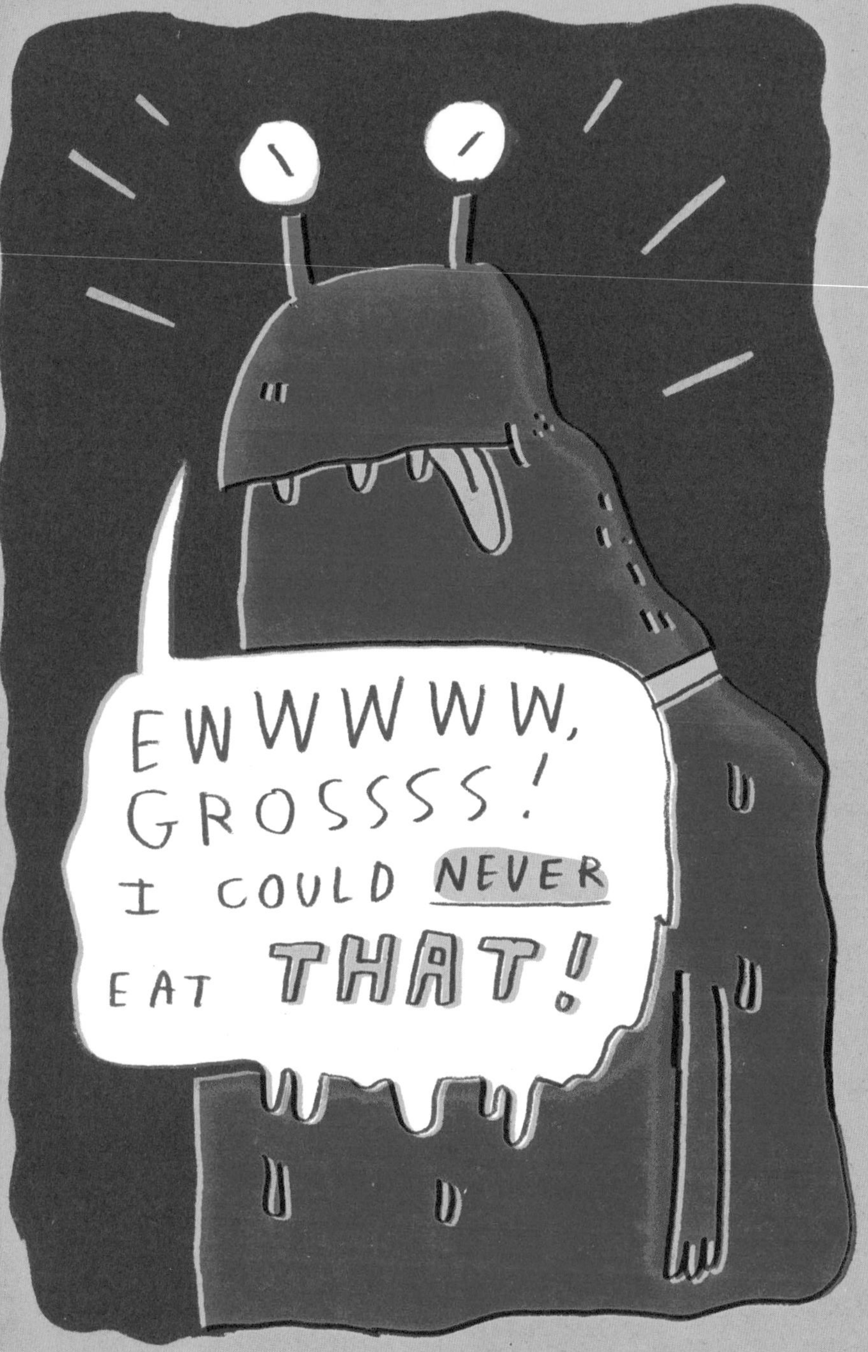
EWWWWW, GROSSSS! I COULD NEVER EAT THAT!

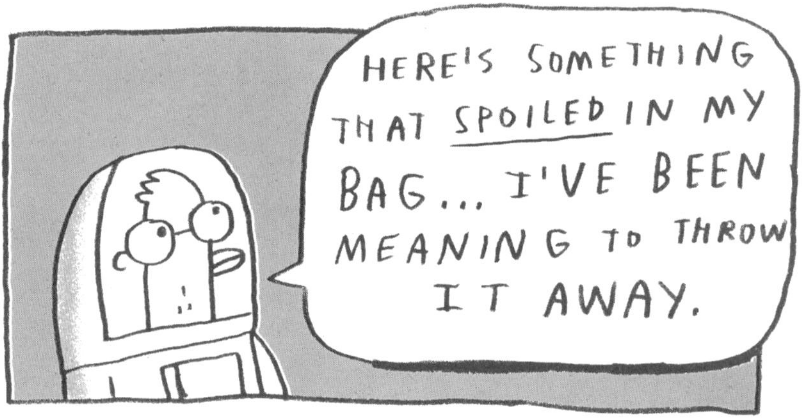
HERE'S SOMETHING THAT SPOILED IN MY BAG... I'VE BEEN MEANING TO THROW IT AWAY.

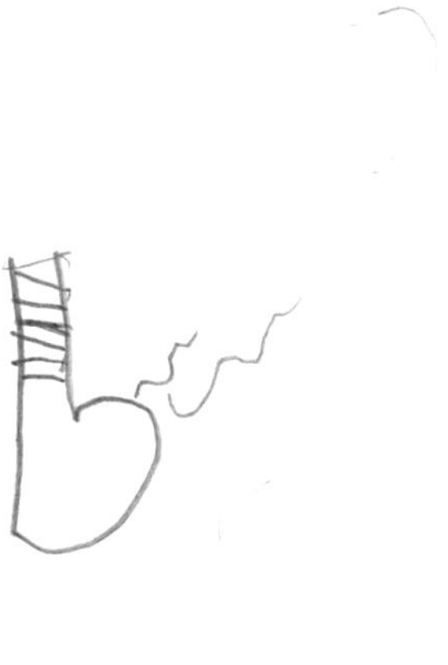

DRAW THE STINKIEST THING YOU CAN IMAGINE!

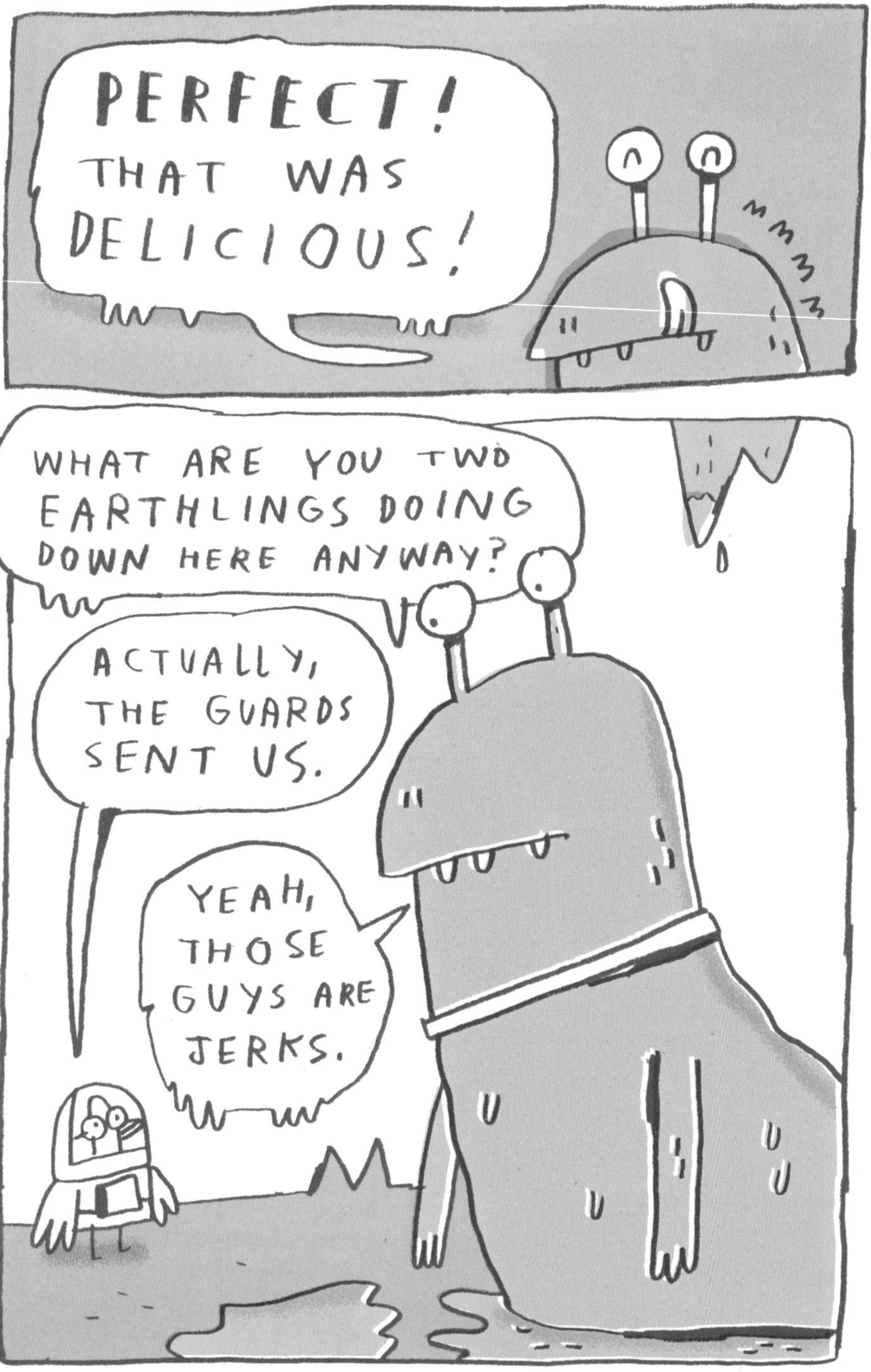
PERFECT! THAT WAS DELICIOUS!
MMMMM
WHAT ARE YOU TWO EARTHLINGS DOING DOWN HERE ANYWAY?
ACTUALLY, THE GUARDS SENT US.
YEAH, THOSE GUYS ARE JERKS.

BUT I KNOW A WAY OUT. THERE'S
A PIPE UP THERE. I DON'T
KNOW WHERE IT LEADS, BUT
YOU COULD GIVE IT A TRY.

IT'S HIGH, BUT I BET IF
YOU STACK THOSE, YOU COULD
CLIMB UP TO IT.

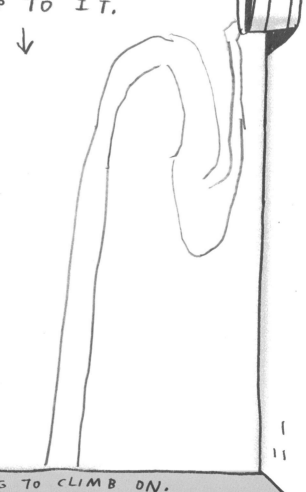

DRAW SOMETHING TO CLIMB ON.

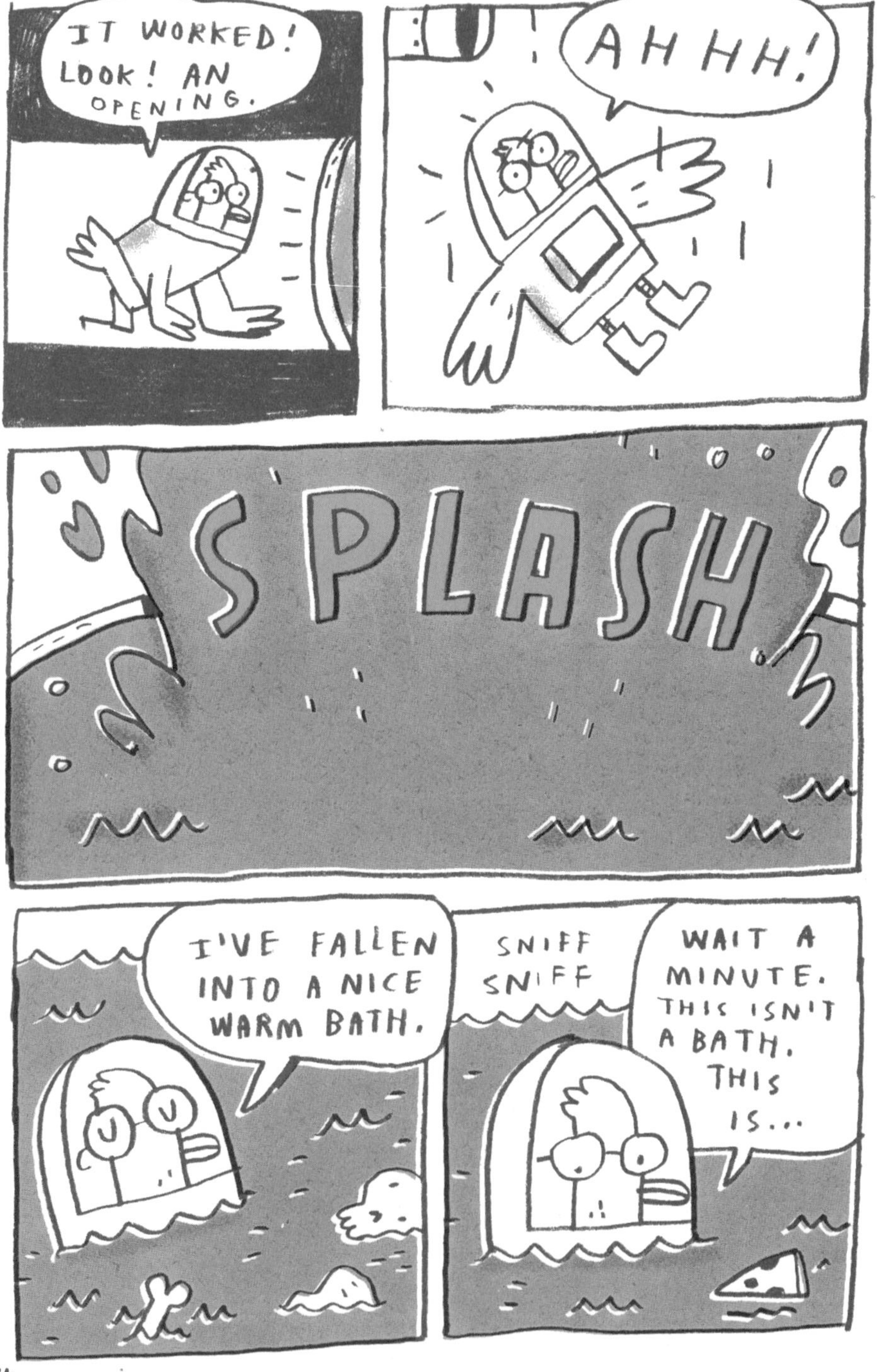
IT WORKED! LOOK! AN OPENING.
AHHH!
SPLASH
I'VE FALLEN INTO A NICE WARM BATH.
SNIFF SNIFF
WAIT A MINUTE. THIS ISN'T A BATH. THIS IS...

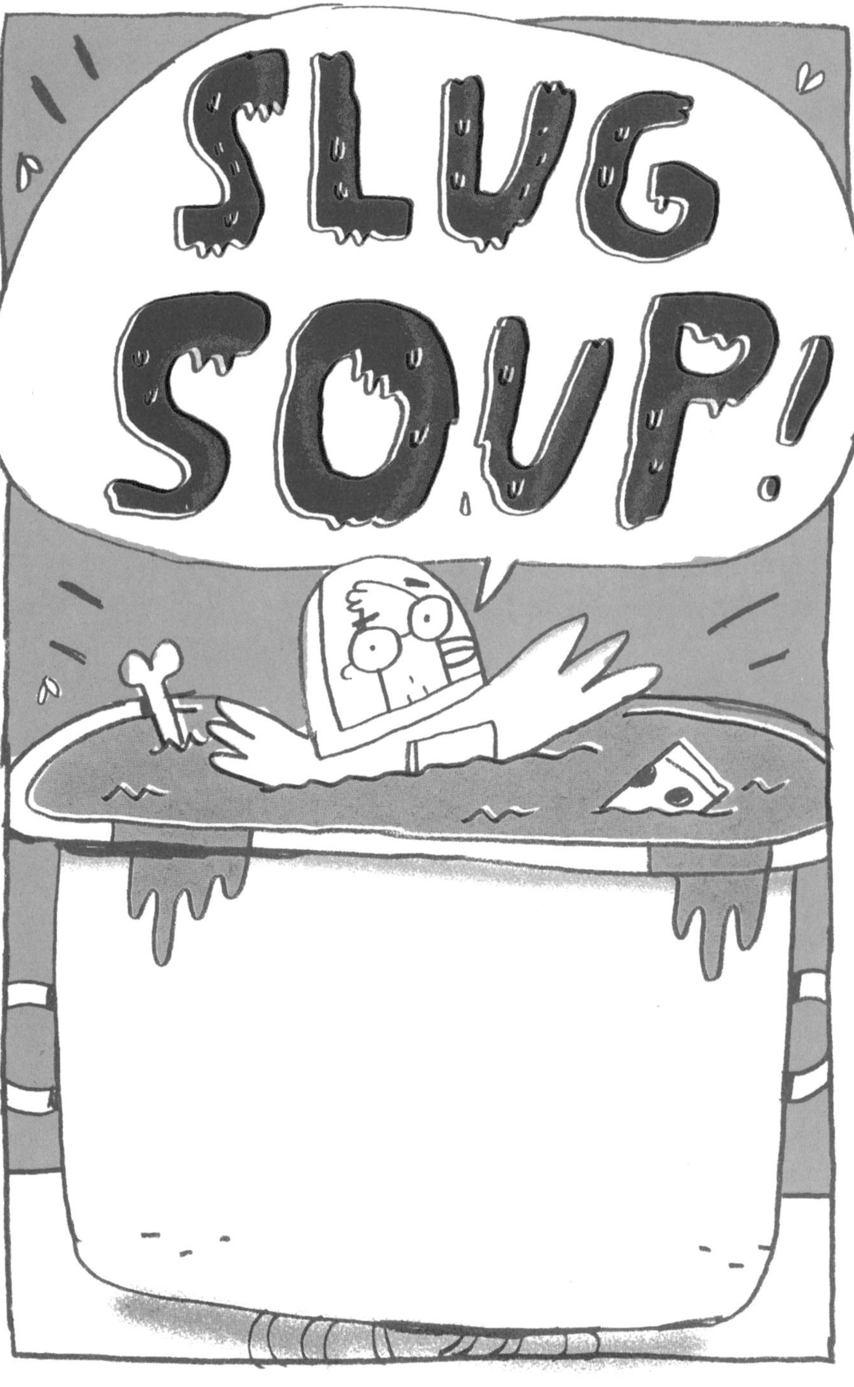
SLUG SOUP!

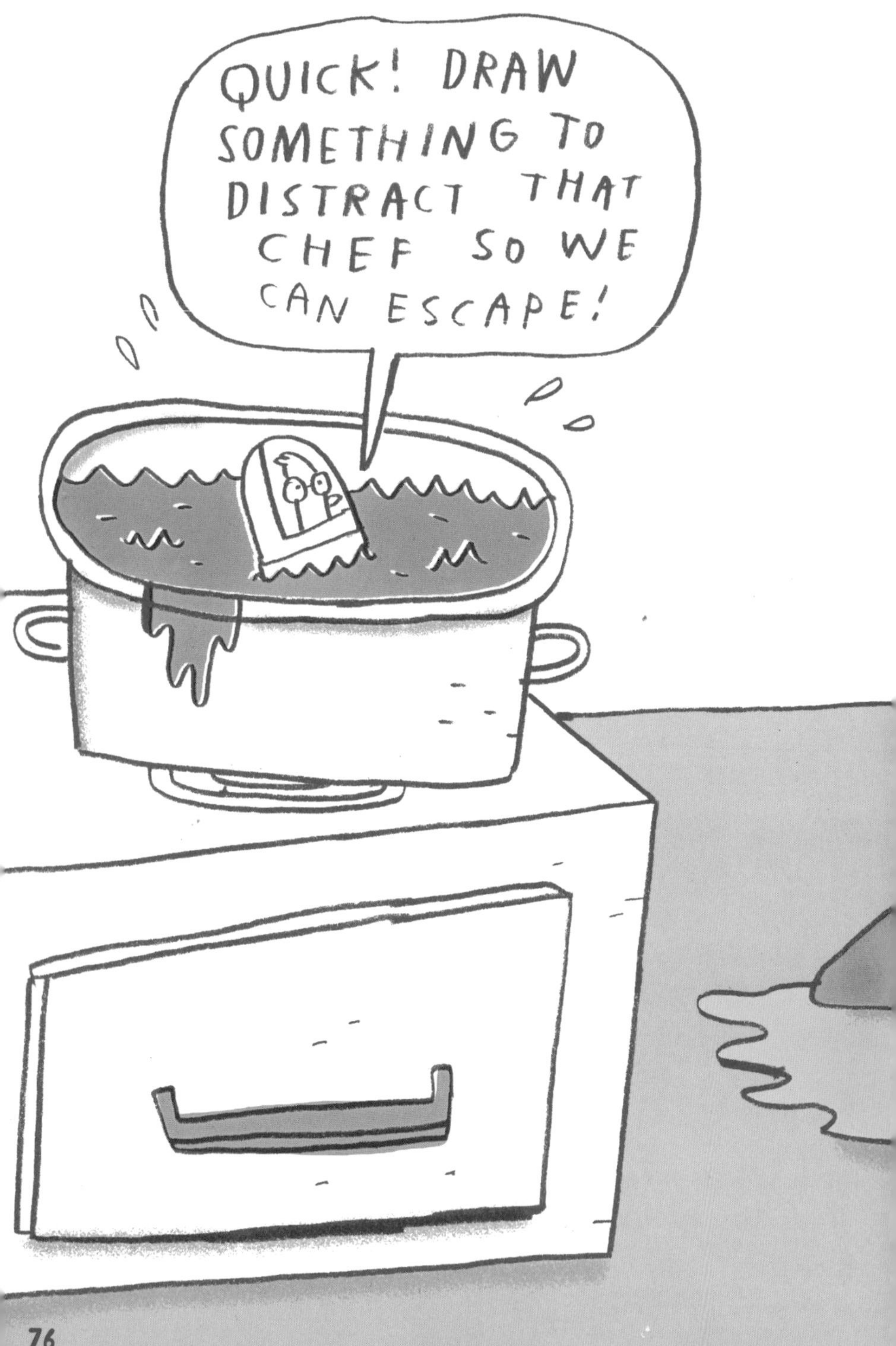
QUICK! DRAW SOMETHING TO DISTRACT THAT CHEF SO WE CAN ESCAPE!

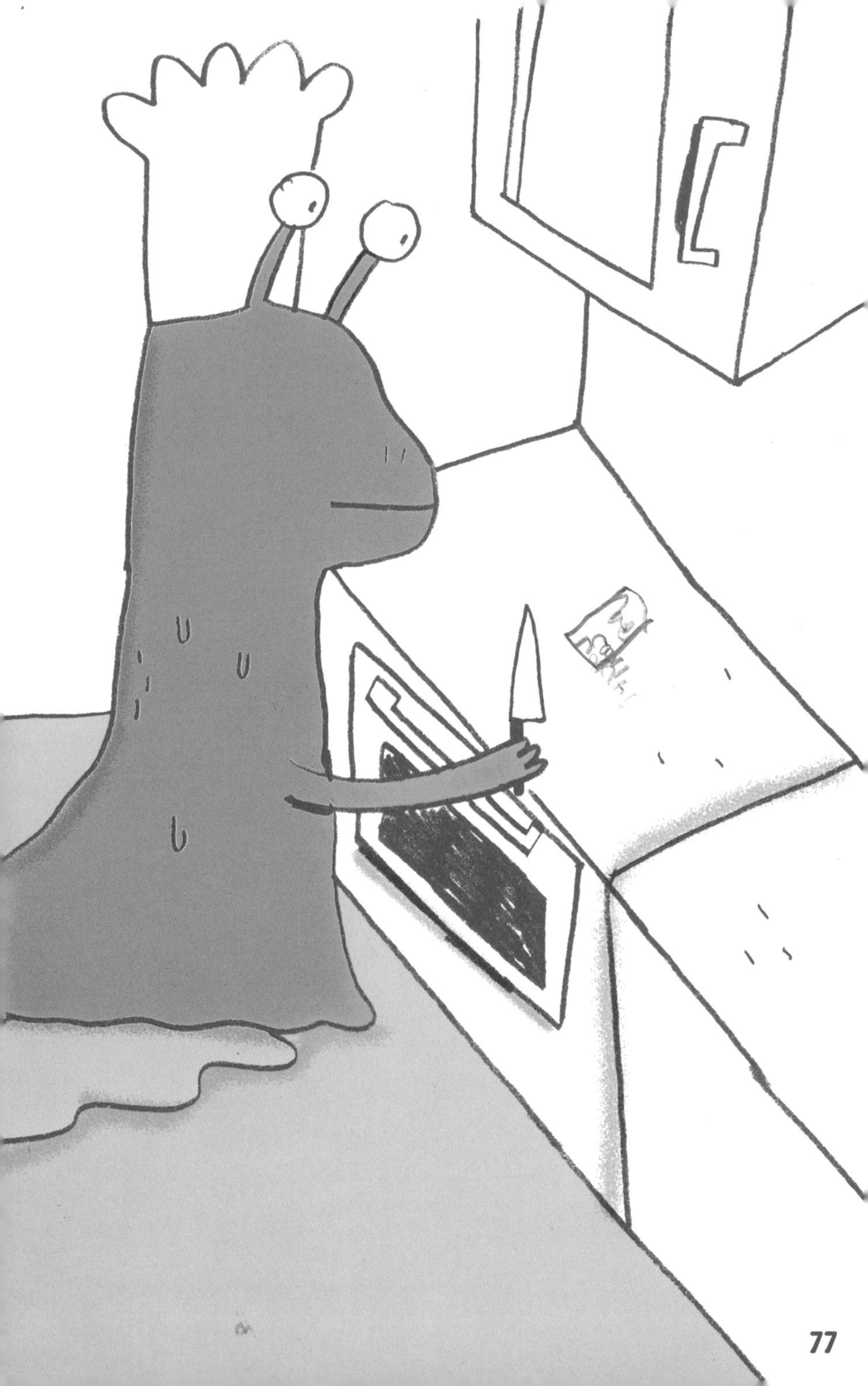

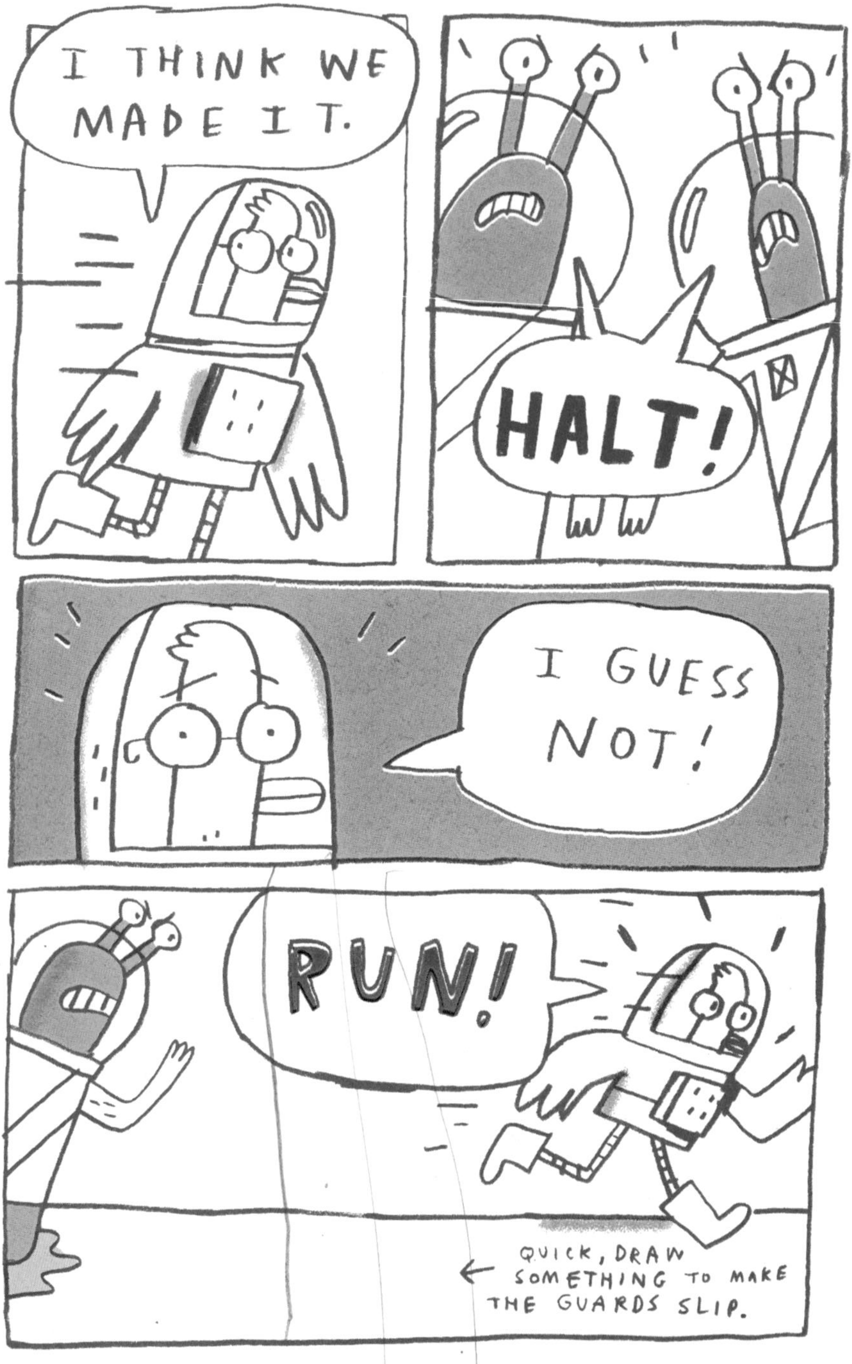
I THINK WE MADE IT.
HALT!
I GUESS NOT!
RUN!
QUICK, DRAW SOMETHING TO MAKE THE GUARDS SLIP.

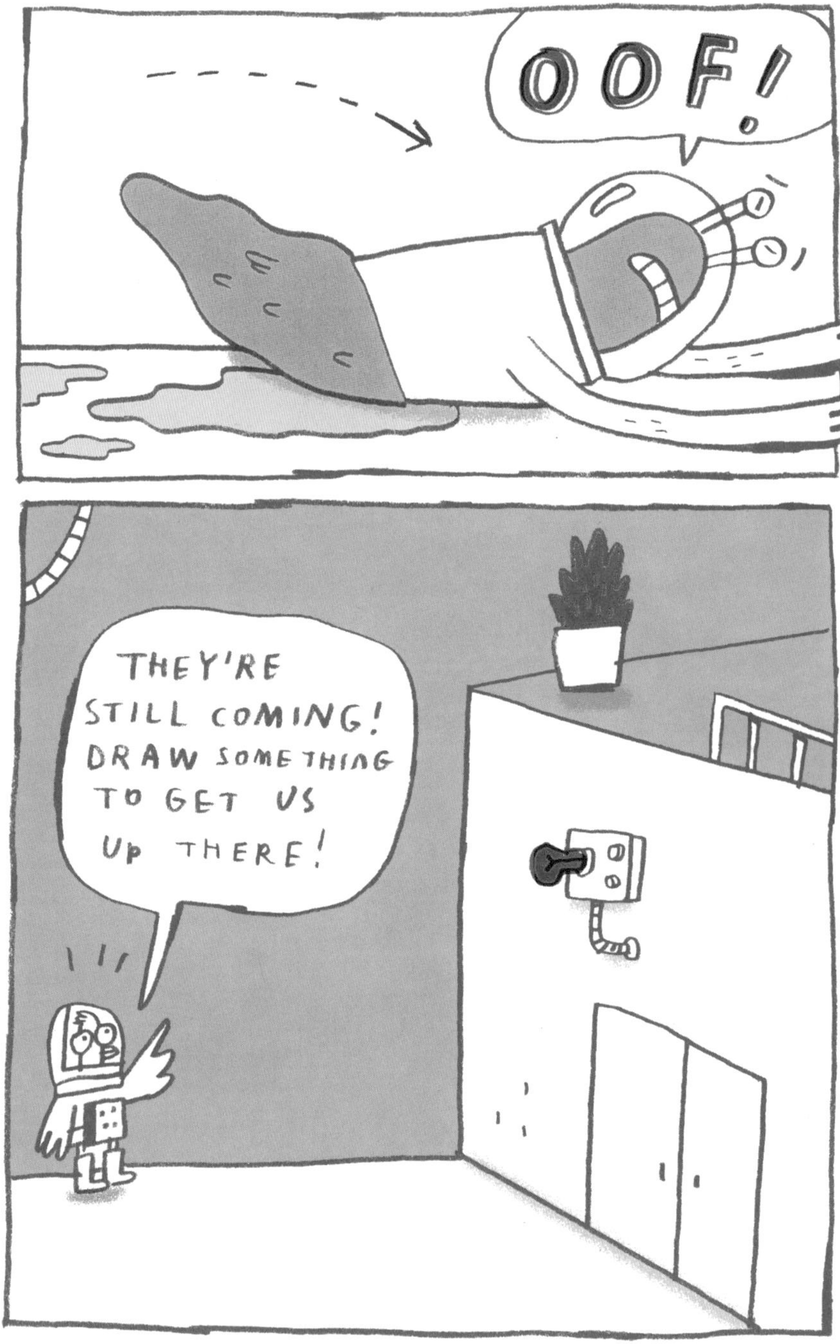
OOF!
THEY'RE STILL COMING! DRAW SOMETHING TO GET US UP THERE!

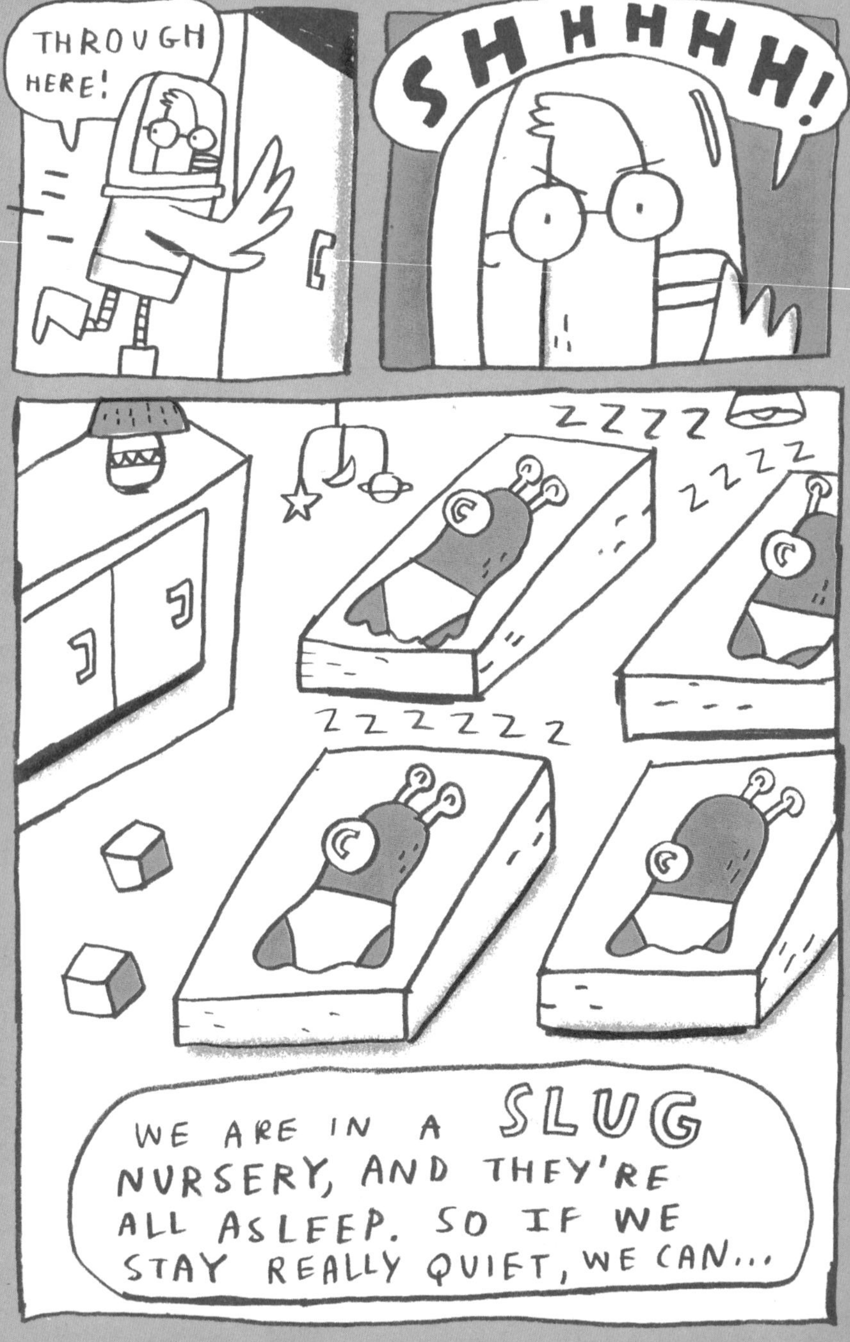
THROUGH HERE!
SHHHHH!
ZZZZ
ZZZZ
ZZZZZZZ
WE ARE IN A SLUG NURSERY, AND THEY'RE ALL ASLEEP. SO IF WE STAY REALLY QUIET, WE CAN...

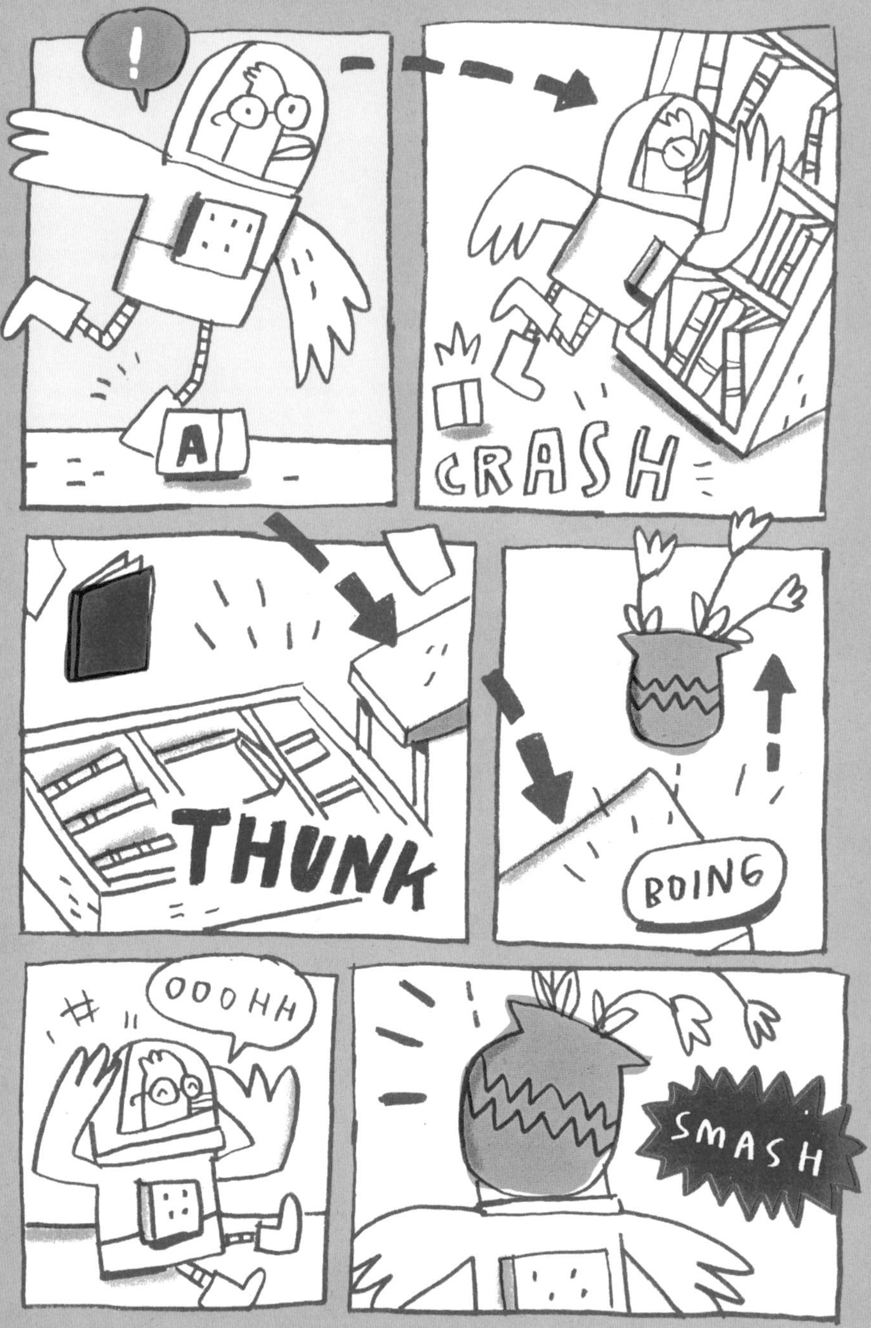
!
A
CRASH
THUNK
BOING
OOOHH
#
SMASH

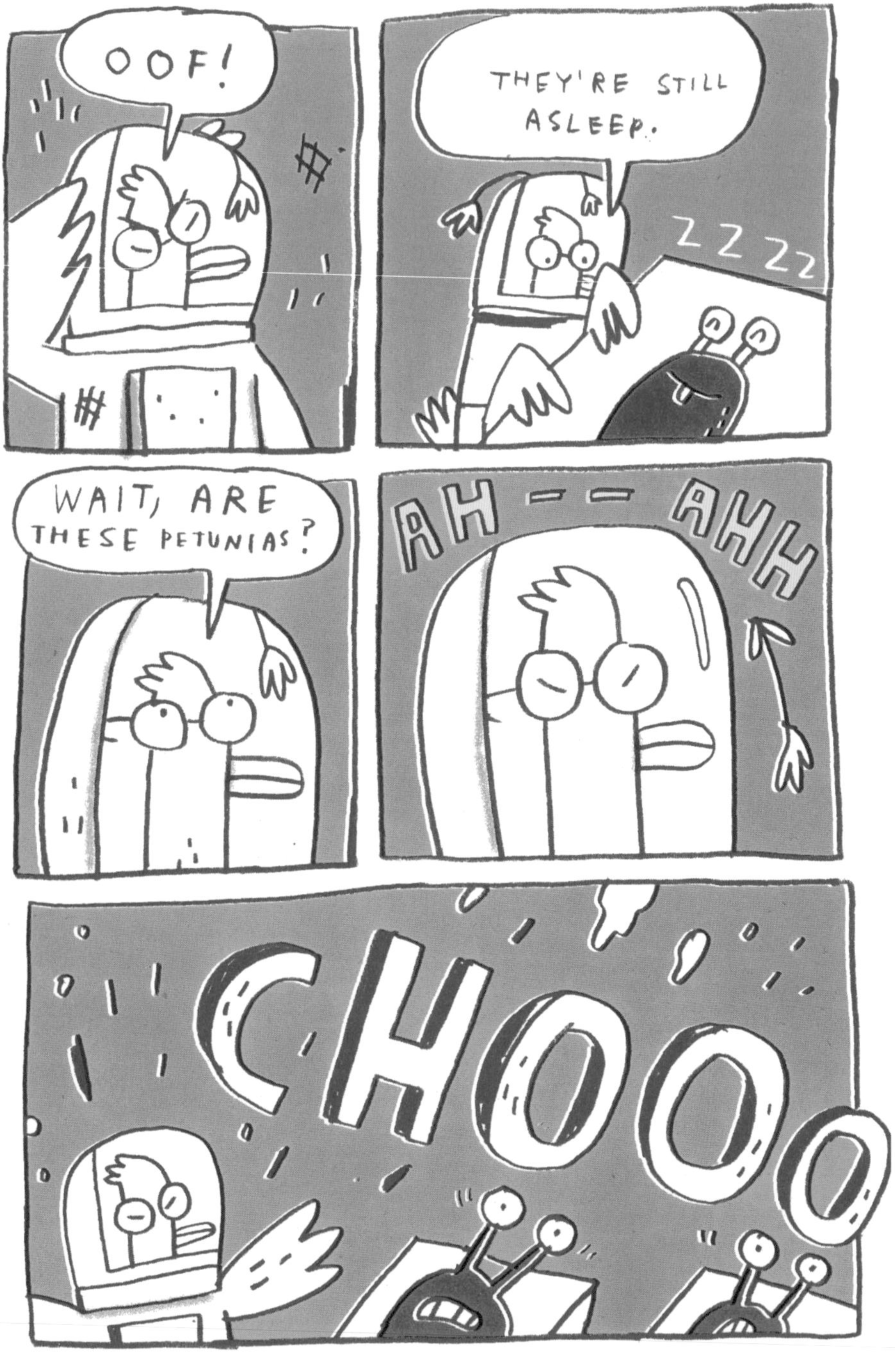
OOF!
THEY'RE STILL ASLEEP.
ZZZZZ
WAIT, ARE THESE PETUNIAS?
AH -- AHH
CHOOOO

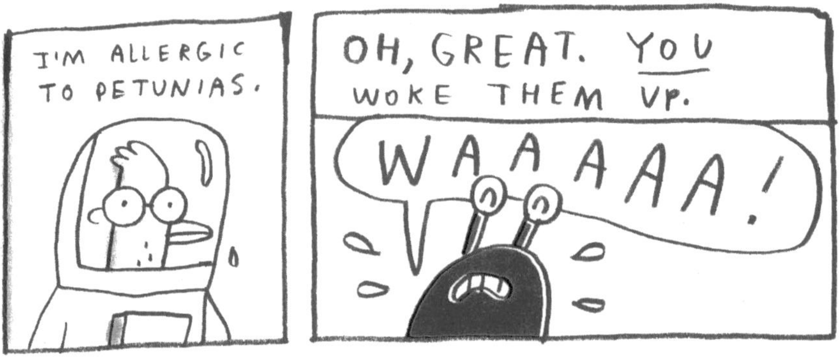
I'M ALLERGIC TO PETUNIAS.
OH, GREAT. YOU WOKE THEM UP.
WAAAAAA!

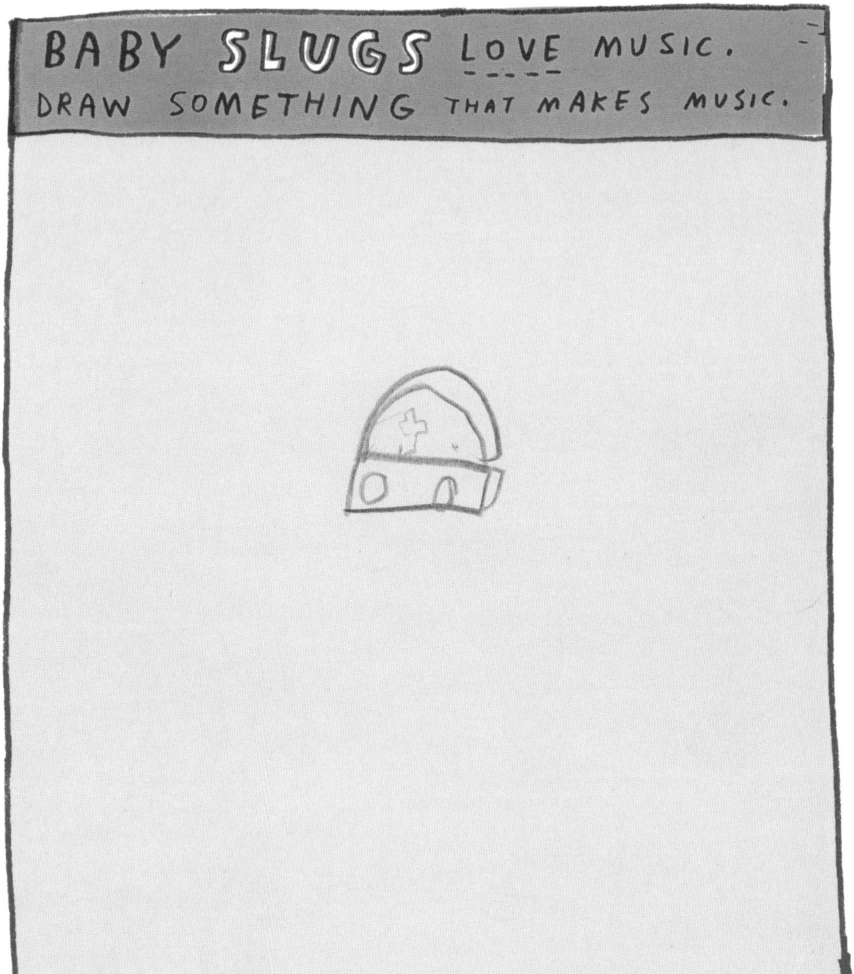
BABY SLUGS LOVE MUSIC.
DRAW SOMETHING THAT MAKES MUSIC.

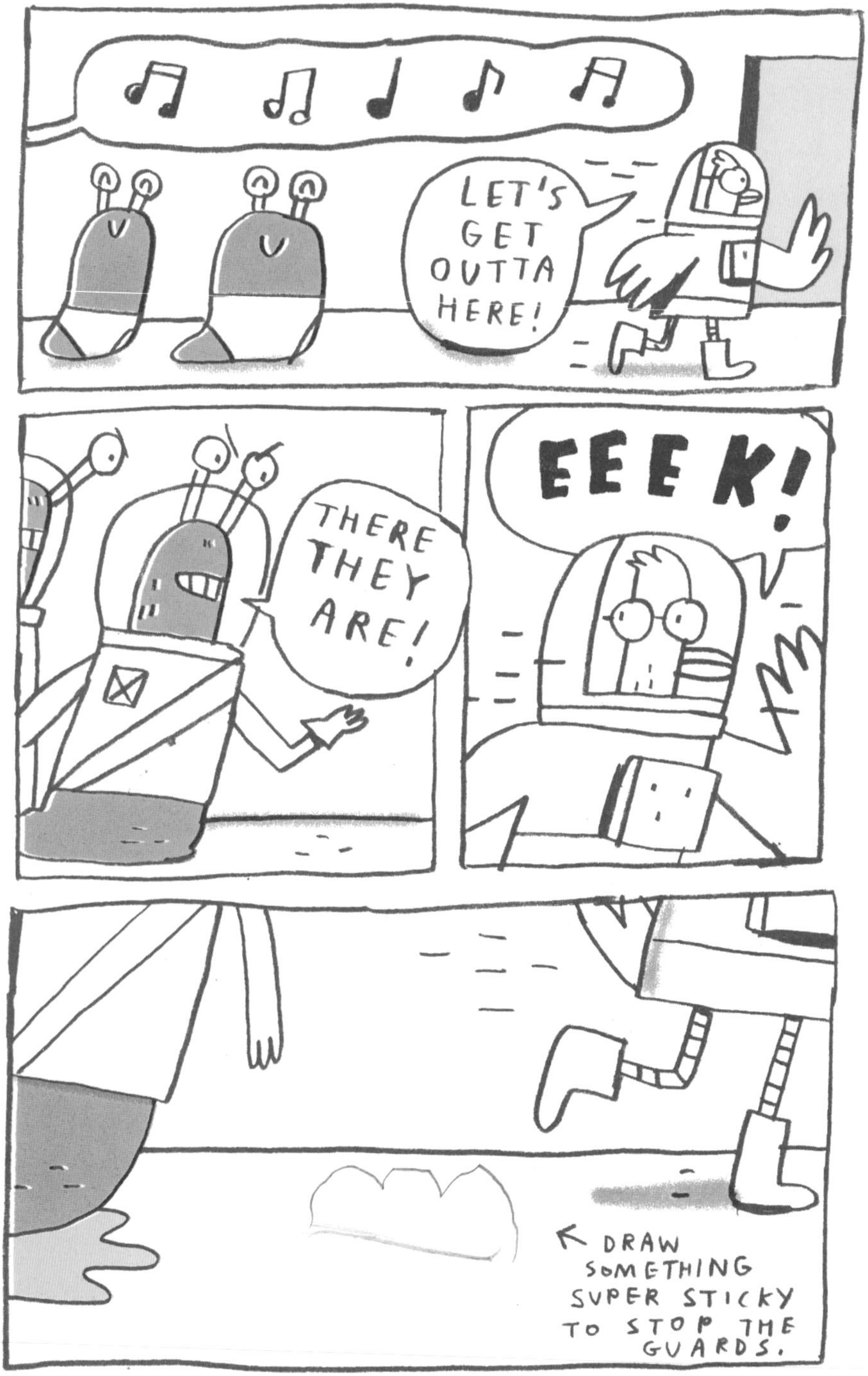

LET'S GET OUTTA HERE!
THERE THEY ARE!
EEEK!
DRAW SOMETHING SUPER STICKY TO STOP THE GUARDS.

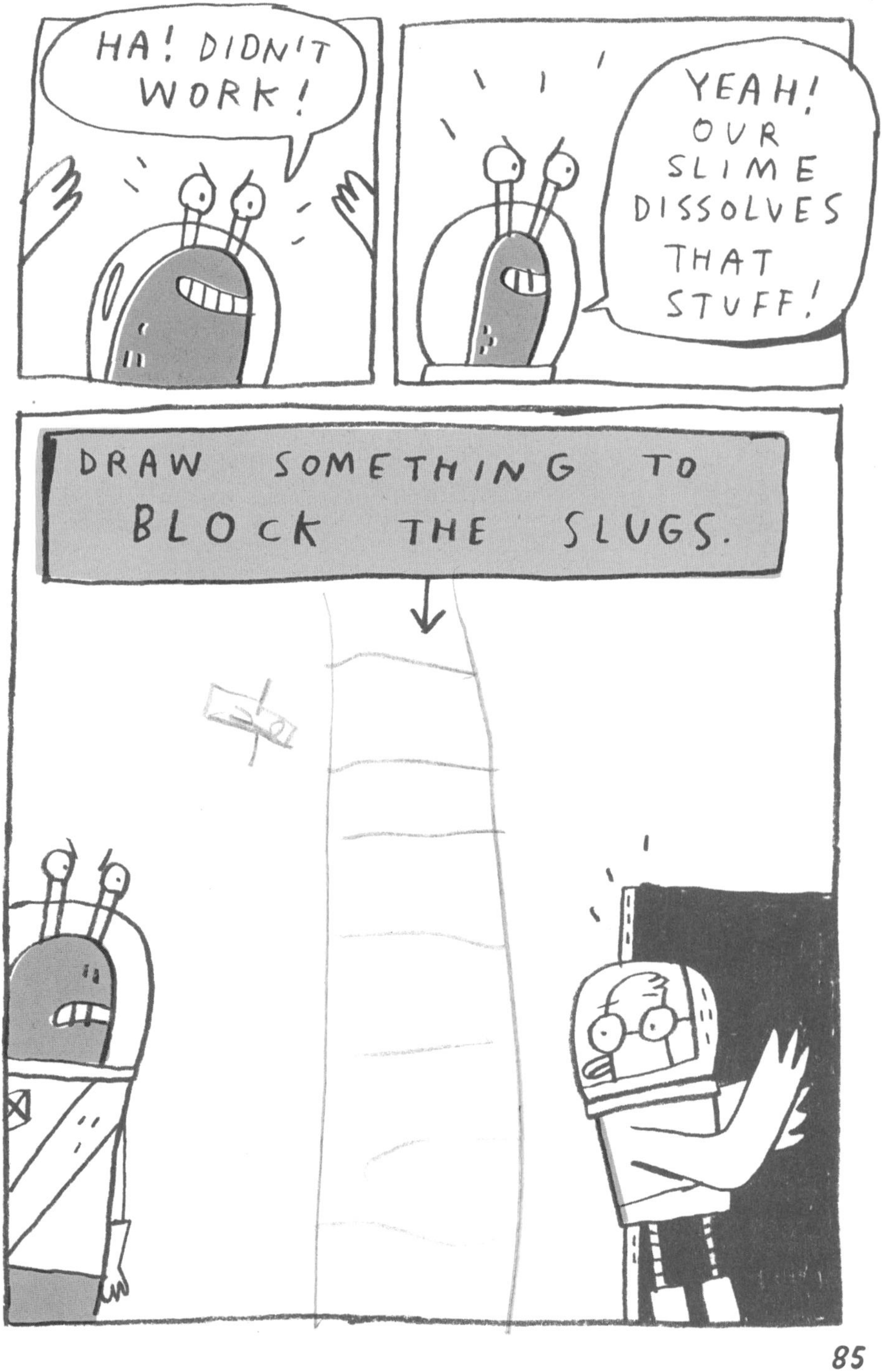
HA! DIDN'T WORK!
YEAH! OUR SLIME DISSOLVES THAT STUFF!
DRAW SOMETHING TO BLOCK THE SLUGS.

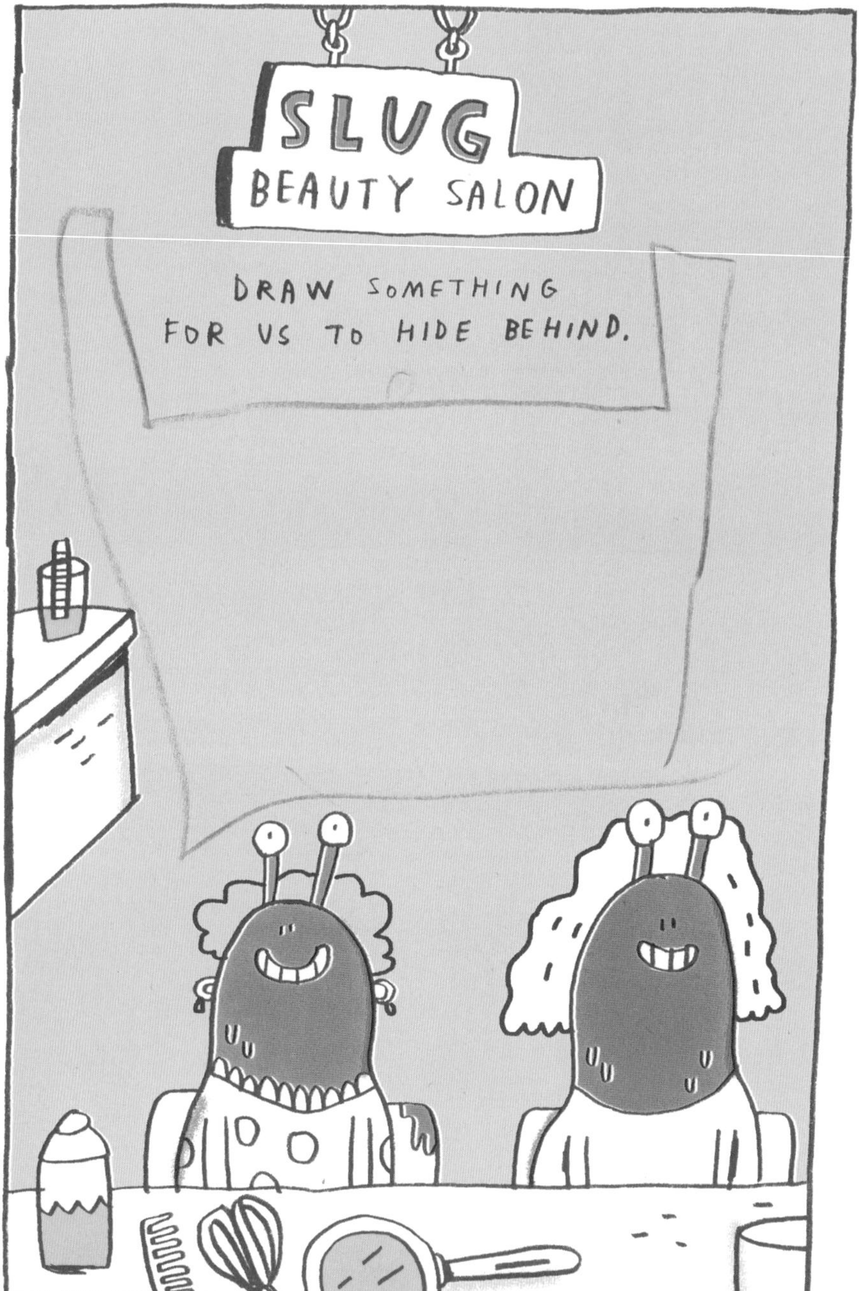
SLUG
BEAUTY SALON
DRAW SOMETHING FOR US TO HIDE BEHIND.

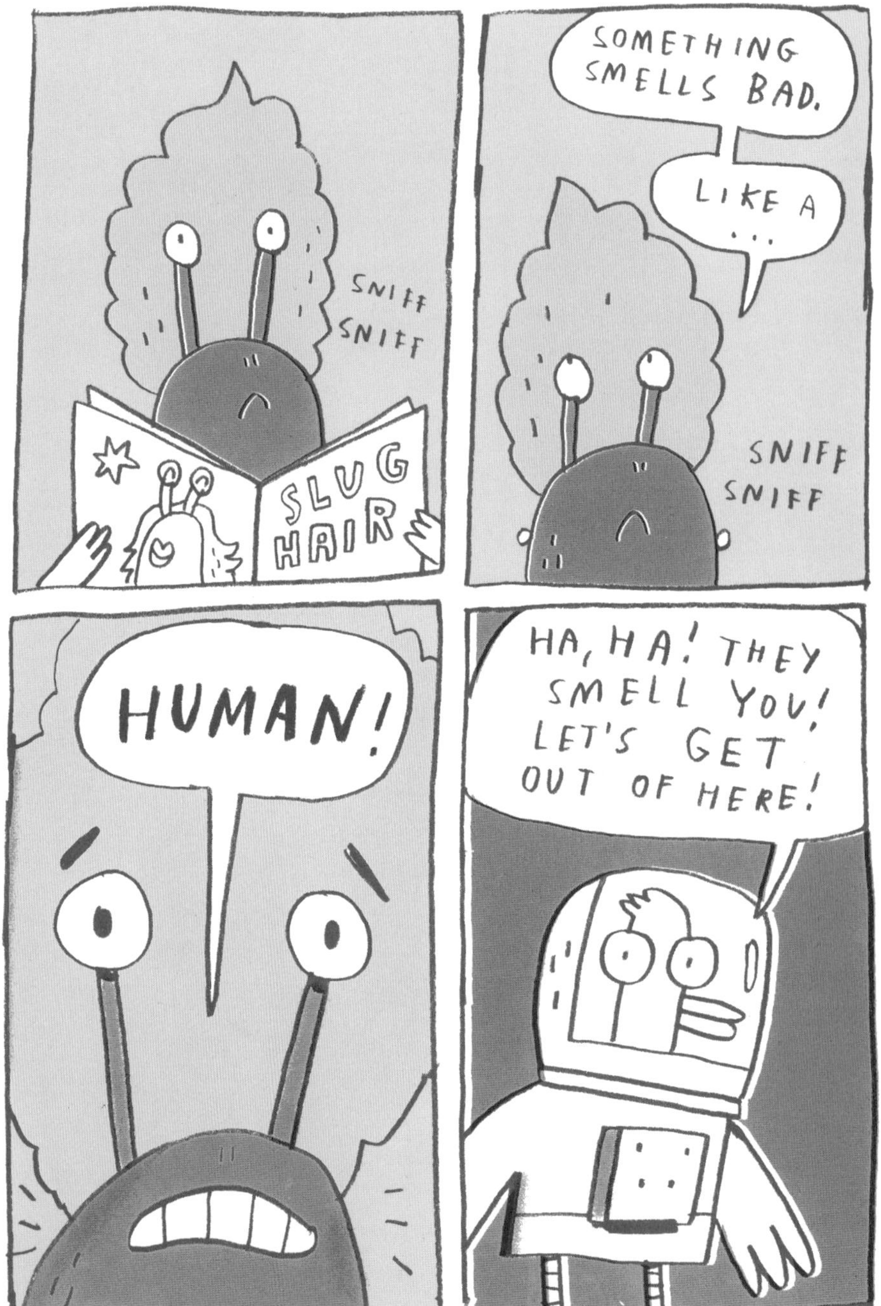
SLUG HAIR
SNIFF SNIFF
SOMETHING SMELLS BAD.
LIKE A . . .
SNIFF SNIFF
HUMAN!
HA, HA! THEY SMELL YOU! LET'S GET OUT OF HERE!

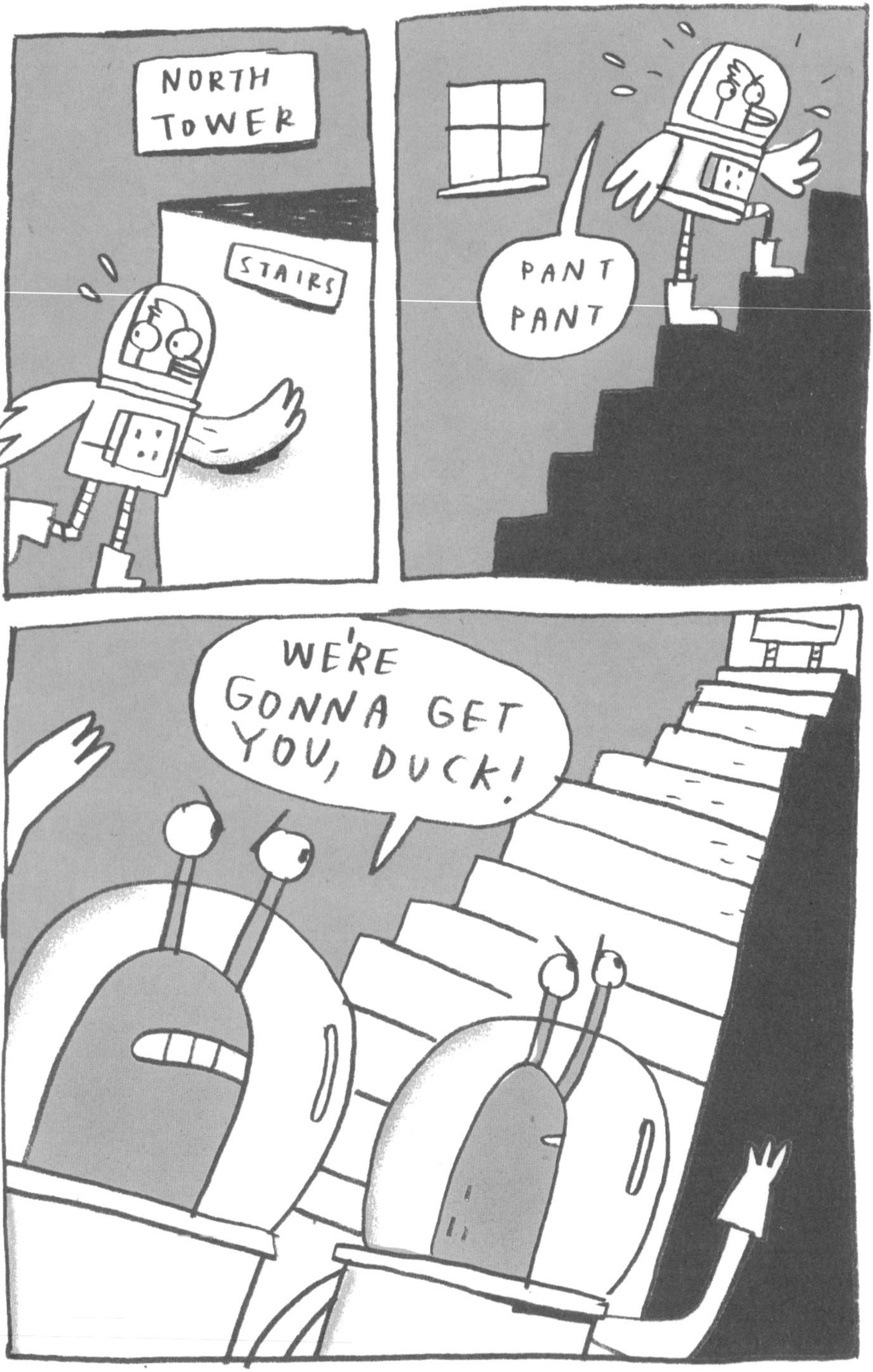
NORTH TOWER
STAIRS
PANT PANT
WE'RE GONNA GET YOU, DUCK!

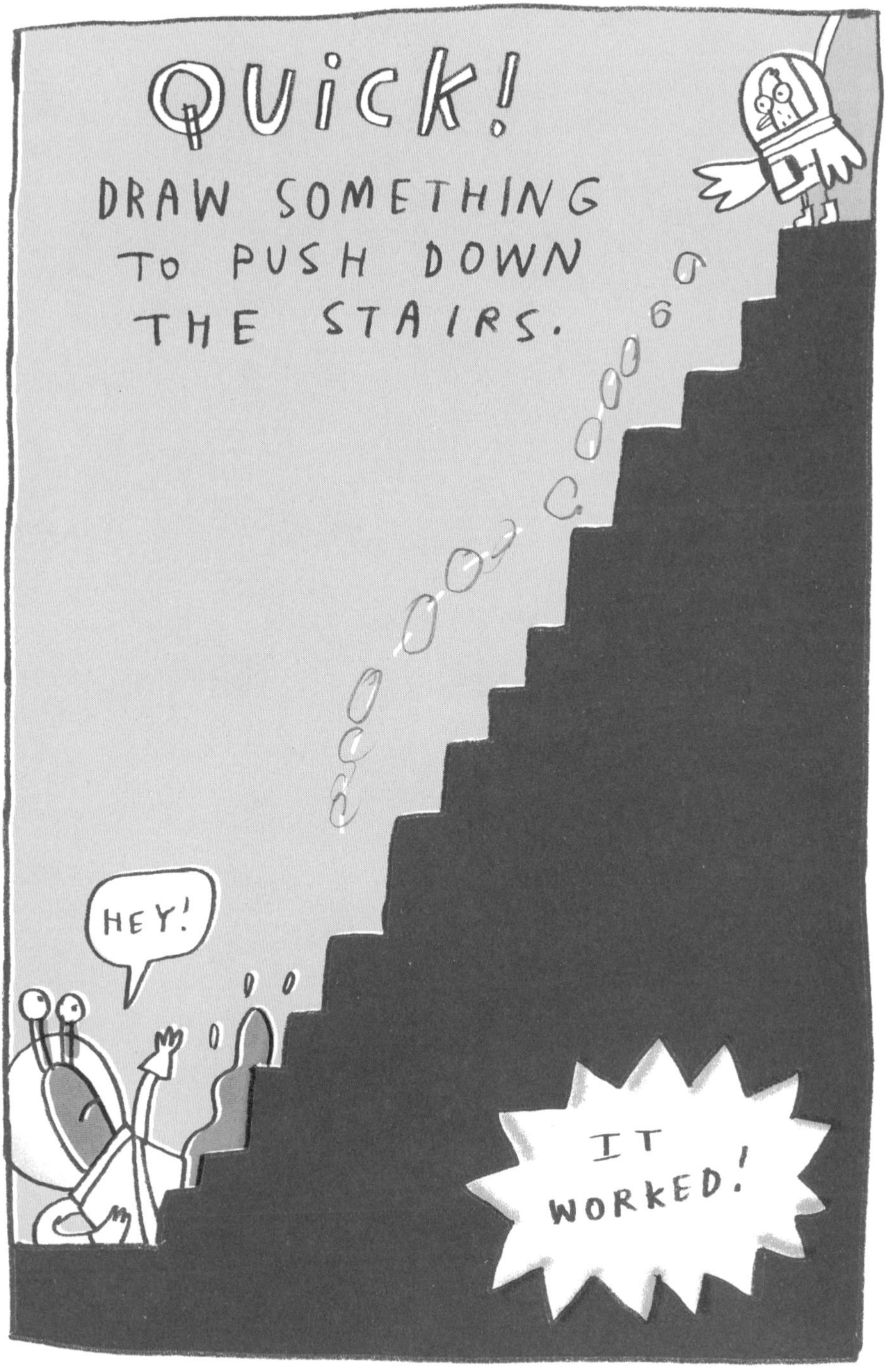
QUICK!
DRAW SOMETHING TO PUSH DOWN THE STAIRS.
HEY!
IT WORKED!

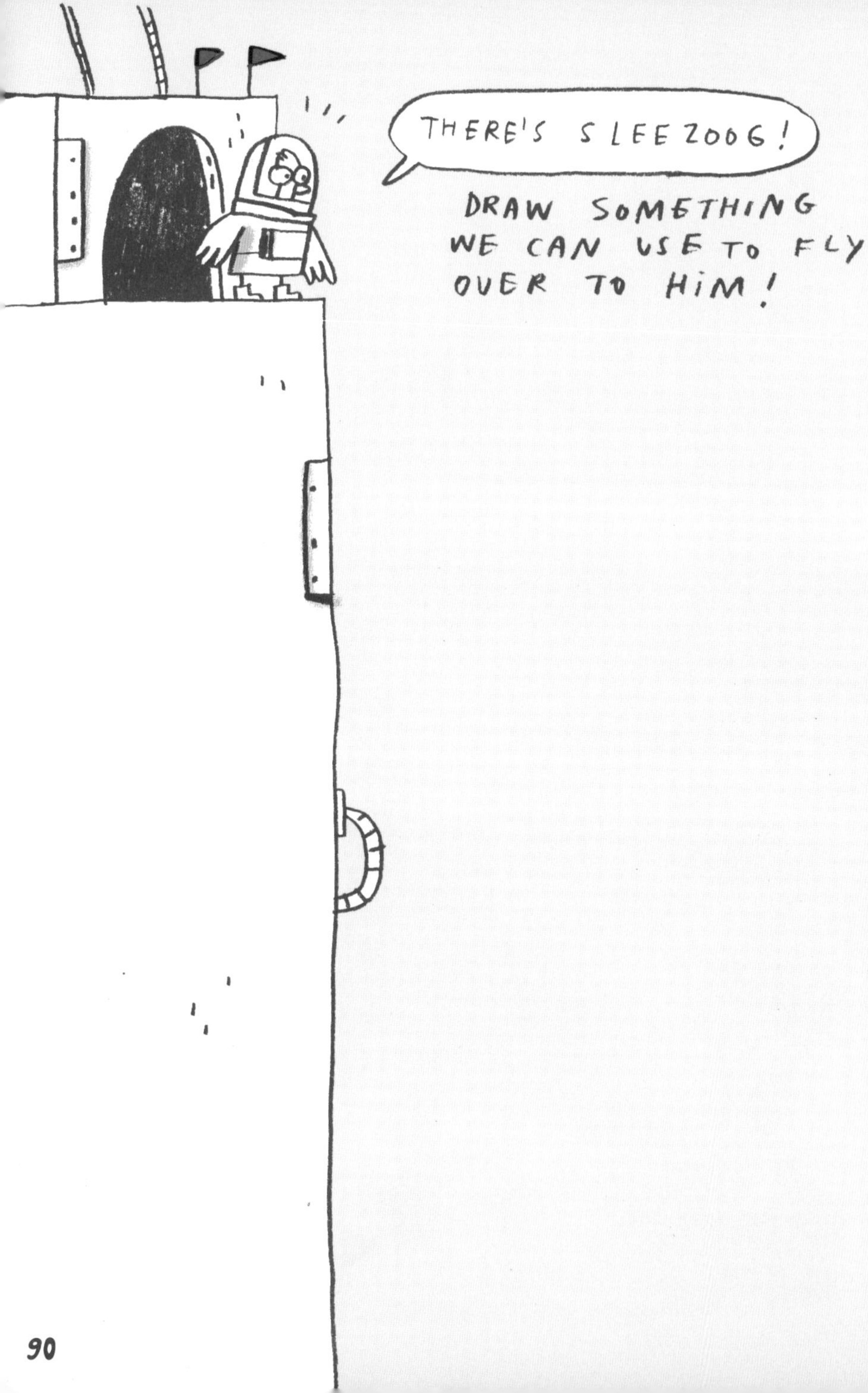
THERE'S SLEEZOOG!
DRAW SOMETHING WE CAN USE TO FLY OVER TO HIM!

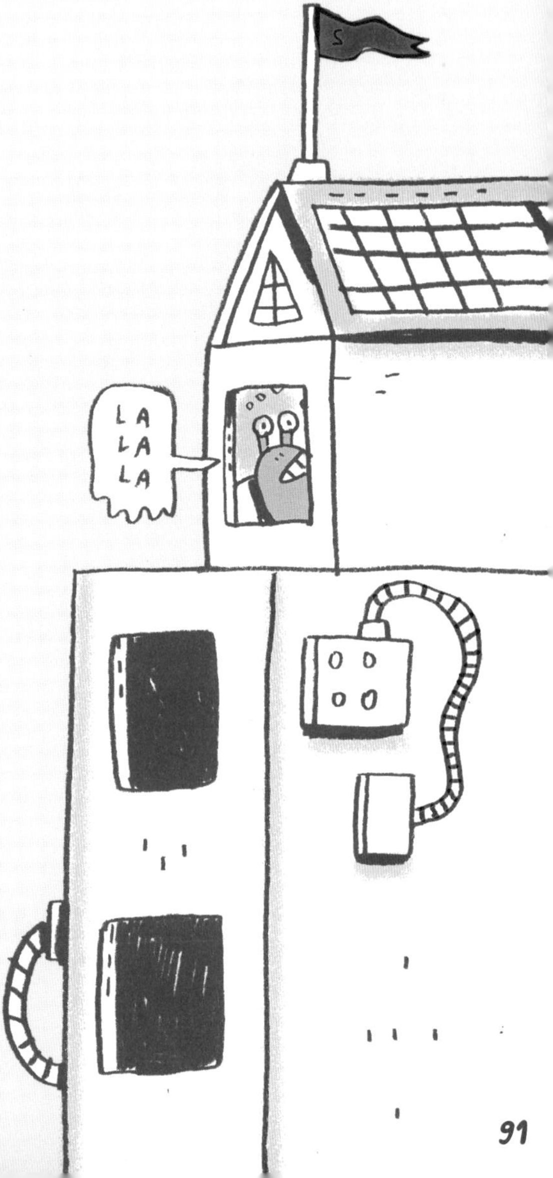
LA LA LA

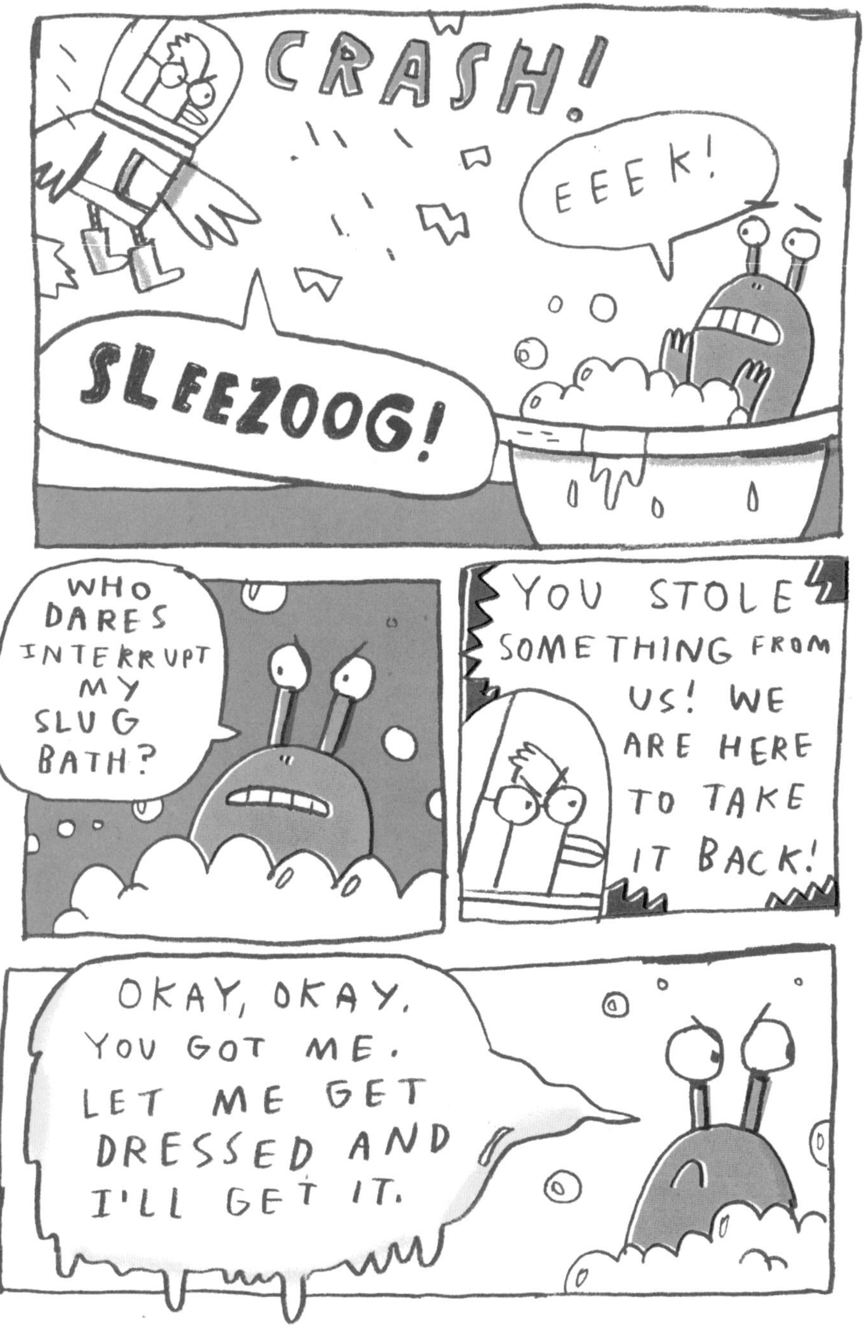
CRASH!
EEEK!
SLEEZOOG!
WHO DARES INTERRUPT MY SLUG BATH?
YOU STOLE SOMETHING FROM US! WE ARE HERE TO TAKE IT BACK!
OKAY, OKAY. YOU GOT ME. LET ME GET DRESSED AND I'LL GET IT.

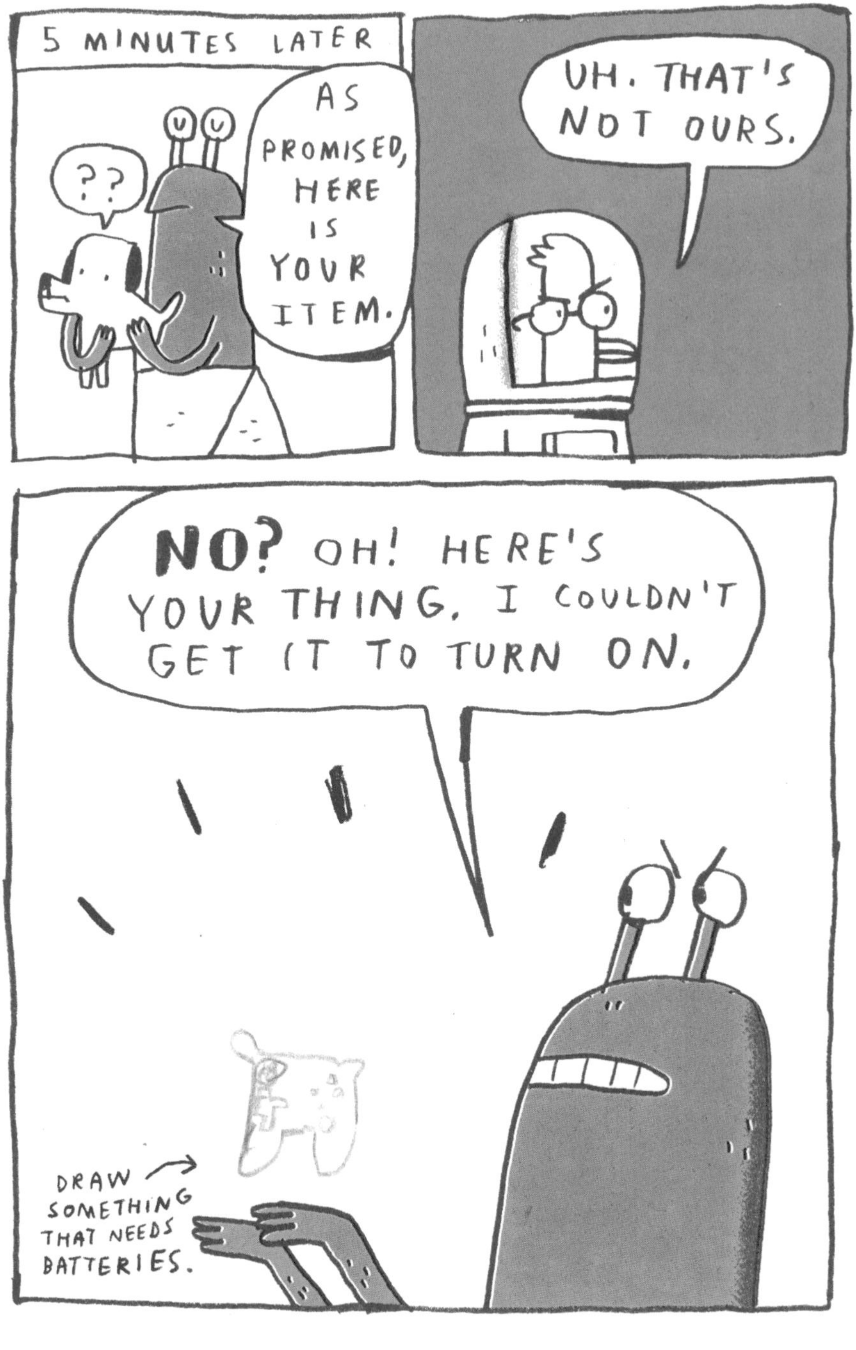
5 MINUTES LATER
??
AS PROMISED, HERE IS YOUR ITEM.
UH. THAT'S NOT OURS.
NO? OH! HERE'S YOUR THING. I COULDN'T GET IT TO TURN ON.
DRAW SOMETHING THAT NEEDS BATTERIES.

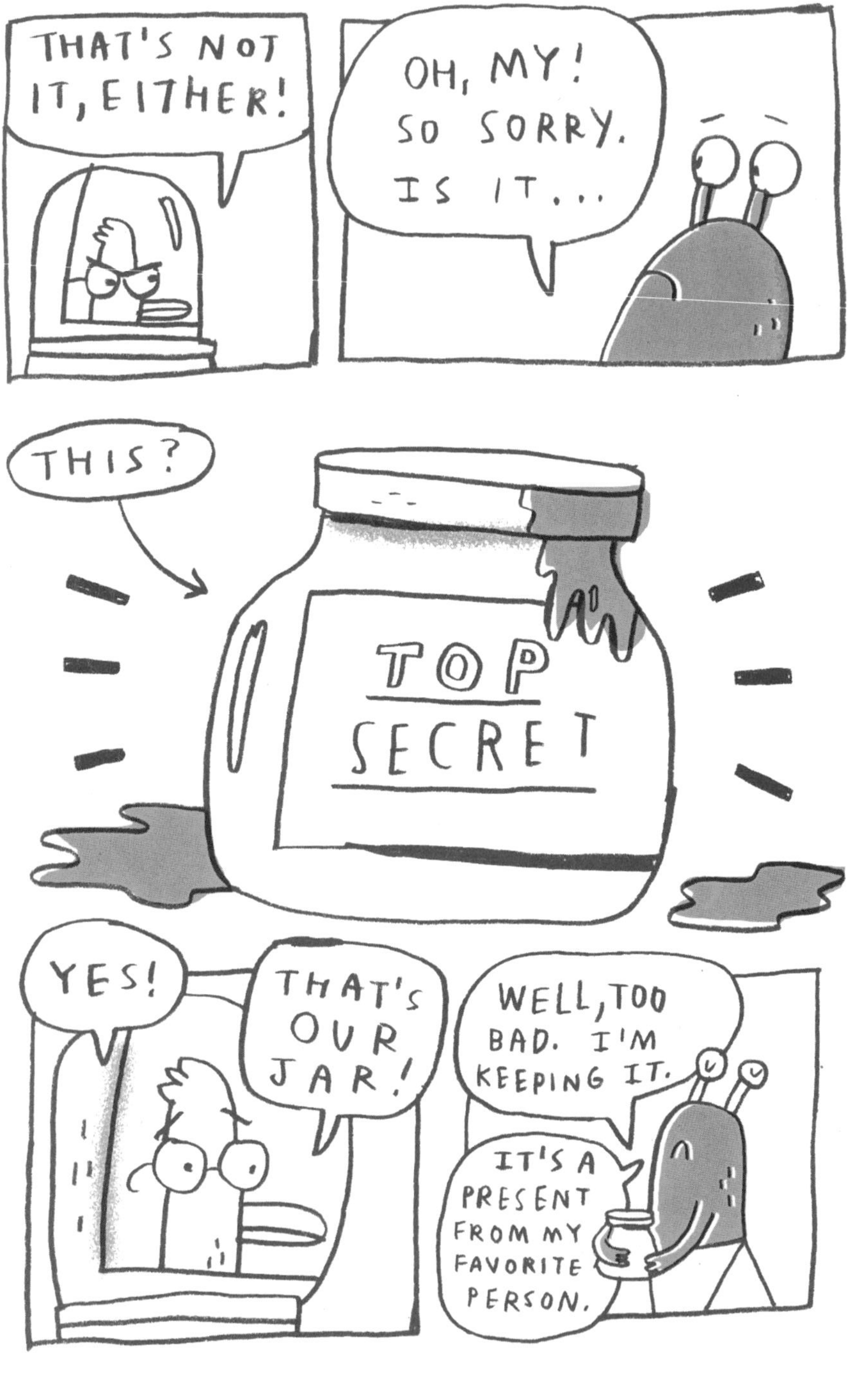
THAT'S NOT IT, EITHER!
OH, MY! SO SORRY. IS IT...
THIS?
TOP SECRET
YES!
THAT'S OUR JAR!
WELL, TOO BAD. I'M KEEPING IT.
IT'S A PRESENT FROM MY FAVORITE PERSON.

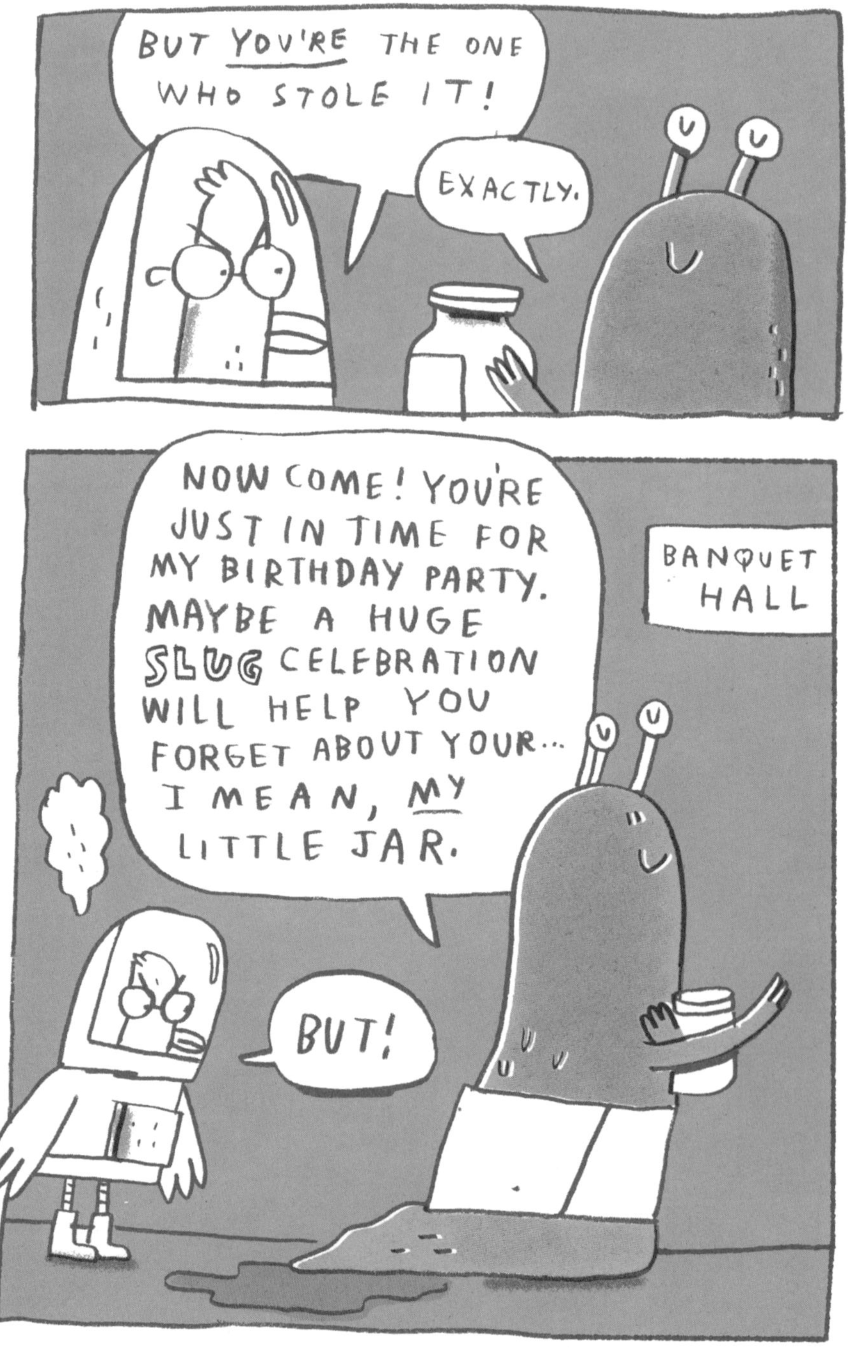
BUT YOU'RE THE ONE WHO STOLE IT!
EXACTLY.
NOW COME! YOU'RE JUST IN TIME FOR MY BIRTHDAY PARTY. MAYBE A HUGE SLUG CELEBRATION WILL HELP YOU FORGET ABOUT YOUR... I MEAN, MY LITTLE JAR.
BANQUET HALL
BUT!

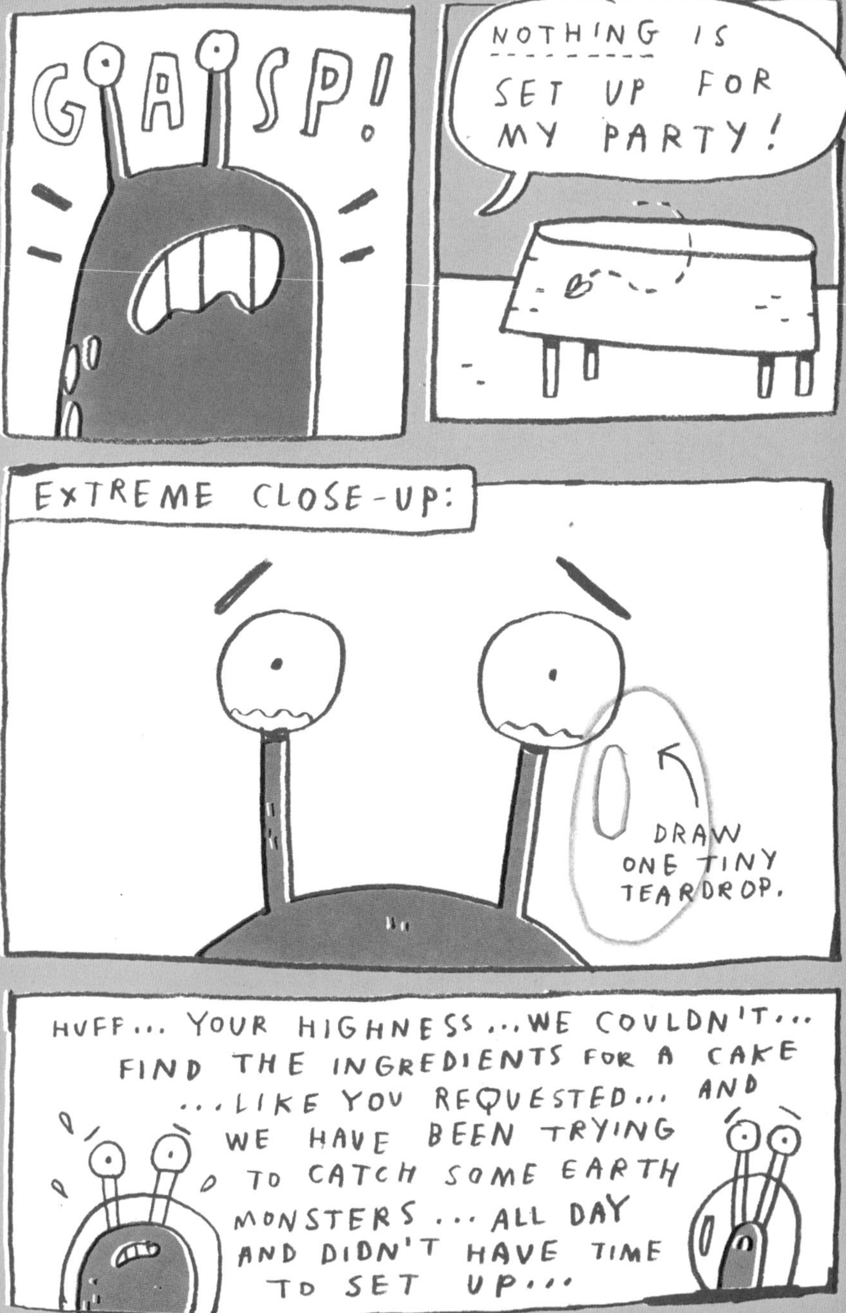
GASP!
NOTHING IS SET UP FOR MY PARTY!
EXTREME CLOSE-UP:
DRAW ONE TINY TEARDROP.
HUFF... YOUR HIGHNESS...WE COULDN'T... FIND THE INGREDIENTS FOR A CAKE ...LIKE YOU REQUESTED... AND WE HAVE BEEN TRYING TO CATCH SOME EARTH MONSTERS... ALL DAY AND DIDN'T HAVE TIME TO SET UP...

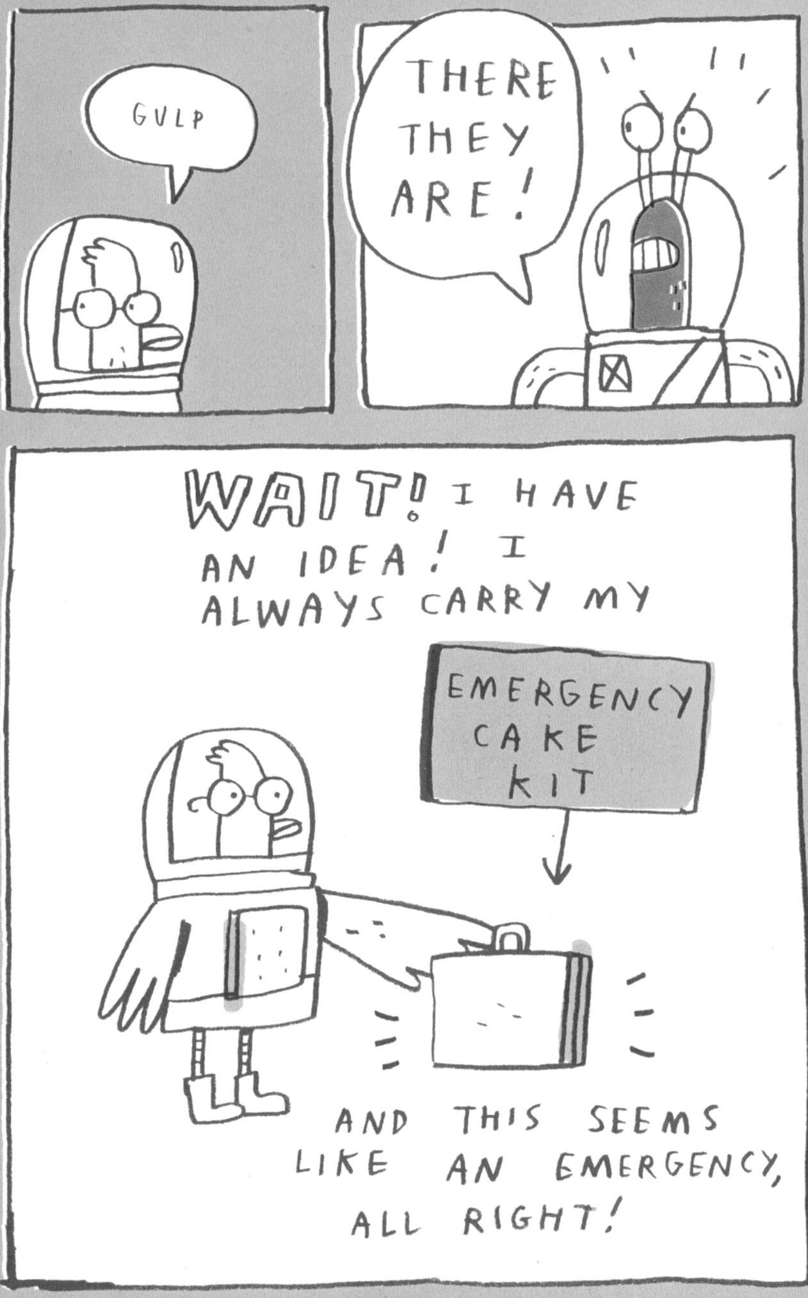
GULP
THERE THEY ARE!
WAIT! I HAVE AN IDEA! I ALWAYS CARRY MY
EMERGENCY CAKE KIT
AND THIS SEEMS LIKE AN EMERGENCY, ALL RIGHT!

DECORATE THIS PARTY
WITH HATS AND BALLOONS
AND OTHER FUN STUFF.

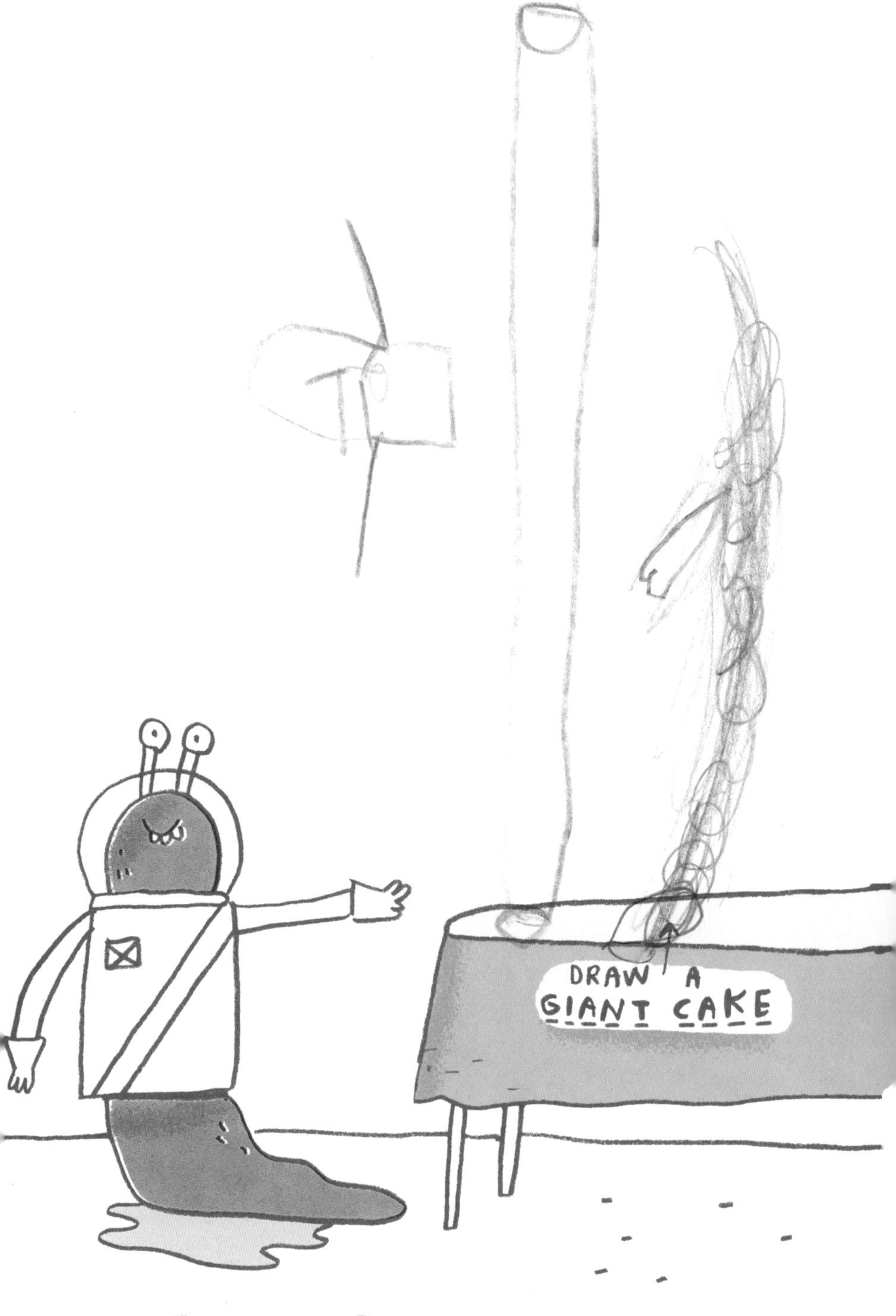
DRAW A GIANT CAKE

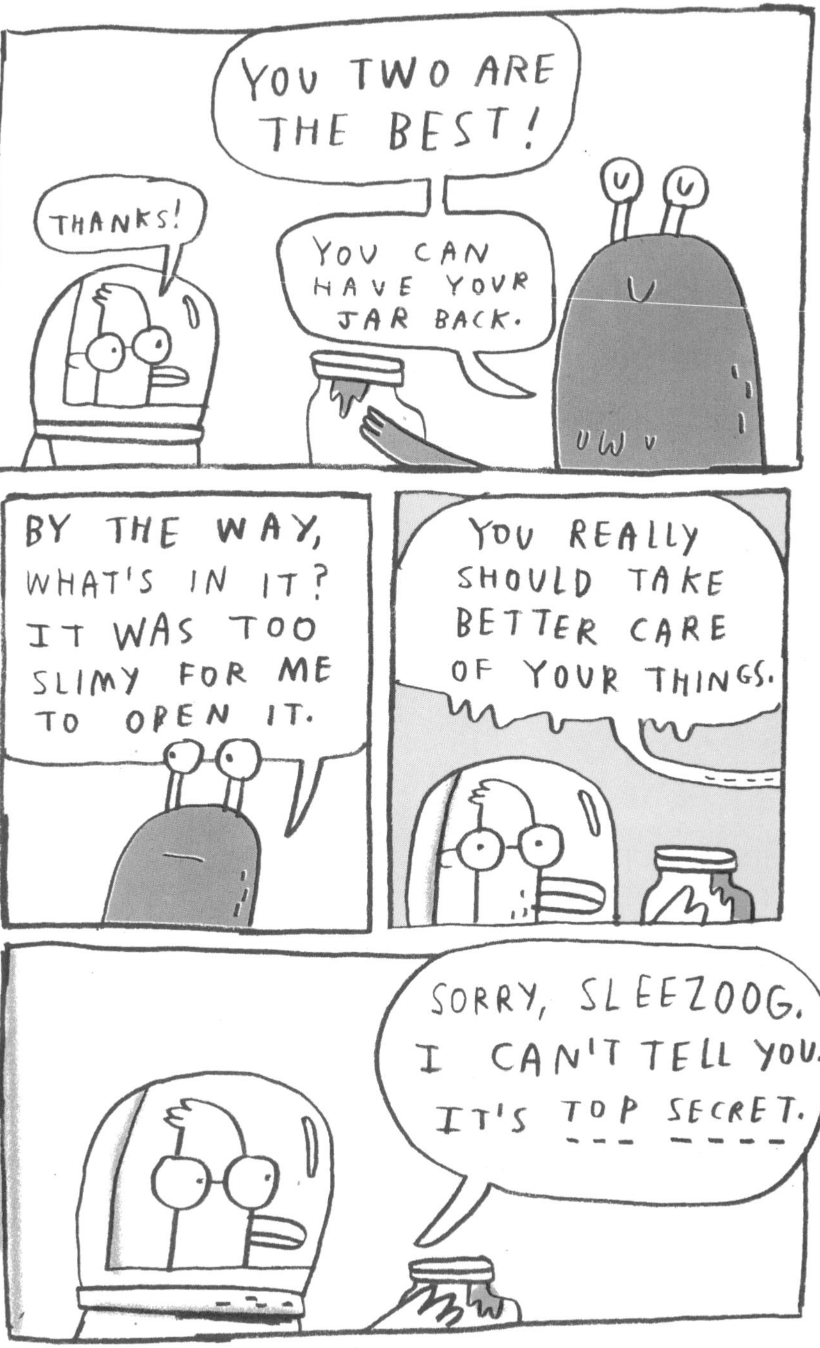
YOU TWO ARE THE BEST!
THANKS!
YOU CAN HAVE YOUR JAR BACK.
BY THE WAY, WHAT'S IN IT? IT WAS TOO SLIMY FOR ME TO OPEN IT.
YOU REALLY SHOULD TAKE BETTER CARE OF YOUR THINGS.
SORRY, SLEEZOOG. I CAN'T TELL YOU. IT'S TOP SECRET.

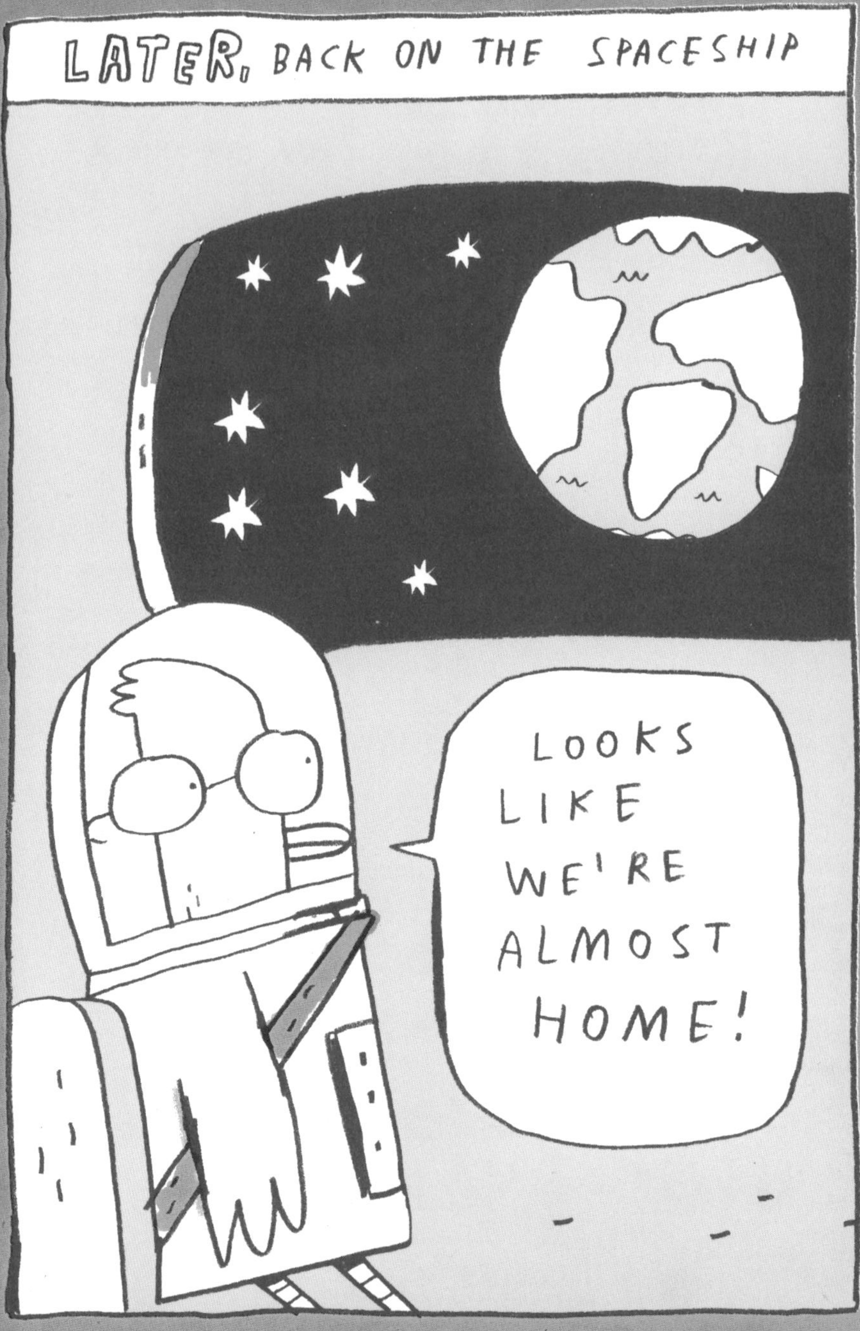
LATER, BACK ON THE SPACESHIP
LOOKS LIKE WE'RE ALMOST HOME!

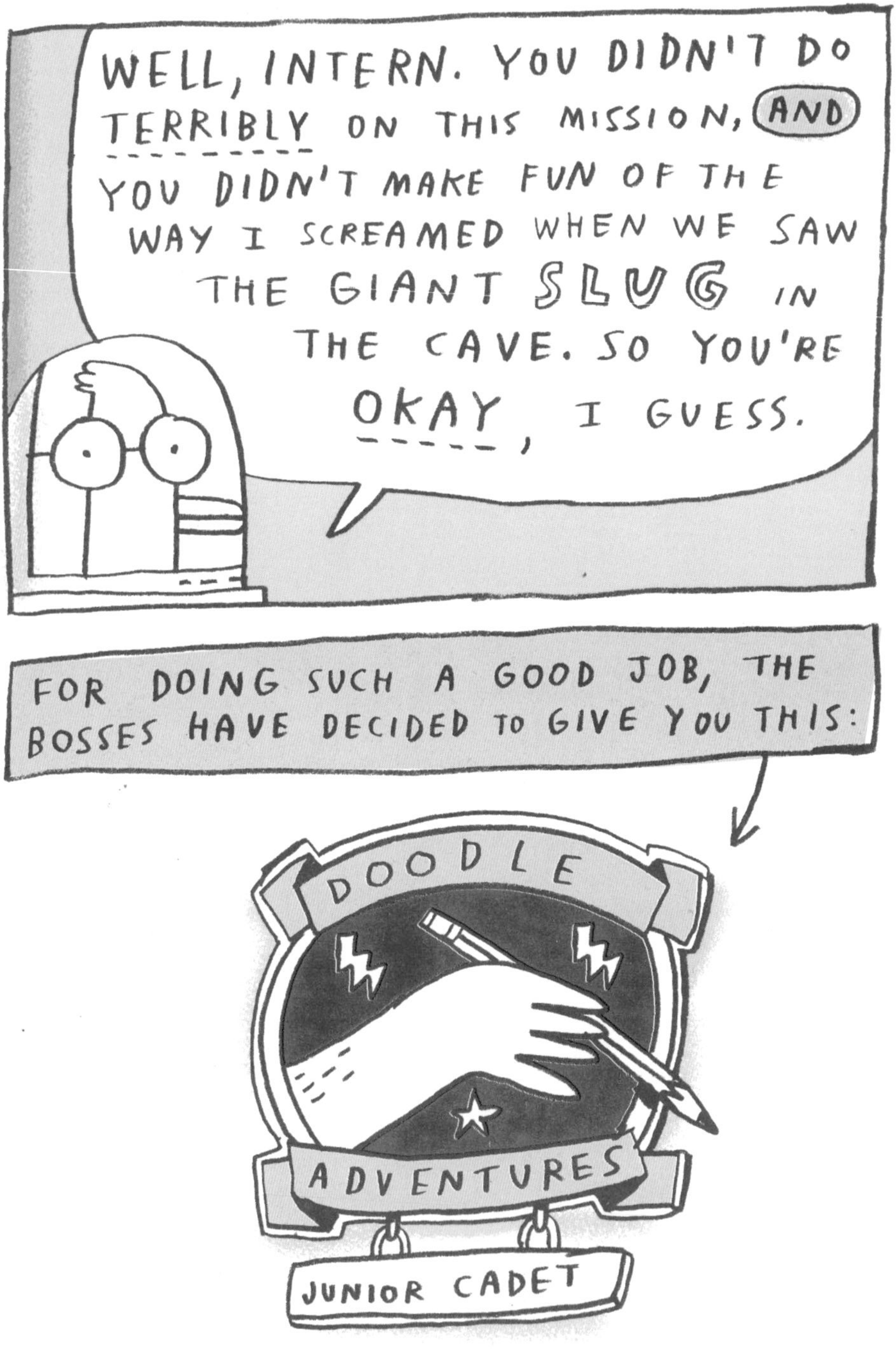
WELL, INTERN. YOU DIDN'T DO TERRIBLY ON THIS MISSION, AND YOU DIDN'T MAKE FUN OF THE WAY I SCREAMED WHEN WE SAW THE GIANT SLUG IN THE CAVE. SO YOU'RE OKAY, I GUESS.
FOR DOING SUCH A GOOD JOB, THE BOSSES HAVE DECIDED TO GIVE YOU THIS:
DOODLE
ADVENTURES
JUNIOR CADET

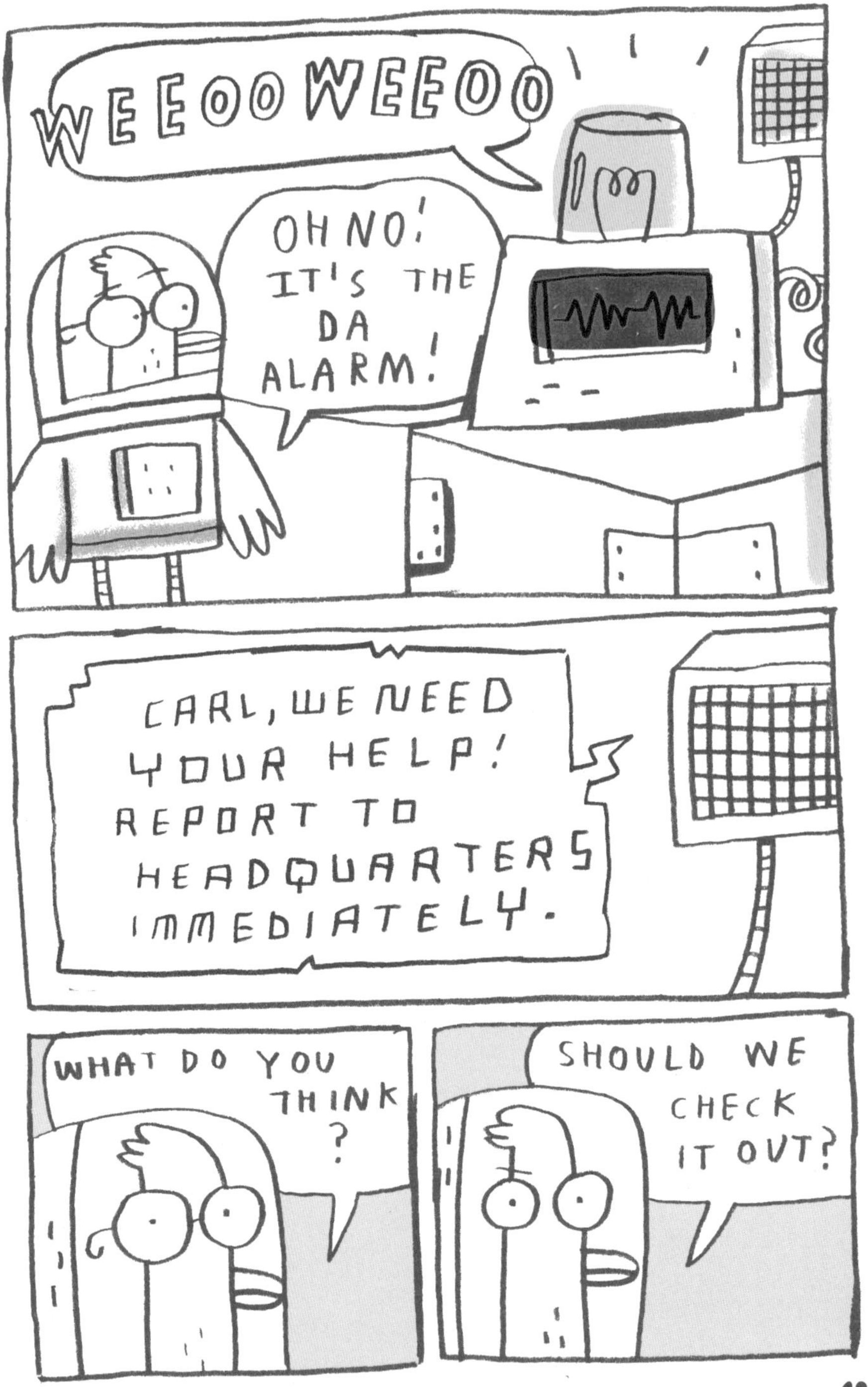
WEEOOWEEOO
OH NO! IT'S THE DA ALARM!
CARL, WE NEED YOUR HELP! REPORT TO HEADQUARTERS IMMEDIATELY.
WHAT DO YOU THINK?
SHOULD WE CHECK IT OUT?

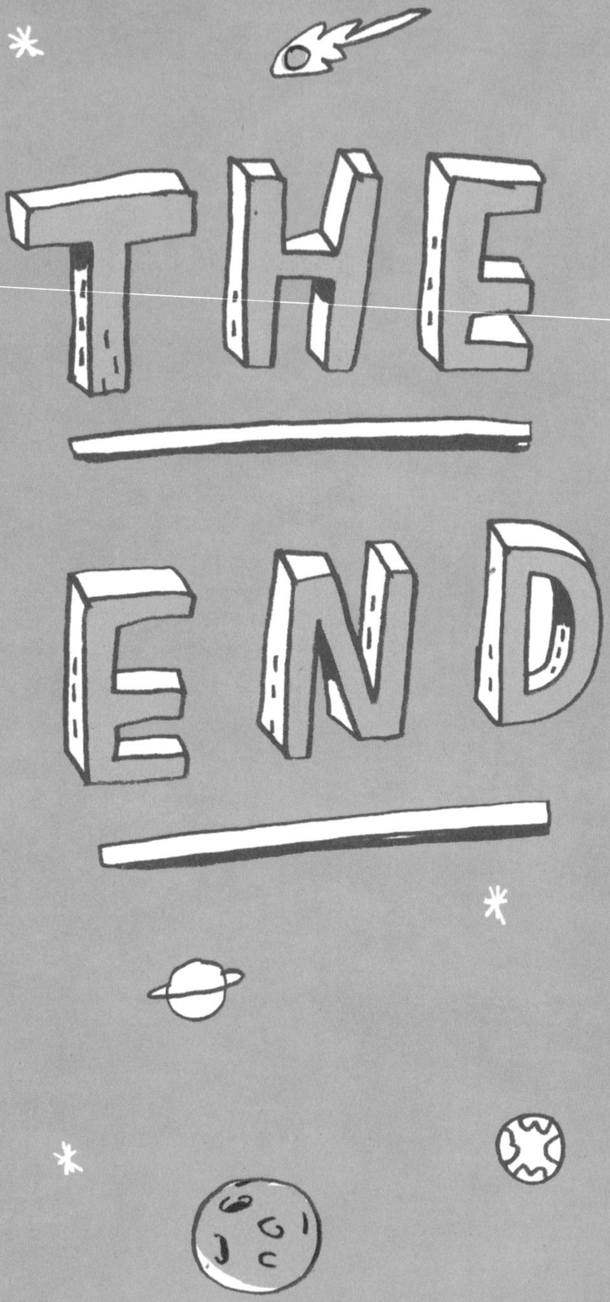
THE
END

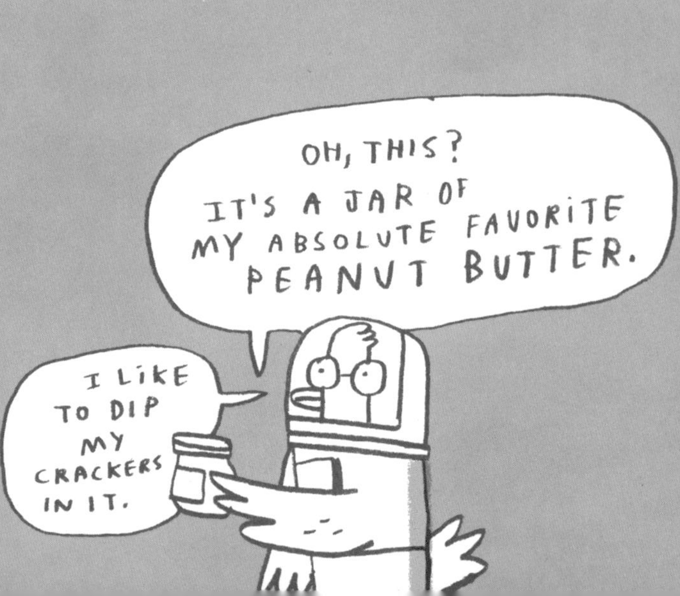
OH, THIS?
IT'S A JAR OF MY ABSOLUTE FAVORITE PEANUT BUTTER.
I LIKE TO DIP MY CRACKERS IN IT.

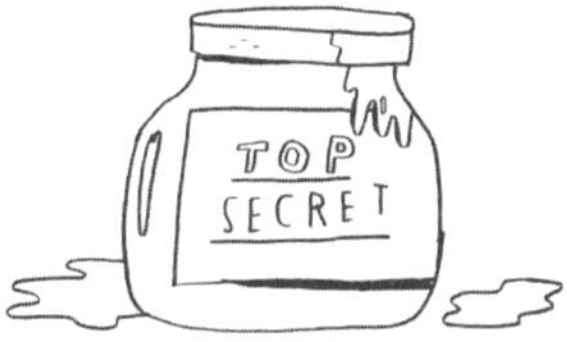
TOP
SECRET

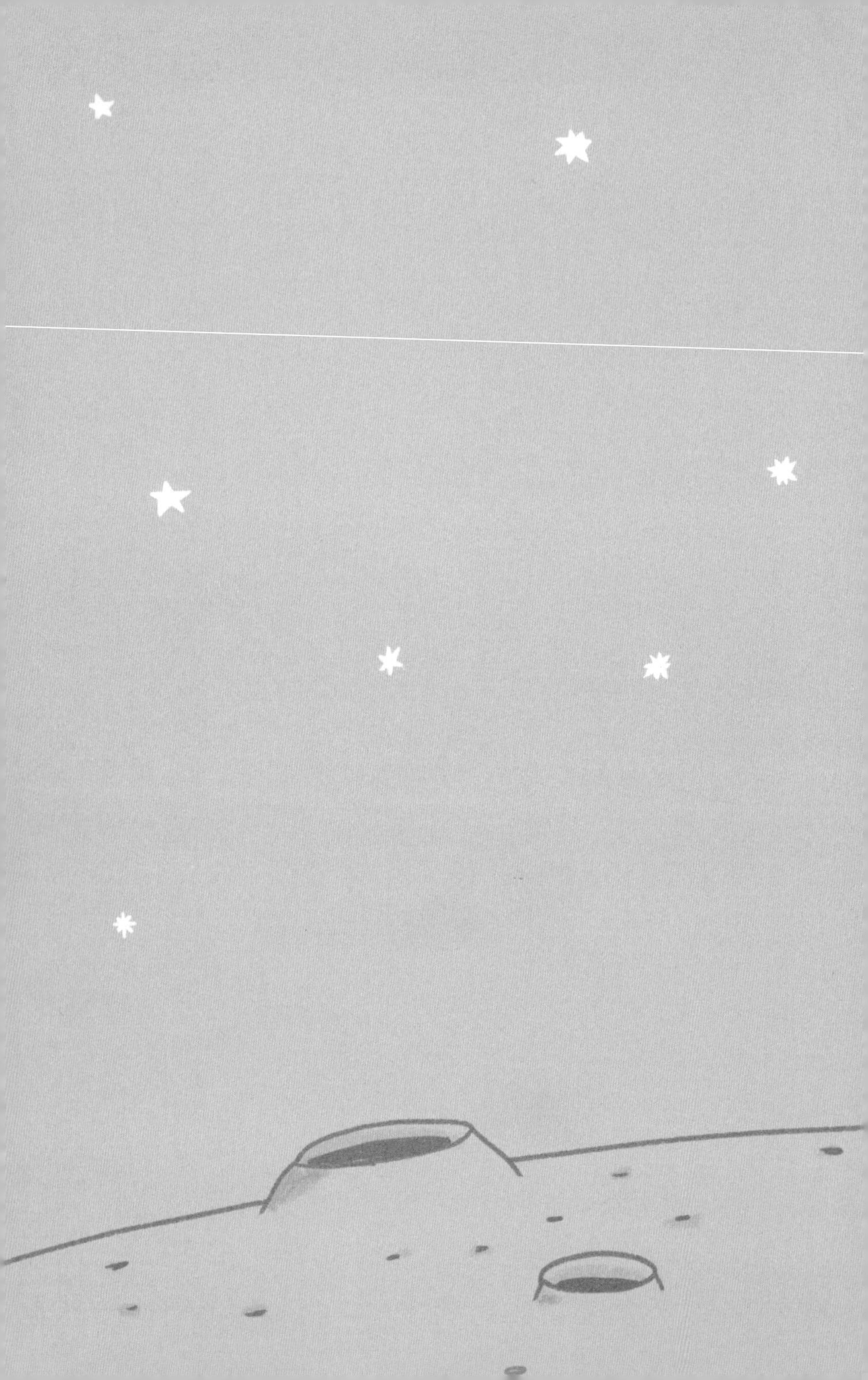